BORN OF THE SUN

I think continually of those who were truly
great—the names of those who in their lives
fought for life, who were at their heart the fire's center.
Born of the sun they traveled a short while
towards the sun and left the vivid air signed with
their honor.

Stephen Spender: *I Think Continually*

A
NAMIBIAN
NOVEL

BORN OF THE SUN

Joseph Diescho
with
Celeste Wallin

FRIENDSHIP PRESS • NEW YORK

LIBRARY OF CONGRESS

Library of Congress Cataloging-in-Publication Data

Diescho, Joseph, 1955-
  Born of the sun: a Namibian novel/by Joseph Diescho with
Celeste Wallin.
    p. cm.
    ISBN 0-377-00188-0: $14.95. ISBN 0-377-00187-2 (pbk.): $6.95
    I. Wallin, Celeste. II. Title.
PR9408.N363D54 1988   88-11980
823—dc19   CIP

Copyright © 1988 Friendship Press

Editorial Office: 475 Riverside Dr. (772), New York, NY 10115

Distribution Office: PO Box 37844, Cincinnati, OH 45222-0844

Printed in the United States of America

Dedication

To the Freedom Seekers
of Namibia and South Africa who are
United in tears, purpose and action;
Those Men and Women
Either dead or alive
Who have fought
are still fighting
and who will continue to fight
For Our Liberation
Our True Liberation
for the Freedom of Our Minds
Liberation beyond building personal castles
That is
That the People make and unmake governments
That Liberation will make
Africa "Afrika"
Yes, all Africa!
Once and for all
Knowing that
We shall Be Free
And Only We
Can Make Ourselves Free!

J.B.D.

My co-accused and I have suffered. We do not look forward to our imprisonment. We do not, however, feel that our efforts and sacrifice have been wasted. We believe that human suffering has its effects even on those who impose it. We hope that what has happened will persuade the whites of South Africa that we and the world may be right and they may be wrong. Only when South Africans realize this and act on it, will it be possible for us to stop our struggle for freedom and justice in the land of our birth.

Andimba Toivo Ya Toivo:
Court Speech, 1968.

ACKNOWLEDGMENTS

My heartfelt thanks go to:

- my collaborator Celeste M. Wallin, who, in the process of typing and editing each draft of the manuscript, contributed her valuable ideas and insights and, as such, co-wrote much of the story;

- the United Church Board for Homeland Ministries for its financial assistance towards the initial word processing of the drafts of this book;

- Letty Grierson who read the story first and discovered its readability;

- David Frederickson for further editorial work on the manuscript;

- Audrey Miller, William Gentz, and Bo Young of Friendship Press for final editorial work on the manuscript;

- Henning Pape-Santos for his time and effort word processing the manuscript;

- the Council of Churches in Namibia (CCN) for the translation of the (South) African Anthem into Namibian languages;

• members of my family back home in Namibia, who, although they have not always known where I was going and what I was doing, assured me of their care and support, (to them I say: *Kurara kwambwa, mughono kwahekudyendi*);

• all the sons and daughters of Mother Afrika who, often through the loss of their own lives, have realized and reminded us that duty is ours in God's events;

• and those who say, and mean, that our True Liberation Shall Arrive.

A Luta Continua!
"Joe"
New York, 1988

NOTE:

The names of places in the story are real but the names of the characters are purely fictitious. Any resemblance to real people is totally coincidental. In addition, the portrayal of the Roman Catholic Church does not necessarily reflect official church policy and is more accurate for an earlier period in history than for the time frame in which this novel is placed.

The author is fully cognizant of the debate surrounding the usage of such anthropological words as, "hut" and "kraal", and the derogatory meanings they have acquired. However, these words are here employed deliberately, in part due to a paucity of better words in the English language, and for the purpose of re-establishing their positive character. The intention has been to convey a vivid picture of African rural life.

CONTENTS

Illustrations on the Part title pages and on the jacket/ cover are by Adebisi Fabunmi.

Cover photo courtesy of *The Namibian*

PART I: RELATIONS

CHAPTER 1

"*Kirikiki, kirikiki,*" the village cocks sing as they begin the second round of their morning choir, signalling that the work-loaded day is around the corner. The commotion of the creatures around the hut and in the neighborhood alerts the young man, Muronga, that the night is changing into day. Still lying on his back on his bed, he feels the day breaking as he stares up at the grass roof of his mud and stick hut. Hearing the cattle stirring as the fowl greet the first rays of the sun, he sighs contentedly. His work in the fields has become a routine to him, as to Haushiku, his father, and his Uncle Ndara, who taught him that Monday, the first day of the week, is also the first day to mount work for the week. It is all fine, he thinks to himself as he rolls over on his flat *kafungo* made of long sticks held together by ropes. Supported by eight large vertical sticks, the bed is covered by a thin reed mat. His wife Makena is not sleeping with him these days. For about three weeks, she has been sleeping alone on the dirt floor on another mat near the fire that separates them now. The elder wives in the village told them that now that Makena's baby is soon due, they must sleep apart. It is not only Makena's protruding belly that makes it hard for them to share their small bed, but the elders teach that a husband and wife should not sleep together when the wife is with the moon and when she is due to give birth.

Yesterday, Sunday, Muronga went to their village church. He told Pater Dickmann, their local priest, that Makena could not come to church with him because her head was ill. It is always hard to convince Pater Dickmann that someone has stayed away from church for a good reason, unless it is illness, Muronga thought as he was formulating a reason for the priest yesterday. Pater Dickmann wants to see every person he knows in church; otherwise he thinks that something is wrong, and heathen practices are the first thing in his suspicious mind. If someone does not go to church for a reason that is good as far as we in the village are concerned, Pater Dickmann must be given some Christian reason, otherwise he believes that you are either still a heathen, or that you are showing some tendency to turn back to heathenism— a disease these missionaries say they came to eradicate.

But Makena was definitely not sick. She had been given some medicine by Shamashora, the best-known *nganga* in the village. According to the good healer, Makena was not supposed to move about as the child she was carrying was due any time within the next few days. And what the *nganga* says is more important to the young couple than all the sermons and admonitions of the priest.

Muronga and Makena go to church every Sunday because they are attending catechism school in preparation for Baptism and "a Christian wedding." On his way to church yesterday, Muronga thought to himself, things are no longer as they were in the days of our forefathers. To get married in the church, with a Christian name— or just to acquire the name—gives you more respect and better opportunities if you want to go to work in the white man's mines or on the farms in *thivanda*, the outside. Besides, it is fashionable these days to be married in the church. Everybody sees you all dressed up and they know you are now a Christian. The priest himself gets to know you and your spouse better, and sometimes presents and gifts go with the Christian wedding. Oh, and another good thing is that the priest gives the marrying couples their wedding rings. It is wise to consider things like these, Muronga reasoned. So why not get baptized? Why not go to this priest and get everything done—just get seen?

So, Muronga decided to tell this man, this priest, that Makena's head is still ill and that she will go to the clinic tomorrow. That is what he wants to hear. Well, he will get exactly what he wants—finish! Then the next thing you know he will baptize us, marry us, and baptize our child, too. Oh, and give us the rings, of course. He thinks about the church service yesterday, and particularly about how he told the priest a good lie. Yes, he thought, if you must tell a lie to make these white people happy, then tell it.

Rolling onto his back again, Muronga can now see through the grass roof that the sky is becoming clearer and clearer. Stretching his muscular body, he sighs contentedly and thinks, soon I will have my own child. He can see himself gently holding his child in his arms and looking into its eyes. It is a heart-swelling thought. His greatest wish is that the child will be a boy. What more could he hope for?

Makena moves around on the mat near the dying fire on the sand floor. She is a beautiful young woman who was untouched until she lost her maidenhead through her husband's manly deeds before the last rains. She is his child's mother-to-be—a giver of life and perpetuator of the race. Even when asleep, Muronga can hear her slightest movements since he is totally with her in spirit.

Her movements now suggest that she is in pain. Muronga turns softly in the direction of his wife. "Did you sleep well, Makena? Are you still fine?" Muronga asks

anxiously in a low voice. At the same time, he wriggles
out from under the grey blanket that covered and kept
him warm all night, and sits upright trying to see Makena.
It is still dark in the hut and all he can see of Makena
is her silhouette. Straining his eyes, he can see that she
is sitting, bent forward with her hands pressing on her
stomach. "Makena, my. . . . !" he exclaims. Leaping like
a mad fellow from the *kafungo* he lands almost on Makena,
but manages just in time to place himself next to her.
"What is the matter. . .ehm. . . .?" he asks sympathetically.
"Should I call Mama Rwenge."

"I am fine, thanks," Makena says calmly, her soft doe-
like brown eyes betraying her. "I am only feeling the pains
that I have been warned to expect. You remember what
Mama Rwenge said. . . Please call her. . . ooh, ooh, it is. . .
it is kicking in my stomach. . . " she pleads, with one
hand clutching the underside of her belly, the other
gripping Muronga's forearm.

Before she can finish, Muronga tears himself away, grabs
his shirt, and dashes out of the hut, running barefooted
to Mama Rwenge. He has never run so fast out of his
hut before. Muronga was to run and fetch Mama Rwenge
as soon as Makena said the word—any time, day or night.
He is very proud to do this for Makena and the child.

Mama Rwenge, the tall old midwife, hears Muronga's
quick footsteps approaching her hut. As usual, she is awake
in the early hours of the morning, contemplating her
schedule for the day.

"Mama Rwenge! Mama Rwenge!" Muronga, breathless,
calls while hastily buttoning his shirt and tucking it into
his shorts. "Are you there? It's me. . . Muronga! Can you
hear me? Please. . . "

"Yes, yes! I heard you coming. It sounded like a lion
was chasing you!" she replies with a laugh.

"Mama Rwenge. . . please, don't laugh. It's Makena. She is in great pain. . . pain! Come quickly! Oh, God. . .Hurry!" he pleads, hopping from one foot to the other.

"Calm down, young man. There is nothing to worry about," she says, easily. "You men are all the same. You boast of being strong, but the slightest pain makes you shiver like a reed," she continues confidently, emerging from her hut.

"Oh, please, Mmmmmama Rwenge," he stutters. "This is not a question of who is strongest. Makena is in pain. . . now! She needs you! And you said I should come anytime, day or night."

"Yes, all right. Run along now and help Makena to the women's hut. But don't panic. I am coming. I knew this would happen any day now."

Muronga doesn't wait for Mama Rwenge to finish. All he needed to hear was that she was on her way. Smiling and shaking her head, Mama Rwenge watches Muronga sprint back to his hut. Reentering her hut, she picks up a small bag of medicines and adjusts her shawl around her shoulders. Quickening her step, she heads in the direction of the women's hut, knocking on the doors of several elder women to inform them that Makena is in labor.

When Muronga arrives at his hut, out of breath, Makena is nowhere in sight. Panting, he calls out, "Makena, where are you?" There is no reply. He listens to the silence in the hut. Maybe she has gone to the women's hut by herself, he thinks, going outside again. He looks on the ground outside the hut and sees her footprints in the sand. Mak..., oh, she must already be there! Dear God of Our Forefathers, help her, help us. Give us our child, Muronga prays. Mama Rwenge, the best-known midwife in the village, told Makena to move into the nearby hut as soon as she felt acute pains. This was, she said, very important. Muronga is once more impressed with his wife. She makes the right decisions at the right times. Muronga knows too that she has a very wonderful common sense. He counts himself lucky to have Makena for his wife. He loves his wife. He reminds himself not to think about taking a second or third or fourth wife, as other men often do. Makena is worth more than ten, twenty wives put together. All these thoughts run like lightning through Muronga's mind.

Still standing outside his hut, he listens to make sure Makena is in the hut—the serious hut. Ah, yes. He can hear Mama Rwenge in the hut talking to Makena. Everything will go well from now on, he sighs, pacing back and forth. The deep orange sun is now resting on the African horizon. Soon he hears more women's voices in the good hut, the hut of joy, of life. Two more elder women have come to Makena's aid. Good. This is how it is done in the village. Women help one another at times like this. Birth is their business, and men must stay away until they are told by women what to do. Then they can act manly. But now they have no business there. Muronga goes back inside his hut to rest on his *kafungo*. His mind, however, is in the other hut with Makena. His child is there, too, isn't it?

There is a moment of absolute silence in both huts. Muronga tries to figure out what could possibly be happening. He closes his eyes and tries to remember how Makena looked and how it felt to touch her the last time they spoke as husband and wife—before they were separated and before all this. He recalls Makena's shy but vibrant smile when he made jokes about the days before they were married, when they did not look at each other as husband and wife, but as third cousins through Muronga's mother. These were the days when Muronga looked at Makena as a child, a small sister, since he was many moons and twelve rains older than Makena.

Makena, who was of the correct lineage, had been selected at an early age as a prospective spouse for Muronga and prepared by the elders to be a good wife and mother. Upon reaching puberty, she, in her turn, like each of the other girls in the village, was whisked away from the *kraal*, the fenced-in area of the village comprising huts for a number of families. Makena was surrounded by dancing, ululating elder women who gave her a hoe, a symbol of woman's role as provider, and escorted her to the forest, where the rituals began.

The secluded spot was off-limits to all males, who knew that if they dared go near the initiation place, their hair would fall off. But they could hear the singing of the women. Through songs, dances, and stories, she was told about female sexuality, about her rights and responsibilities as a wife and a mother, and about the hardships she would have to endure throughout her life.

About two weeks later, at the crack of dawn, she was taken to the river, where she was bathed. Then she was returned to the *kraal*, where the elder women presented her with gifts of necklaces, arm and leg bracelets, and belts made from small beads, river shells, and pieces of ostrich egg shells. A large fabric apron hung from a huge belt and a skirt made from the skins of wild goats and decorated with more shells and beads was wrapped around her narrow hips. Her hair was tressed with cords made from the roots of the Stinkwood tree and then partially packed with a mixture made of powders, clay and the oil of the *Mono*-tree seed. Finally her smooth, supple, dark brown skin was glazed with a thin coat of herb-scented oil. As an adult woman she would be expected to maintain her new appearance, and to comport herself as she was taught, as a virgin, until the day of her marriage.

Now, only a little over a year later, Muronga smiles as he remembers the day of his and Makena's traditional wedding. Dressed in new but everyday clothes and bared to the waist, they were taken by his uncles and her aunts to Makena's parents' *ghutara*, a large, flat, grass-roof canopy near their hut. Under the canopy burned a new fire, built with the long-burning wood of the *ghupupu*-tree, which Muronga had fetched earlier in the day. This was one of the groom's duties. In front of the blazing fire, on a new mat given to them by one of Muronga's uncles, they sat cross-legged with Muronga's right leg resting on Makena's left, their little fingers hooked. In the company of their guests, they listened attentively to the instructions given to them — first by Uncle Ndara and then by Mama Rwenge, as she poured oil on the places where their bodies met.

After the ceremonies, they were led by the jubilant guests to the hut Muronga had built for his bride, and deposited there to begin their life together. Alone together for the first time, the fire dying in the darkened hut, they nervously made small talk until Makena found an opportunity to rub against Muronga as she had been instructed to do.

Remembering the joy of that night and of the months that followed, Muronga now feels Makena's absence keenly and wishes that he could participate in her pain— the pain which he in fact caused. Although excited by the thought of creating life, he is forlorn as he thinks of Makena's pain at this time. I wonder what is happening now, he thinks anxiously with his arms folded on his chest.

"*Kwithe, kwithe* . . . Apply yourself. Be strong until your baby comes," come Mama Rwenge's encouraging words out of the women's hut. "It will all be over soon. Yes, yes, go on doing that . . . yes . . . you see!"

I wish I were there to hold Makena's shoulders, Muronga thinks woefully. But the laws of our people do not allow us to do certain things. If it were not for Mama Rwenge, who has complete control over situations like this, then what? But now, there is no need to worry! Muronga says to himself, nodding his head.

A child's cry! Muronga sits bolt upright. His heart is suddenly beating wildly. His blood races and he cannot blink his eyes as if he can hear with them. He is bewildered by the sound of the child . . . his own child. The child is silent again and the women can be heard murmuring in the hut. Muronga cannot hear the exact words, but the women sound contented.

Oh, God, can it be true, really? I hope it is a boy. And if it is, he is going to be as great as my Uncle Ndara. No . . . greater. I will make him great, greater, greatest! That is certain. My forefathers will help me in this. They have told me this in my dreams many times.

Happily, Muronga lies flat on his back again, his eyes studying the grass roof and the light coming through it, until he hears footsteps approaching his hut. He listens to the footsteps curiously as they come closer. One, two, three, four, five, six, seven, and eight. Then the voice of Mushova, the mother of his friend Karumbu, or *Nyina-Karumbu*, as she is commonly known, comes through the thatched door.

"Are you asleep, father of the child?"

"Oh, no," bellows Muronga. "What is the news . . . ehm?"

"Ah, it is about Makena and . . . a successful birth. She is a very brave woman." She pauses to keep Muronga in suspense. He can hear the smile in her voice. "And the old man gave a hunter's kick as he reached my hands. He is strong like a lion's cub."

Muronga jumps from his *kafungo* and begins to dance by himself. He shrugs his shoulders swiftly to and fro in the traditional rhythmic dance of joy.

"I have heard you, *Nyina-Karumbu*. Thank you for everything you and Mama Rwenge have done. I will hunt you a hare one of these days."

Humming to himself, Muronga continues to dance as yellow rays of sunlight bathe the room. A boy! It is a boy! Muronga repeats *Nyina-Karumbu's* words over and over to himself. God of Our Forefathers be thanked! Prancing a little while longer, he finally comes to rest on his *kafungo* again, wondering what he will do with himself for the rest of the day. It is Monday, after all. *Mandaha* . . . the first day to mount work for the week. Outside the huts the other village men can be heard milking the cows and preparing to leave for the fields. But Muronga will not do any work today. A new father is expected to stay home on the day his child is born to wait for news from the elder women. If any problems arise he is instructed by them what to do. Relaxed, Muronga listens with his eyes and ears for the slightest sound of approaching footsteps.

Muronga had long since decided if the baby was a boy he would name it after his brave Uncle Ndara. Everybody in the village has heard stories of how Ndara killed a lion with a stick when he was young—when he was only a few rains old, as they say. Muronga also knows that the people who chose Makena for his wife made no mistake. And it was Uncle Ndara who had the final say in the choice of his wife. His uncle is a very wise man. Even the chief and the Bantu Affairs Commissioner know him. He speaks often at their elders' meetings and he once gave the white commissioner a headache when he asked many questions about the new land and tax regulations.

Ndara. . . yes, Muronga says to himself. It is a good name—a wise name. But what shall the child's nickname be? Muronga asks himself. Hmm. . . of course. . . the child will be called Mandaha, Muronga decides. It is our custom that a child is given the name of the day of the week it is born on. So, baby Ndara will also be known as Mandaha. Content with his decisions, Muronga waits patiently in his hut as news of the baby's birth spreads quickly from one person to another in the *kraal*. Going about their daily chores of gathering wood, fetching water, and preparing the food for the day, the women exchange greetings and pass on the news of the arrival of the youngest member of the *kraal* and community. After quite some time, Muronga finally hears footsteps approaching. He hopes that it is *Nyina-Karumbu* or one of the other elder women bringing news from the women's hut.

"Child's father? Are you still there?" sings *Nyina-Karumbu*. "I have brought you some food. You must be hungry, since you have no work to keep you busy today."

"Oh, yes, I am here!" Muronga exclaims as he dashes to the door. "Do you need me? What's the news? Is anything wrong?" Opening the door he sees *Nyina-Karumbu's* smiling face and two bowls of steaming food in her hands. "Oh, thank you," Muronga replies as he takes the food from her. "Both my child and I are being well cared for by you good people."

"Everything is fine. The birth is complete. Both the child and his mother are well and sleeping now. Mama Rwenge has said that you can return to the fields tomorrow, and soon your Uncle Ndara will come to see you."

"Very good. I am happy, and I am sure Uncle Ndara will be pleased to have a new namesake," Muronga replies with a broad smile. As the elder woman turns to walk back to the women's hut, Muronga shuts the door. Sitting on a low stool near the now-dead coals from the fire, he dips his fingers first into the bowl of hot porridge, *yithima,* and forming a small lump, he then dips the *yithima* into the meat stew and begins to eat.

Muronga knows that for the time being he will be taken care of by the elder women until Makena is allowed to return to the hut with the baby. She will be confined to the women's hut for a few days, until she is strong again. When the baby's umbilical cord begins to look like it will fall off, preparations will be made to reunite the couple and introduce the child to his father and the other members of the community. Once a woman has rejoined her husband, she can sleep under the same roof with him, but not under the same blanket. For about six weeks after she has given birth the baby sleeps with her and the couple stays apart until the womb has closed up again.

Later in the afternoon, Uncle Ndara, who has just returned from the fields, pays Muronga the expected visit. After consulting his wife on the condition of Makena and the baby, Uncle Ndara, beaming with joy, walks the short distance to Muronga's hut with an unusually quick step. Whistling a traditional children's song, he announces his arrival. Entering the *ghutara*, close to Muronga's hut, he pulls two low stools near each other and seating himself on one, calls to Muronga.

"*Shambushange,* Father of My Namesake, . . . we are here." Stretching leisurely, Muronga walks proudly out of his hut. Uncle Ndara continues, ". . . the women have told me that my namesake is a strong man." Standing up and shaking Muronga's hand, the older man joins him in the *ghutara*. Uncle Ndara pats Muronga on the shoulder as they sit down on the stools. With a twinkle in his eyes he then goes on to say, "I am not sure whether the new man is strong because of his good parents or because he will bear the good name of his wise ancestors. What do you think, Father of the Child?"

"Oh, no. I am sure the child's strength comes from his brave mother and from the one whose name he will bear. The whole village will agree with me."

The two men continue to talk for a while until a young boy, Wetu, who has been sent by Uncle Ndara's wife, comes running to tell Uncle Ndara that there is a visitor waiting for him at his hut. Muronga bids Uncle Ndara good night and returns to his empty hut.

At sunrise the following day Muronga is awake as usual and ready to resume his work and communal responsibilities. As he joins the other men headed for the fields, they greet and congratulate him on the birth of his son. Although they greet him in the same manner as always, Muronga feels their greater respect. He now feels more comfortable in the company of the elder men, who regard him as a man, a father like the rest of them.

After a few more days have passed Muronga is once again on his way to the fields when he meets *Nyina-Karumbu* on the road. She has emerged from the bush where she has gathered a handful of *dishashanogha*, The sticky juice from this aloe plant that is applied to the umbilical cord until it falls off.

"You are up early today, child's father," *Nyina-Karumbu* greets Muronga, looking at the sun on the horizon.

"Yes, and so are you. Did you sleep well? What are you doing out here so early?" He looks knowingly at the bundle of plants in her hands. "How is. . . "

"We are all fine, but we have run out of this good medicine, so I came out to fetch some more. It looks as if the cord will fall off soon and then you will be able to see your child."

"How is he now. . . and his mother?" Muronga asks inquisitively.

"You will see soon enough. Now, I must be getting back to them. We will see you soon."

"Go well, *Nyina-Karumbu*, " Muronga says.

"Work well, child's father," the elder lady replies as she walks swiftly on towards the village. Muronga stops now and then to look back at the receding figure as if to see his wife and child in her.

What *Nyina-Karumbu* has said is indeed good news. He will be happy when Makena comes home again but he knows he must not have sexual contact with her while she is healing. Luckily he has only one wife, otherwise a special ritual would be needed in order to enable him to pursue his normal life with his other wives. Since Makena is his only wife he must remain celibate for the time being. If he does not, his newborn child will become ill, or may even die, and the baby's illness will tell everything about his father's doings and moral behavior. This is *thidhira*.

Once in the fields, Muronga goes about preparing the land for planting. Thinking to himself, he gathers the *mahangu*, the millet stalks from the ground. It is taboo for a man to touch a woman while she is having her period. It is taboo for a woman to ever say her father's name to anyone, or for a man to say his mother's name. This is *thidhira*. It is taboo for a man or woman to sit or sleep where his or her in-laws have slept. This is *thidhira*. It is taboo to swear at a person of the opposite sex; for women to sit on chairs; to discuss sex in public; or to marry without the consent of the elders. This is *thidhira*.

Since there have been no complications during and after the baby's birth, the day after the baby's umbilical cord drops off is chosen as the time for uniting the family and naming the baby. Early in the morning, the young women in the *kraal* begin pounding millet into meal from which porridge will be made, while the young men are sent to fetch wood for the ceremony later in the evening.

When the sun begins to set, all of the married people in the *kraal* assemble in Uncle Ndara's *ghutara*. Meanwhile Uncle Ndara sends for Muronga, who arrives just as the last couples take their places around the fire. At last Uncle Ndara signals one of the elder wives to run and fetch

Mama Rwenge, *Nyina-Karumbu*, Makena's and Muronga's mothers, Makena, and the baby from the women's hut, where they have been waiting. As the group approaches the *ghutara*, Mama Rwenge begins the ululations, which are joined by the women around the fire. Holding the baby as she dances, Mama Rwenge leads the procession of dancing and singing women into the shelter. There they take their places around the fire opposite the men.

Uncle Ndara stands and says, "I am happy that you have all come tonight to meet the youngest member of our family. I rejoice every time we do this. This is how we were all greeted by the older people. Now, where is the person whom we are receiving into this big world?"

Mama Rwenge hands him the baby to whom he says, "You are my namesake. Your name is Ndara. . . the name I was given by your ancestors. This is a well-respected name. Respect this name and never bring shame upon it." Then he looks into the faces of the attentive group and says loudly, "You have heard me charge this child with honoring the name of my grandfather. It is your duty also to see that he keeps this pledge. And to you, his parents, who are responsible for raising him for all of us, I say, this child is the spirit of our ancestors and a gift from the God of Our Forefathers." Sitting down on a chair, he hands the baby to his wife. She rocks the baby in her arms and blesses the child before passing him on to Makena's father. He closes his eyes tightly, and with the baby in his arms, prays so that only his lips can be seen moving. After a few moments he passes the baby on to his wife who blesses it and then hands it to Muronga's mother. After singing a short song to the baby she blesses it and hands the child to her husband who dances the warrior dance with it before giving it to his son, Muronga, the child's father. When the child is put into Muronga's arms for the first time, the crowd rises in ululation and dancing while the women sing a rain song, a symbol of life.

Everyone eats and talks until quite late. Baby Ndara is asleep in Makena's arms when Mama Rwenge comes to escort the young parents to their hut. The welcoming fire is already burning and she reminds them, "Do not hesitate to call me if you need me." She blesses Muronga, Makena and the new baby one last time, then leaves them for the night. Alone together again, Muronga and Makena are too tired to say much more than, "Good night. . . sleep well," before they retire to their beds. With the baby cuddled in her arms, Makena falls asleep on the mat near the fire. In the glowing light of the fire, Muronga watches the sleeping mother and child. The fire soon dies down. Unable to see them, Muronga finally falls asleep.

"Are you coming with me *Nyina-Mandaha*?" asks Muronga, addressing Makena by her newly acquired title as Mandaha's mother. He washes his face from a bowl of water under the shade of his *ghutara*.

"Coming with you where?" she responds, half-surprised, her hands on her hips. She has put Mandaha to sleep on a little mat under the *ghutara* and speaks softly so as not to disturb the sleeping infant. "I said, where do you want me to go with you? And why are you washing your face this time of the day?"

"Oh, I thought that you might want to come with me to Pangandjira's hut, in the headman's *kraal*. When I left early this morning, I went to his *ndjambi*. There were fifteen of us who went in canoes to the islands to cut grass and reeds for his hut. Now we are going to sit together and drink. The other men are bringing their wives and I thought it would be good for us to go together. It has been a long time since we went to things like this together. I am sure the other people would like to see you carrying the baby. It's not far from here. You know where the headman lives. It is four *kraals* from here," he continues. "And you know, Tawa, Pangandjira's wife makes excellent beer. She is the woman Mama Rwenge talks about all the time. Let's go and spend time with other people. Then you don't have to cook dinner tonight, hey?"

"You are such a good man! Or should I say you know how to make a woman happy?"

"Come on, woman. Are you saying you don't want to come?"

"Oh, no, I am coming. I have not been out for a long while. It will be good to take Mandaha for a walk too."

"Yes, as long as he doesn't cry and want to be given beer. Can you imagine a night with a drunken baby?" They both laugh loudly, teasing each other as they prepare to leave.

Makena picks up Mandaha. The baby starts to cry and Muronga plays with his fingers. His wife rocks the baby in her arms and hums a baby's song close to the baby's ear. Mandaha falls asleep again. Makena hands the child to her husband and walks over to a small mono tree. She selects several large leaves and lays them one on top of the other, making a small pad. She picks another handful and, as she is arranging them in a stack, she enters the hut. She returns with a large dark piece of cloth to where Muronga is waiting. With two of the straps from the fabric she carefully ties the cloth around her waist and spreads the pad of leaves against her left hip. Muronga gently places Mandaha against her back as she leans forward. Pulling one of the remaining straps over her right shoulder and the other under her left arm, she makes a baby pouch in which Mandaha will ride comfortably during the short walk. The three then start out for the headman's *kraal*.

After they have walked past three *kraals*, they begin to hear voices speaking in loud conversation. There are many people gathered there already. They walk faster, wondering if they are not too late for the occasion.

"Listen, *Nyina-Mandaha*, can you hear the noise? I told you that Tawa makes good beer. By the sounds of it, people are getting happy already. One or two cups of that woman's beer can knock you down in no time!"

"Are you talking from experience, child's father? And when did that happen to you? I hope long before you met me."

"I heard from older men. You know that I was not allowed to drink alcohol before I became a man and before you married me," Muronga laughs softly, touching the baby's forehead that hangs out on Makena's side.

"I am just teasing. I know that my family would not have consented to our marriage if you were seen drunk before."

When they arrive under the *ghutara* where the others are assembled and drinking, there is a happy mood all around. Everyone is talking about cattle, marriages, deaths, future rains, elopements, births, and love stories. The women are together on one side of the *ghutara* while the men are on the other. Makena joins the side of the women and Muronga spots Kaye who came earlier to partake, even though he didn't go to the islands to help in the morning. It was not uncommon for people to go for the drinks only, with the understanding that next time they would participate in the work.

"How are you, lazy man?" Muronga says in greeting to his friend Kaye, taking a seat on the ground next to him.

"Oh, I am fine. Why do you call me lazy? Because I did not go to the islands this morning or what? I knew you went and I knew that there would be plenty of beer here. No, I am joking. I did bring my part. I brought three bundles of grass from what I had left over from building my new hut."

"Oh, yes, I remember. I was beginning to wonder why you were looking so comfortable if you didn't bring any contribution. How is everything?"

"Everything is going well, as you can see on these elderly people's faces. The beer is very good, for small chests like yours and mine. Do you see the young man behind the headman, there by the pillar in the corner? He just emptied two cups in a row, and see how he is now. We could all leave now and I bet that he would not hear us."

"His head must be spinning very fast," Muronga responds, laughing audibly.

"Muronga, you are here," shouts the *muhindi*, who is busy serving. "I was wondering what happened to you. The first cup here is for you, my friend. Did you bring your wife with you?"

"Yes, she is sitting behind you, next to Shonge, with the baby on her back!" Muronga shouts back in order not to be drowned out in the loud conversations.

"Good. What, your baby? You are a man then. You get an extra cup for that. You made it. What is the baby's name? Did you name it after me?"

"Ndara,. . . named after my uncle. You know him!"

"Yes, I do. Who does not know Uncle Ndara in this area? Who would not know himself?" he laughs. "Is he here today?"

"I don't know. I am sure you would have seen him. Oh, yes, he is here," Muronga responds, looking around. "He's sitting there beside the headman. On your right!"

"Yes, I see him. How couldn't I?"

"Maybe you are not giving all the cups away!"

"You can say that again. I feel different already, but I am enjoying it!"

Both Muronga and Makena are given their respective cups at the same time. Before Muronga drinks from his, he looks around at the elderly men. He spots Ganiku, an old man to whom he is related through his mother's totem line. He is one elder who Muronga can make traditional jokes about and tease.

"Old man Ganiku, you are sitting there like an owl. Drink from my cup first and take the poison away. I am so happy that you are here. You even have a new shirt on. Where did you get it? Why don't you give it to me? It will look better on me," Muronga shouts at him.

"You are so good to me, Muronga," responds the giddy old man, stretching his hands to take hold of the full cup. "I would be very upset with you if you did not remember me. Oh, the shirt was given to me by my sister's son who just returned from *Thivanda*. He brought us clothes and, as you can see, this shirt and this hat are new," he continues, pointing to the price tags that are still hanging onto the sleeves of the shirt and the front of the hat. Then he takes three long sips, pauses a while and begins to shrug his shoulders rythmically before giving the cup back to Muronga who finishes it.

Suddenly a sharp ululation permeates the crowd. Two women stand up to dance. They are followed by two more. Then three. Then two and then three men. In a while every man and woman has joined in the singing and dancing. Chairs are moved aside to make space for dancing. Kaveto, Wawo and Manyando, three young men in the headman's *kraal*, go to fetch drums. Before long, everyone is dancing under the *ghutara*, the men on one side and the women on the other.

"Is Muronga here?" asks Manyando, looking around and squeezing the *dinongo*, the drum wax, in his hands, before rubbing it carefully on the center of the drum. "Muronga is the best head-drummer in this area. Is he here?"

"Yes, he is here," shouts a young woman who is known to be the best dancer. "I just saw him here. He is really good. Give him the head drum."

Kaye and Manyando carry Muronga to the *ngoma*, tie an ox leather rope around him and the drum and pat him praisefully on the shoulders. The two of them take the other drums. With Muronga in the middle, they begin beating to the song.

Muronga is known for getting carried away by the drum beat when he plays. As soon as the song, the drums and the dancing get fully synchronized, Muronga, his eyes closed as usual, enters the circle with the drum between his legs. Falling onto the ground, he rolls onto his back. His legs in the air, he continues to play. The women surround him, ululating loudly. An old man, Shangoma, who taught Muronga how to play the drum, pours water on Muronga's face. In ritual fashion, the old man takes his jacket off and covers the quivering Muronga with it. Muronga belches, stands up, and without missing a beat, goes back to the rear of the *ghutara* and continues to play.

They dance until late into the dark night. Muronga never tires of playing the drum. It is said that he was given *mbero*, an anti-exhaustion medicine by Shangoma when he was very young. For the rest of the dance, Muronga beats the drum, showing no signs of weariness. His wife and family are very proud of him.

When the dance is over, Muronga walks home with his wife, Uncle Ndara and other kraalmates who cannot stop talking about the wonderful day they have had and Muronga's standing in the community.

"*Wiha-Mbushange*, father of my namesake, do you realize the good words so many people say about you mean something in your life?" Uncle Ndara asks Muronga, walking in front of everyone on the narrow path.

"What does that mean?" replies Muronga.

"When people, particularly old people, have good words to say about someone as young as you, that means your forefathers have plans for you in the future. I can tell you some of the good things that I remember old people saying about a young man. You know our chief Dimbare? He is a young person. Before our people chose him to be chief, my friends and I knew that he was going to succeed his uncle, chief Dimbu."

"Really? I always wondered what happened to the old chief, since he only died a few years ago. According to our customs, a chief stays a chief until he dies. Not so, Uncle Ndara?"

"That is very true. It was always like that. Our people have always been honorable people. A chief who did not rule according to the wishes of his people was dethroned by the people. You see, big people do not like to tell stories that are not good lessons for the young ones. Now that you are big, I can tell you," continues Uncle Ndara, looking about to be sure there is no stranger around.

"Go on," Muronga says.

"Chief Dimbu was very greedy. He wanted everything for himself, and not for his people. When a chief is given the chair, everybody is promised that he is there for the people, not for himself. This one did not listen. As soon as he was in power he became very, very. . . well. . . bad. I don't like to say such things."

"What did he do?" Muronga inquires, inquisitively.

"According to our traditions, a chief could do whatever he wanted. The chief was considered the father of the whole people. But Chief Dimbu did not act like a father. He had a little heart. And he had too many children, too. Sometimes he made people give him cattle even when they were not guilty of any crime. In earlier times, when the chief came to our *kraal* my father or one of the men in our *kraal* gave the chief his wife to take care of him.

When I was a boy, this was a very common practice. It was an honor to give the chief your wife."

"Did you hear that, *Wiha-Mandaha*?" Makena teases Muronga.

"Yes, I did. I would not want to have to give *Nyina-Mandaha* to another man, not even if he was the chief," Muronga says, relieved.

"That is why chief Dimbu was removed. He was so greedy and careless that he expected teachers and church-goers to share their wives with him. They did not like it and finally one of the teachers told the commissioner and a big meeting was held. Strangely, the people agreed with the commissioner and the teachers. It was a very bad experience for the elders. But you see once again, things are not the same anymore. There are some things we have to accept that we do not like. When an old elephant can no longer reach the highest branches, it lets the young stretchy ones do it. And that is why chief Dimbare was elected. The people wanted a chief who could hold a pen. He is good, this man of the pen. He is here for the people whose tongue he speaks. He is very clever and his head is full of ideas. He goes to this thing, this church to speak to the white man's God. He is very strong because he gets his power from our God, *Nyambi*, and from the church God. He knows the white man's tricks. Are you listening, *Wiha-Mbushange*? The elder people used to say good things about him and dream about him, too."

"Uncle Ndara is right. People say many words, good words," two women say, almost in unison.

"You, *Wiha-Mbushange*, were also meant for something special. We don't know what yet, because you are not from the chiefs' clan and you have never gone to school. But one day, these people's words will mean something," Uncle Ndara says with conviction.

Muronga doesn't say anything. He looks straight ahead and continues to walk behind Uncle Ndara. For a long while no one says anything. They get to Uncle Ndara's hut and say good-night to him as they all break up to go to their respective huts.

Back in their own hut, Muronga and Makena both make the fire that lights up their hut and together put the baby to sleep. Staring at the embers of the wood fire, Muronga goes into a daze until his wife shakes him by his nose.

"I am here ... What are you dreaming about? Mandaha is here, too."

"I was just thinking."

"About what? Drums? Not here!"

"No, about the future. And many things."

"Oh, by the way, there is still *thishongero*. We still have to go to the mission to attend classes before we are baptized. Have the drums made you forget?"

"No, no, no, we shall go. We are so far into it now that we may as well finish it."

"You seem to be doubtful about this thing, this Baptism, aren't you? It is you who started it. You dragged me into it."

"Yes, and I have not changed my mind. We are going for classes and we will be baptized. We should go to sleep now. I have to milk the cows tomorrow morning."

"Yes, I need to get some sleep now, too, before this man beside me wakes up. There is just no way to sleep when he is awake," Makena says with a yawn, as she crawls under her blanket while Muronga, from the *kafungo*, watches the fire fade away as the sun does when it leaves the earth before darkness.

CHAPTER 2

On Sunday, Muronga walks along the river on his way to church, alone but for the company he keeps with the animals who live in and by the mighty rushing waters of the Kavango River. Hippos, crocodiles, iguanas, and a host of creatures greet him as he passes by. Walking along the narrow dirt path beside the river, he watches the half-submerged hippos yawn lazily as they bathe in the muddy river. Rustling noises in the underbrush warn Muronga that he is disturbing the many creatures that share their space with him. He stands still and watches as a crocodile dives into the cold water.

The path leads him closer to the river, where he invades the territory of a flock of pelicans who preen themselves in the mid-morning sunlight. The large white birds, and other smaller ones, fly from their perches at the first sign of his presence. Muronga, just as startled as the birds, stops momentarily to watch as they swoop and land on the water, losing themselves in the brilliant reds, pinks and purples of the water lilies. Quickening his steps, he strides on, imagining what life would be like if he were an animal living in the forest.

Suddenly, a silvery lizard scurries across the path in front of him, chased by another one. He jumps back, and lands on a rock. The pain is sharp and he stops to rub his bare foot for a moment before going on. It's good that it wasn't a snake, he thinks to himself. If a *dituruandhira*, the dreaded poisonous treesnake, had crossed his path it would have been an omen of a death in his family. Relieved, he utters to himself, "The God of Our Forefathers be praised," but he realizes that he should be thanking a different God now. The God in the white man's church. He has been going to church regularly for the past few weeks, ever since he and Makena started attending *Thishongero* to get ready for Baptism.

Muronga and Makena have two more catechism sessions to attend before they can be baptized. Only then can they be married in the church. But according to their own customs, Muronga and Makena are already married. They made their wedding vows before the elders, and were anointed as husband and wife. However, the Catholic Church, the only church established in their community, does not recognize tribal unions. Every Sunday the priest repeats the church's stand against such marriages. He calls them heathen unions, or pagan practices, or cohabitation. They are sin in the eyes of the church.

Watching the two playful lizards racing past again, he grins, imagining what they will do when they catch each other. Ah, this is how life should be, Muronga reflects, following the course of the shimmering lizards with his sharp eyes. Free, and without fear or shame. I wish Pater Dickmann and his missionary workers were here to see how life goes on without the church. We were as free and fearless as these lizards before the white people came. We don't need to be ashamed because we take care of one another. But the missionaries see only the sex in our unions. They believe that a man only wants sex when he takes a wife according to our rites. Pater Dickmann says that only after kneeling before the candle-filled altar can a man and woman have God-blessed sex. Otherwise sex is "an act which brings shame". Without the priest's blessing and handshake, sex is sin and the consequences are obvious—Hell!

But Muronga and many of the other churchgoers are not intimidated by the tales told by the priest. He does not believe the stories about the black devil with long nails and long horns. How can a devil who is black be so bad, and not the sweet white angels? Muronga wonders. It is the white missionaries who are bad. Not the black people in our village. It is the missionaries who do not understand the importance of other human beings. We are the people who have souls. We were born once by our mothers. Not only people who have been born by white mothers ought to be respected. The missionaries do not think beyond their long funny hair, he thinks.

Before Muronga knows what has happened, he has arrived at the mission. His father and Uncle Ndara told him how their forefathers and chiefs used to dwell where the mission stands today, and how the white ghosts on oxwagons came and clashed with them. Built on the banks of the Kavango River, with several islands in plain view, Andara Mission was established by the white German missionaries when Muronga's mother's father was a boy. Desiring the most strategic spot for their mission, the missionaries tricked Chief Ndara of the haMbukushu tribe with gifts of guns, mirrors and clothes until he gave them the plot of land on which the mission now stands. Made of bricks from termite heaps and sand, the church and the numerous smaller buildings of the mission are squeezed in against the river bank by the lush green foliage.

Muronga looks around to see if there are any other people arriving. There is no one else in sight. He realizes that the service will not start for awhile. I guess I can go into the church, he says half aloud to himself. He cautiously walks around the church to the main doors which face the river. One of the large wooden doors is open. Not baptized nor being accompanied by a Christian, he is unsure whether or not to enter the church. He climbs up the few steps and hesitantly approaches the open doorway. Pausing, he glances behind him to be sure no one is watching. Peering into the half-lit interior, he dips his fingers into the bowl of holy water by the entrance, just in case someone is looking. Slowly he makes the sign of the cross on his forehead and chest. Cautiously, he takes a few steps forward. Faded by the bright sun, streaks of sunlight pour through the once brightly colored simple stained-glass windows. The fragrant smell of incense mingles with the musty smells of old wood, cold concrete, and candle wax. No one is there. Silently walking up the aisle, his hands pressed together in a gesture of prayer, he kneels piously by the front pew and counts all his fingers and toes three times before getting up. After standing there long enough, he decides to look at one of the pictures of the seven stops on the wall. Flanked by stained-glass windows, the picture shows a bleeding Christ carrying a heavy wooden cross over his shoulder. Its gilded frame has lost its luster. His hands still clasped together, he cannot help wondering how these white people came to be so cruel. Look at this, he says to himself in dismay. And this man is white, too. I don't understand what this man did wrong. Is it any wonder that not many of us want to become Christians?

The missionaries actually confuse the villagers more than they convince them to turn to Christianity. They go to church and do whatever the priest commands them to do because they remember that when the white people came with their red books, they forced everyone to listen to what they called "the Word of God", to the white God from overseas. The missionaries told them that their God of Ages, *Nyambi*, was an evil god and had to be chased away and destroyed with holy smoke. Anyone who did not listen to their Christian laws was tortured and killed "in the Name of God".

Muronga thinks on these things as he sits on a bench near the front of the church. He is not allowed to sit in the pews until he has been baptized. Yes, he thinks, when the white people came, we had the land and they had their red books. Then they started preaching to us and teaching us to hear the words from their Bibles. When we looked around, they had the land and we had the Bible.

Staring at the huge mural of the ascending Christ hanging over the altar, Muronga decides it is best not to question some things that the white people do, let alone resist their power. No, it is too dangerous to resist as our people did in the past. It did no good. White people have guns to shoot fire at the unarmed. Our people were all destroyed as they were about to be converted. Who wants to risk his life now? Muronga remembers the story that is told by some old people who worked in *Thivanda* long ago. Once upon a time, the Hereros, a different group of people who had a different chief, were killed at a church service. The priest was at the altar and huge cardboard boxes that were supposed to be gifts and presents for the new Christians were brought into church. When the priest finally got them to trust him, they relaxed to receive the presents, and the boxes simply opened up. They spat fire, and people died in church. Some old men even tell about a General von Trotha who loved blood. These stories make many people very suspicious about the church.

As the church fills up with parishoners, Muronga slides down to the end of the bench so that Pater Dickmann can see him easily. The service begins. Since Makena is not with him, Muronga says the important prayers very loudly for Pater Dickmann to hear. The priest likes such piety. It is a pity that Muronga cannot yet receive Holy Communion, or he would be the first one at the altar to receive the Host. Muronga is prepared to do anything to show the Father that he wants to be a good Catholic, even though he understands very little of what the priest bombards them with.

After the service, the priest stands at the entrance of the church and shakes hands with his parishioners as they leave. Pater Dickmann's fair skin has become reddish from working around the mission under the scorching African sun. Dressed now, however, in his floor-length black cassock, all Muronga can seen of his pinkness is his balding head and muscular hands. His stomach protrudes as he leans back now and then to wipe the sweat from his forehead and push his glasses on his nose before shaking the next hand. Actually, the priest is checking who did not come to the service. Muronga, having chosen to come out last, shakes the *Muruti's*, the Father's, hand warmly and talks with him since there is no one else waiting.

"Aha . . . What's your name again?" This is the first time Pater Dickmann has taken a personal interest in Muronga. Since he is not a Christian yet, he is still a "lost sheep," a heathen.

"Muronga, *Muruti*. I am attending *Thishongero*."

"Oh, yes, that is right . . . now I remember. You come with that woman you say you want to marry. You don't have a name yet. You will get your names the day you are baptized. And where is the woman now? Is she here? Was she in church today?" he asks in simple Thimbukushu. He tilts his head back, and looking through his glasses, gazes at a group of women who are standing nearby.

"She is not here today, *Muruti*. She . . . uh . . . she . . . ," Muronga stammers.

"Don't . . . don't . . . don't tell me that she gave birth before you have both been baptized," the priest thunders as he shakes his finger threateningly in Muronga's face.

"Uhh . . . yes," he says softly, shuffling his bare feet in the sand. " . . . A few days ago . . . Monday . . . it is a boy . . . " At the thought of his new status as a father, he suddenly lifts his head and boldly looks Pater Dickmann straight in the eye. "The child and his mother are both fine and we are all very happy. I am sorry she could not come with me today."

"But do not forget that you and your woman should come for *Thishongero* soon. Next Thursday I want you both to be here. Understand? And then later I will marry you in the church and I will baptize your child also. You are not married yet, you know?" Pater Dickmann exclaims. Then, glancing at his watch, he turns away and walks off in the direction of the dining room. The conversation has evidently come to an end.

Poised ready to reply, Muronga is left standing alone. He looks around and sees that everyone is going home, and that Pater Dickmann is not coming back. With the sun now high overhead, he begins the long walk back through the forest. All the way home he thinks about what it will be like once he has been baptized and married in the church. Then he will be seen as a man by this priest, and not as something that is lost and not yet found. But he wonders whether he should let the priest baptize his son . . . perhaps that would be going too far.

Lost in his thoughts, Muronga does not notice that the vibrant sun is now swallowed up by gathering dark rain clouds. He quickens his pace as large wet drops hit his forehead. He stops for a moment and breaks a small branch off from a large-leafed tree and holds it over his head. Humming to himself, he hurries through the forest. Small animals run for cover. The faster he walks the heavier the rain becomes. By the time he reaches the edge of the village, the sky is black and roaring. Streaks of lightning shimmer through the thick atmosphere. He drops his tree-umbrella, takes off his shirt, and with it in hand, begins to sprint.

When he arrives home he is drenched. Makena, who is finishing feeding Mandaha, hears her husband's footsteps pounding the wet earth as he approaches the hut. Straightening her simple sleeveless blouse, she meticulously tucks it into her home-made skirt. By this time Muronga has entered the hut. Makena, with the chubby baby in one arm, welcomes him with a smile and without saying a word, hands him a rag to dry himself with.

"Yoh, what a great storm! Let me dry myself before you give me this old man. People will soon start plowing if it continues to rain like this." He shivers and shakes as he closes the door.

"Take your trousers off and give me your shirt, too. Your shorts are on the chair there by the *kafungo*," Makena commands. "Then come and sit here by the fire to warm yourself and tell me about your talk with Pater Dickmann."

"Oh, I took care of him, all right! But he wants to see us soon. Together."

Later, when the rain has stopped, Muronga walks to Mama Rwenge's hut to ask her if Makena can go with him to attend classes at the mission on Thursday. Mama Rwenge agrees with him that since Makena will be fit enough by then, it is better for her to go with him now before planting begins. This suits Muronga well. When they go, Mama Rwenge will look after Mandaha. At other times, Mama Rwenge's most regular assistant as caretaker, Muronga's mother, the quiet, strong, but most caring woman, will also willingly look after the small one. She, too, loves babies dearly. How much more a child from her own son's loins?

Thursday morning, Muronga and Makena are up early. It takes them about two hours to walk to the mission for their *Thishongero*. They arrive with the mission workers who walk miles to the mission every morning. They know white man's time well. The priest and his fellow monasterians are still having breakfast when Muronga and Makena arrive.

After a while Pater Dickmann and the brothers come out of their dining room. They all walk toward the Father's house, except Bruder Goetz who greets the workers and assigns them their jobs for the day. As the workers all go about their work, Muronga and Makena remain alone, seated on the rocks under the *Divuyu*, a huge Baobab tree, in the center of the mission. It was here, right here, under this *Divuyu* tree that my people refused to accept the white man's control, he remembers. And what followed? War, war, war, . . . damn war. But where was all the love and peace they teach us about? Suspended? Forgotten?

Patiently waiting, Muronga sees Pater Dickmann return quickly to the dining room. Only when he comes out again, carrying a book, does he see them. Dressed in a short-sleeved shirt and trousers with suspenders, he puts on his glasses to see clearly. Turning around, he walks towards them.

"Aha, good morning! How did you wake up? Well?"

"Yes, *Muruti*, and how did you wake up?" respond Muronga and Makena simultaneously.

"Listen, wait for me here. I just want to fetch the book of names. And I want to see how many more classes you have to attend before your Baptism." Before he enters the monastery, he looks back and says to them in a loud voice, "Go and wait for me in the church!" Normally, one knows that Baptism is near when the priest changes the place of instruction from under the tree to inside the church. It only confirms what the priest said earlier. They need to attend only two more sessions. This makes them very happy. Like well-fed parrots they can repeat their prayers, the Ten Commandments, the five laws of the Catholic Church, and the rest of the catechism—just as the *Katekete*, the lay religious instructor, and the priest require. Understanding what they are saying does not matter at all.

The priest returns with a thick book and asks a few questions from it. Muronga and Makena get the right answers to all of the questions but one. They have both forgotten who God's representative on earth is. For a while they look down, trying to remember, but they cannot. Nevertheless, Pater Dickmann is satisfied with the rest of their performance, so he smiles broadly and explains it once more.

"I will tell you again. This is very important," he goes on. "God's representative on earth is the Pope, who is sitting in Rome, the holy capital. I told you this before, remember?" They nod their heads. Now they remember. How could they forget? They have been told many times about the Pope. He is the man who wears dresses day and night! Muronga smiles quietly at the thought of this man who looks like a woman, but he says nothing. "And this person, the Pope, cannot make any mistakes. The Pope's laws are binding on all Christians, who are the children of God. This means everybody who is baptized in the church." He tells them more about this person and warns them never to forget what he has told them. "You must always remember that Jesus Christ himself gave the Pope the key to heaven."

Muronga and Makena nod in bewildered agreement as the priest lists the powers of the Holy Father. They haven't the faintest idea about what the Pope is and where Rome is. They cannot even figure out if this "Pope" is male or female. The pictures Pater Dickmann has, show him wearing dresses all the time, as women would, but the priest and *Katekete* speak of him as a man. Maybe the Pope is a she-man, like Shamwaka, the man in the next village, who wears women's clothes and cannot get married, Muronga speculates. But Shamwaka is not the chief. I don't understand how a she-man can be a chief. A she-man could never be a chief, Muronga says to himself. He is tempted to ask the priest or *Katekete* more about the Pope. But he remembers that it was this priest who chased one catechist away from the mission when he asked whether Mary, the mother of Jesus Christ, broke the marriage law by sleeping with the Holy Ghost. That would have explained how Mary got pregnant without sleeping with her man, Joseph. The catechist's question made perfect sense to Muronga, but kept the priest in a bad temper all week long. Muronga decides not to risk asking such dangerously un-Christian questions as, "Is the Pope a man or woman?" for fear that the priest will take it in bad grace.

From that day on they all learned that it was best just to believe what the priest said. They have been taught that believing, or faith, does not necessarily bring understanding. They do not even ask whether the Pope is a white or a black person. He is probably a white man. What else can he be? . . . Like them? No! Impossible! Preposterous!

"Do not ask too many questions about God. God is like 'the wind'," the *Katekete* told them when they first began *Thishongero*. "You will go mad—or be rejected like Satan, the vainglorious Lucifer, was—if you want to understand everything about God." It must be the same with the Pope. Anyway, I don't ever want to meet this person called the Pope—he or she is far too complicated for me, Muronga decides as the priest finishes his litany.

Satisfied that they know enough, Pater Dickmann decides that they are finally ready for Baptism. He announces that they both will be baptized on Sunday. Tomorrow, Friday, they must come early in the morning, as they did today, so that they can rehearse the ceremony.

He also tells them to bring along two people, a man and a woman who are already Christians, to be their godfather and godmother. He explains to them that it is very important for them to have guardians who are already Christians.

Finally he asks them if they have chosen any Christian names for themselves yet. Since they have not, Muronga asks Pater Dickmann if he can assist them in finding two names. It is very difficult for them to choose which names to wear. By tomorrow they should have and know their new names—so the rule goes. Taking out a whole list of names of saints from his book, Pater Dickmann reads through the list while Muronga and Makena keenly observe him. Most of the names sound very difficult, and Muronga and Makena fear that they will not remember any such difficult names. But the few easy ones are too common. Johannes, Thomas, Petrus, Josef, Moses, Andreas, Paulus, Michael, Maria, Veronika, Theresa, Katharina, and the like—are all too common. Every third Christian has one of these names. It is like wearing a mercenary's uniform!

The more names Pater Dickmann reads, the more difficult and confusing it becomes for them to choose "their" names. They simply do not know whether they are coming or going. Pater Dickmann can see that they depend on his direction in such emergencies. He responds impatiently, "Seeing that you cannot decide for yourselves what your names will be, I will give you your Christian names, names of saints. Let us see if we can choose good ones." Both Muronga and Makena smile at the priest while they glance at each other as if they were atoning for their failure to choose the obvious. Everyone is content with this solution.

"That is very good . . . eh . . . very kind of you, *Muruti*," responds Muronga. "Give us any . . . eh . . . our names. We thank you."

The priest runs through the list of names with his fountain pen.

"Now, I have found two good names for you. You are Franziskus, and you are Maria-Magdalena," the priest bellows, pointing at Muronga and Makena as he says the names. "Good names, hey ... saints' names!"

"Yes, they are very nice. Can you repeat them please, *Muruti?*" Muronga asks hesitantly.

Pater Dickmann repeats their names and has Muronga and Makena repeat them after him.

"Franziskus, is my name."

"Maria ... hmm ... Magdalena is my name!" The *Muruti* nods in agreement as they say their names. Excited about their new names, Muronga and Makena no longer feel the strain of the long session. When the Angelus bells ring, they say the Lord's Prayer seven times with the priest. "Don't forget to come back tomorrow," says Pater Dickmann.

"We will come back, *Muruti.* We cannot forget." On their way home, they talk of nothing but their Baptism, and their son Mandaha. They both wonder what the boy's new name will be when he is baptized.

"Do you remember your name, *Wiha-Mandaha?*" asks Makena.

"Eh, yes, I do. My name is Fiasco, right? And yours? Yours was longer than mine. What is it again?"

Makena is not sure at all. "I remember the first part, Maria . . . but I have forgotten the rest of it. You . . . can you remember? You are cleverer than I am. You men are used to these white people's names. Come on, tell me my name. Please, my darling."

Muronga looks proudly at his wife. "Who says I am cleverer than you? Who brought Mandaha into this world?

Not you? What could make me cleverer than you, child's mother?" he says. "Well, I also cannot remember it. It is a jaw-breaker. It sounded like . . . the piece of iron that pulls other pieces of iron to itself. You remember that thing our friend Wetu once brought back with him from *Thivanda*. It is called . . . magnet . . . yes, something like that."

"Yes'" Makena interrupts. "My name is Maria-Magnet. I remember now!"

"That's right!" exclaims Muronga. "But mine is not a nice name; it has no meaning. Yours has attraction in it. What on earth does 'Fiasco' mean? I wish I had a better name."

Once they are home again, Muronga and Makena tell everybody that they will be baptized on Sunday and that they already have been given new names, Fiasco and Maria-Magnet. The other people forget the names as soon as they have heard them. They are only Sunday names, anyway. At home they will still be Muronga and Makena, or, since their child's birth, simply *Wiha-Mandaha* and *Nyina-Mandaha*, Father and Mother of Mandaha.

The other village people are excited about the child and uninterested in the Baptism. After all, the villagers are suspicious about the white people and their church. It is these church people, the white people, who have dislocated their lives. They have forbidden many activities in the village, and they call their forefathers "servants of the devil". The *nganga*, the priest says, is an evil man who must be avoided. However, Muronga and many other villagers have more faith in the nganga than in the priests. These white people have all kinds of medicine, but say that ours is evil, he thinks. Why can they not see sense in our medicines? We use the same trees and herbs, don't we? Furthermore, the priest keeps telling us that we need to be born again. Very funny! How can a man like me be born again? I have a son, Mandaha, but even he, so young, is born only once. It is the spirit that lives on after we die. Our ancestors are with us in spirit, but not reborn! These are the doubts that plague the villagers and hinder them in their commitment to Christendom.

Before sunset Muronga must go and fetch wood from the forest. The baby and its mother need to be kept warm in the night. There also must be enough wood to keep the hut lighted at night, when the child's bottom needs to be wiped, or when the child needs medical attention. It is generally a scandal if a man's wife does not have *mbyata*, marks on the inner thighs and legs caused by sitting close to a burning fire. It is a clear indication that the man is lazy, and there is not enough wood to keep her warm and loved. *Mbyata*, and if a woman is fat, shows that she is obviously happily married.

While Muronga is chopping wood in the forest, Makena is expected to attend to the day's supper. But now that she has this newcomer, Muronga's sister, Kahambo, helps prepare all the meals. In fact, Makena is not supposed to do any strenuous work until she is strong again. The other members of the *kraal* are responsible for her. They work for her, just as she would work for them if they were in her situation.

Finally, Sunday, the day of the Baptism dawns. Makena awakens early and begins to prepare the meat from the goat that Muronga slaughtered the previous day. Preparing the meat with herb seasoning and water, she cooks it in a three-legged clay pot over a wood fire.

They have forgotten their names again, even though Pater Dickmann reminded them again on Friday. This morning, Muronga, Makena, and all those in their *kraal* who are already baptized, and other friends, walk to church. The baby is left with its grandmother. It gives the old lady great joy to play with her daughter's son. She talks to her grandson as if she were talking to an adult. She tells him the history of his lineage, sings songs to him, asks him questions which she herself answers in baby-tongue, dances with him, weeps with him, teaches him all about life.

They have to walk a long distance, past ten *kraals* to get to the mission—but much less than the longer distances they walk when they visit some of their friends and relatives. When they start walking they hear the first church bells ring, a warning that the service is to begin in an hour or so. They walk faster—Muronga in front, followed by Tweya, then Tjapi, Mbamba, and all the women one after the other. When they walk past the fourth *kraal* on their way, they are joined by Heinrich, and Johanna, Muronga and Makena's godparents.

Not long after they have arrived at the mission the bells chime a second time. They are seated on rocks under the Baobab tree waiting and watching as other churchgoers arrive. Muronga and Makena remember what the priest told them. They must wait outside the church with their godparents until all the others have entered.

"Should we wait at the big door at the back, or. . . ?" asks Muronga, hesitantly.

"Yes," replies Makena, "but we must wait until all these teachers and other people are inside. I am too shy to be seen by all these well-dressed people. It looks as if they come to church to show us poor people how rich they are. We poor people feel left out here. They have newer clothes. They even have shoes and we do not. What I need to get is this Baptism of theirs; that's all. I am not even sure if I will come to church often. Or can the priest debaptize you if you don't do your . . . eh?" Makena queries. "Then, does God denounce you as unborn, maybe send you back into your mother's stomach or what happens? What kind of father denounces his children? I cannot imagine doing that to Mandaha. Maybe that is how white people are . . . oh, . . . what a mess."

"You are not supposed to speak words like these on the day of your Baptism; it is not good," interrupts Faustus, an elderly-looking Christian who comes to church every Sunday.

The others are silent on the matter. They frankly do not know anything about debaptism, but the mere thought of it is very frightening. The other people with whom Muronga and Makena have come, leave them with their godparents and join the crowds in the church building. The godfather, Heinrich, suggests that all four of them go and wait by the church door.

As they move towards the door, *Katekete* Nikodemus in his brilliant red gown meets them halfway. He greets them all with a welcoming handshake. "Do you feel excited that you are about to become children of God?" the *Katekete* asks them with a broad smile on his shiny face. You can see he has walked a long distance. The sweat on his face is still drying up. He is a good-looking man—he looks very respectable in his red church gown. He is almost a black priest.

"Yes, *Katekete*, we are very happy to be receiving the Holy Sacrament of Baptism today. We are just about to be b-b-born again." Muronga nods his head and smiles woodenly at the *Katekete* like a puppet on a string. He knows how to give the right answers, at the right time.

The *Katekete* is very impressed with Muronga's well thought-out reply.

"Jesus Christ, but you know your Bible, my friend—and your memory is fantastically good. That means that we have taught you well, is that not true?" The *Katekete* pats Muronga on the shoulder. Then turning to Makena, he asks, "Do you also remember everything so well, eh?"

"Yes, *Katekete*, but perhaps not so well as *Wiha-Mandaha* does. He helps me every time I forget something that you have taught us," she answers, looking at her husband proudly.

"That is not true, *Katekete*," intervenes Muronga. "I do not know of any other woman who is as clever as *Nyina-Mandaha*. She is just praising me because I am her husband. But she certainly has better brains than I have. I often think that God gave her to me ... "

"Very good that you know these things. Oh, excuse me," says the *Katekete*, interrupting himself. "I think it is time for us to go in. Father is ready to start the Mass." Entering from the back of the church and walking nervously down the aisle, Muronga and Makena sit down on the front bench reserved for them. Behind them sit all of the women on one side and the men on the other. The *Katekete* goes through a side door into the Sacristy.

It is absolutely quiet in the church. Merely coughing makes a person feel guilty, for everyone looks in the direction of the disturbing noise. Everyone is seated. Suddenly the bell rings and the priest, in his immaculate white dress over a black dress, led by pious-looking altar boys dressed in white skirts and red blouses, emerges from the Sacristy. They all proceed slowly toward the beautifully decorated altar. The altar bears six tall, glowing candles and a thick paschal candle in the center. "Alpha and Omega, 1966" is inscribed on the paschal candle in vibrant colors.

Before they reach the altar, they all kneel and rise in front of it. Meanwhile, the congregation has risen in deference to the orders of the Church. The priest and his altar boys walk slowly in a colorful procession down the aisle to the main door while the priest sprinkles the congregation with Holy Water. During this time the congregation, led by the priest himself, sings *Asperges me*. Returning down the aisle, the priest and the altar boys take their places around the altar. The priest then leads the congregation in the usual repetitive responsorial Latin prayers.

"*In Nomine Patris et Filii, et Spiritus Sancti.*"
"*Amen.*"

"*Introibo ad altare Dei.*"

"*Ad Deum qui laetificat juventutem meam.*"

"*Adjutorium nostrum in nomine Domini.*"

"*Qui fecit caelum et terram.*"

"*Confiteor.*"

Then the priest and the congregation pray together,

"*Deo omnipotenti, beatae Mariae semper virgini . . . ,*" followed by the *Kyrie eleison.*

The congregation, accompanied by the pianist Venantius, sings a hymn before the priest resumes.

"*Gloria in excelsis Deo!*"

The congregation, accompanied by the priest, prays loudly,

"*Et in terra pax hominibus bonae voluntatis. Laudamus te. Benedicamus te. Adoramus te. Glorificamus te. . . . Qui sedes ad dexteram Patris, miserere nobis. Quoniam tu solus Sanctus. Tu solus Altissimus, Jesu Christe. Cum Sancto Spiritu, in gloria Dei Patris. AMEN.*"

Muronga keeps score on which responses he gets and misses. He knows most of the short responses, but the long ones are too difficult to remember. To show Pater Dickmann that he has learned the prayers, he moves his lips everytime there is a response to what the priest says, even if he does not know the words.

Everyone who has been baptized and spent some time at the mission knows the Latin prayers by heart, but they do not understand what they say in the prayers. What everybody knows is that people respect you if you can join in the prayers. It gives you a feeling of achievement, too, when you can speak other people's languages. Reciting the prayers resembles the rituals conducted by the *nganga* in the village. He also speaks in tongues very often. He is the only one who understands what he utters—if he understands himself at all. During the church prayers the alter boys look different, like little angels—if angels were black—even divine. Only their heads, bowed in prayer and mystic devotion, can be seen. They beat their chests again and again saying, *Mea culpa, mea culpa, mea maxima culpa.*

The *Katekete* steps forward, reads the *Epistola* and says, "This is the Word of the Lord," and everybody answers, "*Gloria tibi, Domine.*" Then Pater Dickmann read-sings the Evangelium, after which Muronga starts to say, "*Kyrie Eleison*" as the congregation responds, "*Laus tibi, Christe.*" The priest smiles at the congregation, focusing on the baptismal candidates.

"*In nomine Patris, et Filii, et Spiritus Sancti,*" he says.

"Amen." The parishioners reply, making the sign of the cross on their faces and chests. One of the regular churchgoers, old man Claudius, is known to all the parishioners for his ability to sleep through the service. Vaguely disoriented, he still manages to awaken just in time to say " Amen" very loudly.

Standing in front of the altar, Pater Dickmann continues with the homily.

> My dear Christians and heathens, we have just heard from the Big Word of God how important it is that every person be born again; born again in the Holy Spirit, and baptized in the Fire. We know that you were all heathens and savages, who were doomed before the missionaries came. The *ngangas* and witchdoctors were leading you on the road to hell

to meet the devil, until these missionaries, these priests who were sent by God to do their wonderful godly works came. They were inspired and blessed by God. Now, those of you who have turned to the Holy Catholic Church have been made white and purified in the blood of Jesus Christ. You have received the Holy Sacrament of Baptism and are now as white as snow. You have become children of God. The two people who are to receive this Sacrament are about to enter the ranks and become members of the rich Christian family—the beloved children of God the Almighty. All the saints are speaking to God on our behalf so that we will join them in heaven. God does not listen to those of you in the villages who give offerings to your forefathers, for He does not know your forefathers. Pray that the saints, Holy Johannes, Holy Nikodemus, Holy Franziskus, Holy Maria-Magdalena, and the others, will pray to God for us. Before one receives the Holy Sacrament of Baptism, one is a lost sheep. It is very, very important to be baptized. Tell all the people in the village to stop playing their drums and come to church where God is waiting for us all. . . . . . Amen. *In nomine Patris, et Filii, et Spiritus Sancti.*

Katekete Nikodemus emerges from the sacristy again and beckons to the candidates to come forward and kneel. "Dear Christians and heathens," he says, "the two persons here in front of us, are today receiving the Holy Sacrament of Baptism. As we know, they are now becoming children of God. We will now stand as they repeat the holy baptismal vows."

Everyone rises with great enthusiasm to say the vows and see the candidates. Muronga and Makena and their godparents also rise. The altar boys bring the holy water and the white baptismal cloth to the priest who comes closer to the candidates. It is an occasion for reminiscing for those who have been through the ritual before. Those who are considered heathens cannot help but envy the white-becoming Muronga and Makena.

"Do you renounce the devil and all his evil deeds?"

"We do."

"Do you believe in God, the Father Almighty, Creator of Heaven and Earth; and in Jesus Christ, His only Son our Lord, who was born and suffered for us; in the Holy Spirit, the Holy Catholic Church, the Communion of Saints, the Forgiveness of Sins, the Resurrection of the Body, and Life Everlasting?"

"We do."

The priest takes the water and baptizes them by pouring the water on their foreheads, saying, "Franziskus, I baptize you in the name of the Father, and of the Son, and of the Holy Spirit. Maria-Magdalena, I baptize you in the name of the Father, and of the Son, and of the Holy Spirit."

It is an exciting moment for both Muronga and Makena. They have never experienced such silent ovation in all their lives. When they got married before the elders, only a few people were there, and all those present knew each other very well. On their wedding day, they felt it was their own celebration, whereas here the exposure makes the occasion feel more like a spiritual crisis. Muronga cannot help but wonder if he is the only one who does not believe in this transformation. Maybe the other Christians believe, he thinks.

After the baptismal ritual, the organist Venantius leads the congregation in the usual baptismal hymn, and everyone who knows it sings ostentatiously.

Ghundambo ghoDiyoghero	(The Bond of Baptism
ghu kare kate kufa.	must stay till death.
Na wana me ndhira dhomoyo,	I have found the way to life,

noneke noruvigha.	I have found mercy and blessings.
Nyambi na kukanderera,	I entreat you, my God,
kuNkirshe dhoye ghuna nitha,	not to let me leave your Church
mbadi mbo ni dhi mwagha.	to which you have called me.)

The Holy Mass proceeds as usual. The congregation says the Apostolic Creed, the Lord's Prayer, the Sanctus, the Agnus Dei, and all the other prayers. The Holy Communion is received by those who are already baptized and who went to Confession yesterday, Saturday afternoon. The service ends. Matheus, old man Claudius' young nephew, nudges his uncle to awaken him.

"*Dominus vobiscum.*"

"*Et cum spiritu tuo.*"

"*Benedicat vos omnipotens Deus: Pater, et Filius, et Spiritus Sanctus.*"

"Amen."

Fully awake now, old man Claudius chimes in with his last Amen for the week.

"*Requiescant in pace.*"

"*Deo gratias.*"

As the people leave the church, Muronga and Makena are congratulated by people both known and unknown to them, some of whom, it seems, expect them to actually look white, or at least different from everyone else. In some ways it feels good to be in the limelight, though Makena, in particular, does not really enjoy such visibility. Almost everyone who comes to shake their hands wants to know what their Christian names are, and they must say everytime, "Franziskus and Maria-Magdalena." Thank

God Pater Dickmann reminded them of their names when he baptized them a couple of minutes ago.

Knowing that Pater Dickmann would like to congratulate them personally on their new achievement, Muronga and Makena approach him as he waits outside the church, chatting to better-known Christians and the new priest who is introduced to the parishioners as the small *Muruti*. Turning towards them, he says in a booming voice, "Na, Franziskus and Maria-Magdalena; be good Christians, all right? Next step, marriage in church, all right? Promise me that you are going to leave all pagan practices, all right? Understand? Happy?" At the same time he pulls them together like children and gives them a pat on their shoulders.

"Oh, yes, *Muruti*. We aspire to be married by you in the church . . . very soon . . . whenever you . . . authorize it. It was so nice today," reiterates Muronga.

With a broad smile, Pater Dickmann bids them good-bye. "So, go well and show all of the other heathens the way to church. Now, don't forget your names, and remember, there are many other sacraments waiting for you," Pater Dickmann says with a patronizing smile.

"Good-bye, *Muruti*. We will try our best," comes a spontaneous response from Muronga and Makena simultaneously, happy to have this Baptism behind them. Now that it is out of the way, they can deal with other problems.

To *Katekete* Nikodemus who comes to congratulate them, Muronga says, "My wife, Mak . . . Maria-Magdalena has prepared some food for our friends who came to our Baptism. It will be nice if you can come, too. Maybe you can pray for us there."

"Very good, thank you. Where do you live? In which village? Who is your kraalhead?"

"Our village is Kake; our kraalhead is Ndara. It is not very far from here."

"Oh, I know where it is. I will be there when the sun sits halfway after midday."

Walking home with the same group of people they came with, they start talking about the baptismal ceremony as soon as they leave the mission premises. One of Muronga's friends who has just attended church for the first time, asks Muronga why the priest was angry and swore at the congregation as soon as he walked into the church. At first Muronga and the other regular churchgoers are puzzled by their friend's question until he asks, "Didn't the priest say *'Dominus vobiscum'*, just like old Johannes does every time he gets angry . . . like when one of his goats runs away, or when he fights with his wife?" Bursting into uncontrolled laughter, the group of friends then understands what he is talking about. Before anyone can explain to him, however, that when Pater Dickmann uses Latin in church he is not swearing, dark clouds can be seen gathering overhead. It will begin to rain soon. Walking swiftly now, the churchgoers soon arrive back in the village and, entering the *kraal*, they go quickly to their respective huts after Muronga reminds them to come to their *ghutara* for lunch in a short while.

Makena reheats the meat which she had cooked in the morning and prepares a thick millet porridge which is eaten with a meat sauce. Muronga, who meanwhile has been playing with Mandaha, takes a few steps outside the gates of the *kraal* to look at the receding rain clouds and spots Pater Dickmann approaching in the distance. Clutching Mandaha tightly in his arms, he sprints back to his wife.

"Quick! . . . Where's Uncle Ndara?" he stammers, somewhat out of breath. "*Muruti* is here! I just saw him on the road, and I am sure he is coming to see us." He looks nervously in every direction.

"So?" Makena replies calmly, "Let him come . . . the food is ready. He is welcome to eat with us." Makena gently takes the fussing baby from her husband's arms.

In a low, strained voice, Muronga retorts, "You don't understand! He is coming to . . . ," but before he can finish what he is saying, Pater Dickmann and the younger unknown white man are led into the *kraal* by a couple of schoolboys. The young white man, a newly arrived priest, is introduced to Muronga as Uncle Ndara and the other villagers begin to arrive. *Katekete* Nikodemus, who seems somewhat awkward about *Muruti's* presence, also arrives. He shakes hands with everyone before he sits on a stool next to Pater Dickmann in the *ghutara*. When Makena comes to greet them, the young priest, who still does not know that women in the village do not sit on chairs, offers his chair to her. Momentarily nonplussed by his rudeness, Makena walks away to finish preparing the food.

With the baby now securely strapped on her back, Makena fills two large wooden bowls, one with meat sauce and the other with millet porridge, and places them on the ground as the men gather around them, sitting on low wooden stools. She fills two more bowls and places them near the children who sit quietly together on the ground. On mats, the women gather around the cooking pots, from which they will eat.

Uncle Ndara, who immediately sent a couple of boys off to fetch two more stools for the white guests, beckons them to join the assembling group of men. The young priest, following the lead of Uncle Ndara and the other men, who carefully pick up a wad of porridge with their fingers and dip it into the meat sauce before eating it, digs his whole hand enthusiastically into the hot porridge, burning himself. Undaunted, he shakes his scorched hand for a few moments, and on the second attempt, manages to pick up the hot porridge and meat sauce, dribbling a little of the sauce down his chin and onto his clean white shirt. Pater Dickmann, declining the offer to join in the eating replies, "Not now, thank you. I will eat with you on the day Franziskus' baby is baptized." Then, pointing his finger at Muronga, he demands, "Did you hear me, Franziskus?" Muronga, having heard Pater Dickmann's words the first time, continues eating but nods his head and smiles. Trying not to stare, the other men, women and children cannot understand Pater Dickmann's rude refusal to eat with them, nor the young priest's bad eating manners.

As soon as the meal is over, Pater Dickmann, somewhat embarrassed by the younger priest's behavior, asks Muronga if he can take him and his companion in his *wato*, a large dugout wooden canoe, to see the islands that separate the waters of the Kavango River.

"I don't think Muronga should go away from his guests here," half-whispers Muronga's godfather to Uncle Ndara.

"Yes, you are speaking the truth. He cannot go. I will take the *Muruti* . . . in my own *wato*," says Uncle Ndara. Without hesitation, Uncle Ndara fetches his canoe paddle and leads the men to where his *wato* lies waiting on the bank of the rushing river. Untying the restraining rope from a low tree branch, Uncle Ndara instructs his two passengers to get into the *wato* carefully, and they set off in the direction of the islands.

While the women are busy cleaning up after the meal, they joke and gossip about the unexpected guests until Uncle Ndara appears a short while later, his trousers soaking wet and his jacket dripping. Shaking his head and muttering to himself, he exclaims loudly, "Yoh! These white people! They don't know how to greet one another, they don't know how to eat. Nothing!" Then, throwing his canoe paddle on the ground in disgust, he continues, "Look at me. Just look at me! I am soaking wet. This young white boy . . . all he wanted to do was to make pictures of the birds with that picture-making box of his. I warned him not to move about in the *wato* or we would capsize. He can't even swim. It's a good thing we all didn't drown! They were too ashamed to come back here and went to their mission. They said you boys must follow them now," Uncle Ndara says to the small boys who had accompanied the priests into the *kraal*. "White people are like children. They want everything to be easy. When I worked far away in the mines, we black men did the hard work while they lazed around and told us what to do. They are afraid to do hard work. It is as if they think they would melt. I just don't know what they would do without black people. It is good for our young men to go and work for the white man. Then you see how they live. Then you understand why these two behave like this. Tell me, you mission boys," Uncle Ndara asks the boys before they leave. "What do you eat at the mission? Do these white people eat with you?"

"No, they eat inside the rooms," one of the boys answers. "We eat outside. And they do not eat the food we eat. It's only for us and the dogs. They have different food that the sisters cook. We're not allowed to eat it." Still mumbling discontentedly, Uncle Ndara heads towards his hut in the center of the *kraal,* while the other villagers shake their heads in amused disbelief.

Kaye, Muronga's friend from the next *kraal,* who never goes to church, walks slowly towards Muronga. He is also amused. "Muronga, what happened to you at the mission that made these white people come? You say you have been washed clean? Why? With what? I don't see any change in you."

"Yes, I have been baptized . . . washed of my . . . sins. But don't let it worry you. I have not changed. It is the white man's thing, you see."

Kaye's eldest brother, Rumapa, who likes to count his cattle on his fingers and toes every night also approaches them with a smile, saying, "It is nice to see white people. They need to be helped—to eat, to go to the river, everything. When are they coming again?"

"They don't come here often," replies Muronga. "They only come here when they want to see something. Anyway, they are gone now. Come, my friends, let's forget about them and enjoy ourselves," Muronga says patting his friends on their shoulders.

As the lunch guests are beginning to depart, Muronga's godfather asks him when he thinks Mandaha will be baptized. He replies, "Well, Ndara will be baptized in the near future. Whether or not it is the best thing to do to the boy, I don't know. I have difficulty with not being a heathen myself. Even though I am now baptized, I am, and will remain, what I was—true to my family, true to my forefathers, and true to my land—not to the saints, I am afraid. I would not want to evict another man from his land by baptizing him. If this makes me more of a heathen than a Christian, then I would prefer to be a baptized heathen. After all, I haven't changed. I am still myself. I am still black . . . and black shall I die."

There is a moment of silence as everyone digests Muronga's words before bidding him and his wife goodbye.

CHAPTER 3

During the two weeks that follow the Baptism, Muronga and Makena attend three more catechism classes to prepare for the church wedding.

The *Katekete* reviews Muronga and Makena's earlier lessons, then lectures them on the meaning of their marital vows. Muronga's marriage to Makena is like Jesus Christ's marriage to the church, he explains.

Now, now, wait, Muronga thinks, wincing momentarily as the *Katekete* goes on to explain further. We've heard enough of these fairy tales. Jesus' wife is the church, a building. That would be like me marrying my hut. My hut? What does he. . . . ? Makena seems equally puzzled, and glances shyly at her husband. But for fear of the repercussions, they stifle their desire to express their curiosity and disbelief. Before the *Katekete* dismisses them, he asks them if they understand. Together they reply, "Oh, yes. Yes, *Katekete*. You explain things very well. We understand. We will remember everything."

After bidding the *Katekete* good-bye, they walk silently for some while along the road to the village. Makena, walking steadfastly behind Muronga on the narrow sand path, finally breaks the silence. "Yoh, *Wiha-Mandaha*, you know they say that we are not married yet. So you still have time to marry a hut if you want to!" She tugs playfully on his shirt from behind. "What do you say, young man?" she jokes.

Muronga stops short and laughs aloud. "Well, I was thinking about it. And what will you marry, a tree?" Muronga gently taps her on her full breast. "There certainly would be no Mandaha if we did that!"

"Now I can see why the priests have no wives and the sisters no husbands," Makena says. "They are married to their houses. But how does it work? The house cannot cook, cannot take care of the others in the village, cannot bear children! Maybe these white people do not understand that you need to marry a person to have children."

"And imagine you sleeping every night with a tree!" Muronga adds, winking at Makena.

This discussion consumes their thoughts as they walk toward the village. Before they know it, they have arrived home. Still laughing as they enter their hut, they agree that it would be best not to tell the other villagers why the white people at the mission have no children. With thoughts of their own child, Makena goes to fetch Mandaha from Mama Rwenge. Makena then resumes her daily tasks and Muronga his.

A couple of days later, Muronga and Makena find themselves sitting in the church listening to the *Katekete's* lecture on sex in marriage. Muronga and Makena attentively listen as he explains how they, after the church wedding, will have God-blessed sex. "After the priest marries you, you will have God's permission to have sexual intercourse. If you have already slept with each other you have sinned. You are sinners in the eyes of God. This is the biggest sin you can commit." *Katekete* Nikodemus has gradually moved towards them until they can feel the heat of his breath in their faces. Confused and startled, they scoot backwards on their bench, until they are almost falling over backwards. "The penalty for that is eternal fire!" he bellows at them.

Does this mean I will go into the eternal fire after only one year of living with my child's mother? Muronga wonders.

Makena, too, thinks about her fate after the elders had blessed their union. Dear Mother, she thinks, I could suffer the flames of the eternal fire, but what about Mandaha, my child?

Muronga wonders whether his elders misled him when they made Makena his wife. No, he says to himself, that cannot be possible. They blessed us. I know. I will pray to our forefathers.

"It is very important for you to remember that you cannot have sexual intercourse more than three times a night. Only three times, because there are only three persons in God. The Father, the Son, and the Holy Spirit. After the third time, it is sin. If you have sex more than one, two, three times, you must go to the priest to confess. This is important. Sex is for procreation only. God said, go and multiply!"

Again, they do not dare to question the *Katekete*, but leave the mission the way they came, totally bewildered. Back in the village, Muronga and Makena feel relieved that this is the last session they have to attend. And they are anxious to get the church wedding behind them.

Standing on the steps in front of the main entrance to the church, Muronga, Makena and a few of their Christian friends wait for Pater Dickmann after the wedding service. Behind them, purple bougainvillea cover the brick facade of the chapel. Above the arched wooden door a small metal cross glints in the sunlight.

Except for a few minor differences in the ceremony, Muronga and Makena's wedding was identical to their Baptism. As expected, Pater Dickmann gave them rings which he had quickly picked out of a small box filled with rings made of thin pieces of shiny metal.

Pater Dickmann, carrying a new white enamel pail, finally joins them. "Congratulations, Franziskus and Maria-Magdalena. To show you how happy I am that you are now husband and wife, I am giving you this new bucket as a wedding present. I have blessed it several times over. Use it and let everybody see it."

As Pater Dickmann ostentatiously hands the bucket to Makena, she curtsies politely while Muronga shakes hands with him in gratitude.

With more admonitions to come to church every Sunday and have their child baptized soon, Pater Dickmann wishes them well. Accompanied by their friends and relatives they go on their way home, relieved to have the ceremony out of the way.

Back in the village, another feast has been prepared to celebrate Muronga and Makena's church wedding, to celebrate not so much the wedding itself, but the fact that it is over and that the church people will now see Muronga and Makena as husband and wife. The day is spent eating and visiting until sunset sends everyone to their huts for the night.

"The feast yesterday was good, don't you think *Wiha-Mandaha*?" With Mandaha asleep in her lap, Makena sits with Muronga on the ground under the *ghutara* he has built to protect them from the often cruel African sun.

"Oh, yes, the feast was fine," responds Muronga. "But I was quite nervous about the whole thing in the beginning. I just wanted the priest to marry us and have it all out of the way. I am glad it is all over now, thank God, . . . I mean the God of Our Forefathers."

"But we still have to go to some more catechism classes, if Mandaha is also to be baptized. You remember *Muruti's* story about the inherited sin, don't you? Mandaha must be washed clean and white, too!"

"Wait, wait, wait . . . we must be careful here. I think we have had enough of this story. I am no less black than I was before we were baptized and neither are you. I see the same, hear the same, taste the same, smell the same, and feel exactly the same as I did before I was baptized. There has been no change. In fact, I love you and my people the same way I always have. No . . . not my son. What Pater Dickmann wanted, he has gotten. What we were made to want, we have gotten—Baptism, a church wedding, and presents, that's all! No more, no less!"

For a while Muronga and Makena silently look at each other as if they are exchanging compliments. Neither of them can forget the hectic ceremony of yesterday. Because the wedding was not long after the Baptism, they feel as if every villager thinks they are fanatics of Christendom.

"But how will you tell Pater Dickmann that Mandaha is not going to be baptized? And what will he do when he hears that? Don't you think there will be trouble?" inquires Makena.

"Well, Pater Dickmann can think what he chooses to think . . . it is up to him! No, wait. I am sorry, I think I am saying very dangerous things now. What will happen is that we will simply keep quiet about it . . . conveniently quiet. Then, when Mandaha begins to hear words, I will tell him stories about our ancestors, about the rains, the fields, the cattle, the children and death. I will teach him to name names. I will teach him that although life is sometimes not like honey, there is a way to find some honey. I will teach my son how to swim through life."

Before Muronga can go on, his best friend Kaye, who was at the wedding feast yesterday, sneaks up from behind them. "Be greeted, Children of Our Forefathers," he says in a loud, cheerful voice.

"Kaye, you come as stealthily as a python," says Muronga, turning around quickly and jumping to his feet to greet his friend. Clasping each other's hands firmly, Muronga entreats his friend to join them. "It is good that you have come to visit us. Come, sit over here," Muronga says as he leads his friend to two tree stumps near the fire opposite Makena. Seated next to each other, the two men begin the traditional African greeting.

"How did you sleep? Well?" begins Muronga.

"Yes, very well, since we parted at the feast yesterday. Leaving here, with my stomach full of good food, I went home."

"Ah, going home is good," Muronga comments in the traditional way.

"Everything at home is fine. The cattle are fine, the old people are healthy, and there is food to eat."

"That's good. Aren't we lucky to have ancestors who help us?"

"Oh, yes, we are. Even when things don't go so right."

"Why, is there anything wrong in your *kraal*, Kaye? Anybody ill? Who?"

"No, no, no, there is nobody who is ill now. My uncle was ill a while ago and everybody in our *kraal* was really worried. Everybody visited him at least once a day. I fetched wood for him every day. And the women brought him food. Not only for him but for the others who came to visit him. Now he is fine. But people are still visiting him. I did not want to tell you about it yesterday because there were some people at the feast who I did not know."

"Yes, some people have evil intentions. And they could have been there too, who knows?"

"There were also those white people at the first feast. I am not used to them. As you know, my family and I do not belong to the churchgoing clans. We are heathens. We do not need their God."

"I know, aren't you lucky?"

"When I left here I walked home with the old man, Kavindja, who told me about an important meeting. The white commissioner is coming. My uncle said he already knows about it and I thought you might also. You and I like to know what is happening and share what we hear."

"Yes. You have spoken good words. We do."

"I was thinking about this meeting, especially after being with the white people here the other day. And I thought, ah, why not visit my friend and talk? And now I am here. How did you sleep? And she and the big man?"

"Oh, they are very well. Isn't he a big man? Doesn't he talk to us almost all night?"

"I thought so. He is a very healthy human being. Like his . . . " Kaye pauses, a glint in his eye. He can tease his good friend Muronga, while still paying him the customary compliment. " . . . his father?"

"No, I do not think so. It is his ancestors."

"And what about this priest thing?"

"What thing? Not my child!"

"I mean, did *Muruti* not say that Mandaha will be baptized like you?"

"No, not Mandaha. We feel forced into this. We were taught things that we were made to memorize without understanding. I will not have that for Mandaha. If *Muruti* forces the issue, we will go somewhere where there are no priests. Perhaps where you come from."

"Good words. Good words, Muronga! We were not born to please these white people. We are heathens and we like it that way. We will stay unchanged, but convince them otherwise, if that is what they want. These white people, who cannot even swim!"

"Saying things to make me think, aren't you, guest?"

"Yes, we think together. This is why I came. I came so that we might think together about serious matters. Remember what the old people always say, trees that grow together ... "

" ... cannot help but rub each other."

The two man laugh loudly, pleased at finding such a good saying to conclude their greeting, and pleased to be able to join each other in laughter, in talk, in life. As they finish their greeting, they shake hands again before they continue their usual conversation.

The day is getting older and the evening dark. Muronga fetches more wood from behind the hut to make a bigger fire. In the meantime, Makena has prepared supper in two three-legged pots over a smaller fire. Both Muronga and Kaye pull their seats nearer to the fire to warm themselves.

"Are you people ready to have supper? It is good that you came, Kaye. *Wiha-Mandaha* hates eating alone, and he just does not like eating with women," Makena says as she stirs the food in the pots one last time.

"Then he is just like me," responds Kaye. "I do not enjoy eating by myself either. Eating with others, sharing food from one plate—that makes eating make much better sense. Otherwise, I feel like an animal that just eats, and eats wantonly."

"You are perfectly right, Kaye," adds Muronga. "We exist, and live for one another. So we must eat together. That is the way we have been brought up. But I understand that white people do not eat out of the same plates. They avoid each other when they eat." He pauses to consider. "How can people live together if they cannot share plates of food? I cannot understand, can you, Kaye?"

"No, I cannot. Why don't they share their food? Are they afraid of each other? Maybe that's why they are such lonely people," replies Kaye, as he looks at Makena who puts the plates of food on the ground in front of the two men.

As Muronga and Kaye eat from the one plate Makena has given them, she, with Mandaha still asleep in her lap, eats from the pots the food was prepared in, the way women usually do. The two men's fingers touch in the plate as they eat contentedly and with gratitude for the hands that prepared the food.

Finished eating, they sit silently as the fire burns with comforting flames. Now and then, Muronga pushes fresh pieces of wood into the center of the fire, where they turn into glowing coals of different shapes. All six eyes enjoy watching the fire as the coals decay and become ashes. As Muronga watches the fire he thinks how the human body goes through the same process of degeneration. He wonders what Pater Dickmann would say about the fire, this beautiful and essential fire, and the devil's role in it. Smiling slightly, he looks up at the other two faces and wonders what life would be like without fire.

"What are you thinking about, Muronga?" inquires Kaye, looking up suddenly. Then, pursuing his own thoughts, he goes on, "Let's talk about this meeting with the commissioner. You have heard that the Bantu Affairs Commissioner, Master Kruger, is coming to meet with all of the men in this area tomorrow, haven't you?"

"Yes, I have heard that, although I do not know what the meeting is about," replies Muronga. "All I know is that the meeting will be very big and important. Apparently the commissioner is going to make some very important announcements. The chief messenger of the headman told all of us earlier today that it was necessary, indeed imperative, that every man worth his name be there. So, I think it is better that we go and hear what the commissioner has to say, otherwise he may send policemen to come and take us to the meeting," continues Muronga, knowing very well that at times these khaki-dressed fellows are ruthless when the white man sends them.

Muronga also knows that it is at such meetings that his uncle, Ndara, often speaks up for his people. The commissioner does not like Uncle Ndara because he thinks he is too big for his shoes. The commissioner does not like people who talk unless they say what he wants them to say.

"Yes, I agree. I think we must go to this meeting tomorrow. It will not do us any harm to go and hear what the white man is going to do to us and our land. I can come and meet you first thing before the sun rises tomorrow morning and we can go together. Is that alright with you? *Nyina-Mandaha,* I hope you will not mind if we go off to the meeting tomorrow. We will discuss our women there, too."

"No, no, no," answers Makena. "You men have things to do. Go if you want to. Good men go to meetings anyway, so that they do not act on hearsay."

"Hearsay is like women's gossip," retorts Muronga. "I have always wanted to hear things for myself. I have gone to three meetings in a row now, and I am not going to stay at home tomorrow and have other people come and tell me what the new laws are. All right, Kaye, come here tomorrow morning, early, and we will go to the meeting together. I am sure Uncle Ndara will be there, too. In fact, I wonder why he did not tell me about the meeting today." Pausing for a moment, he rubs his forehead before saying, "Maybe he was told that the meeting is for the elders only. Not us. Anyway, we shall go."

It is already late in the evening, so the friends end their discussion and part company.

The following morning, as Kaye approaches Muronga and Makena's hut, he loudly announces his arrival. Everyone in the *kraal* can hear him, but of course everyone in the *kraal* knows everyone else's friends.

"Good morning. Did everybody sleep well?" he calls out.

"Yes, we have slept very well. How about you?" Muronga's strong voice permeates the hut. "Wait, I will be with you in a few moments. You are so punctual, my friend. It is as if you slept here with the cocks."

"Well," says Kaye, "a man's word is his honor. Is that not what we were taught?"

"You are absolutely right." Finally ready, Muronga joins his friend. "I am ready now, so let's go, shall we? Did you see any other people on the road as you were coming?"

"No. I am sure they were still wallowing in their *kafungos*, deciding to get up."

"Then we will be the first ones there today. In fact, it will be very good to be there early, so that we can sit near the commissioner. That way, we will be able to hear what he says."

"You mean we will be able to hear what the translator, Makaranga, says," replies Kaye.

"Yes, he is the one from whom we will get the message, since the white man speaks a strange language that sounds like *vsvsvsvs*. Then we must be near Makaranga."

The two men walk until the sun is halfway up in the sky. They pass many other men, mostly older men, walking in the same direction. They know they are all going to the same event. As Muronga and Kaye come up behind two older men, they hear them discussing taxes. They sound rather upset about these meetings with the commissioner and say that, every time he comes, he only announces "new laws, new taxes" without creating any new jobs. At least, they suggest, there should be road construction work for the men to do so they can earn the money to pay the taxes. Otherwise, where else can they get the money? Must they peel it off their skin?

"Be greeted," bellow Muronga and Kaye to the older men.

"Be greeted, too," the elders reply in unison.

"Are you coming to the meeting, too?" asks one of them.

"Yes," replies Muronga.

"That's good. It is good for you young men to go and hear all about the new laws, the white people's laws."

"These laws always come, come and come to us. From where, we don't know," adds another elder.

The meeting place is a wide half-moon of open ground between the three Stinkwood trees at the commissioner's official camp. Other white visitors stay there also when they come from who-knows-where to visit the land and the trees for reasons unknown to the villagers. Generally, the villagers stay away from the camp, for whenever they go near it, the white children there run away. The children in the village are more attracted to the camp than their parents, because the camp smells of diesel fuel, petrol, soap, and spices. The village children like to pick up the empty tin cans and soft papers that lie about the camp after the visitors have left. But it is different now, because the commissioner has appointed Mukuve and Mukoya to watch over the camp and keep it clean. The camp has recently been fenced, too, to keep the villagers away from the visitors. The watchmen, Mukuve and Mukoya, are called "Happyboy" and "Longman" by the white people who come to the camp and treat them like children. Even white children refer to them as "boys."

The commissioner does not come out of his hut until all the men are seated in the meeting area. A loud buzz of deep voices emanates from the seated crowd. No women are present. Each man has a partner, with whom to exchange speculations and uncertainties about what is going to happen this morning. After a while, Makaranga, the interpreter, who has been brought from Rundu, a nearby town, to translate for the commissioner, comes out of the oldest hut, better dressed than anyone else at the meeting. His appearance alone shows him to be much better off than the others. On top of that, he is not a muMbukushu. He is a muKwangali from another tribe far down the river. He does not even speak the language spoken by the villagers. It makes it hard for them to understand what is said at meetings.

"Good morning, good morning! Did you sleep well, all of you?" Makaranga announces. "The commissioner, Master Kruger, will be joining us in a moment. Just sit where you are and don't make any noise. We in my tribe, the vaKwangali, have learned to keep quiet and respect guests. The commissioner, and myself, are your guests. We are observing, once again, how you people in this part of the country behave."

A choral response to the greetings comes from the crowd. "Be greeted, too!" Luckily most of the men understand some Rukwangali—enough, that is, to keep from being sold. Maybe it is a good thing that women are not at such meetings. They, like most of the men who haven't made long journeys, wouldn't make head or tail out of the commissioner's *vsvsvsvs* or Makaranga's language that sounds like *ngoroorongorooro*—they would think Makaranga was talking about the Fisher bird, when he was just saying "etcetera, etcetera."

At last the salt-and-pepper haired commissioner emerges from his hut. Puffing on his pipe, he walks slowly towards the crowd, waving the open palm of his right hand to them. His once pale skin is red and blotchy from being exposed to the hot African sun. The baggy over-sized shorts of his ill-fitting khaki safari suit almost touch his knobby kneecaps. The commissioner's appearance gives him an air of incompetence, yet all the men with hats on, yank them off at the sight of him. At the demonstrative gesture of Makaranga, they all stand up to welcome the commissioner with vigorous nods of their heads and false smiles. This is part of showing hospitality to white people, they believe.

The commissioner joins Makaranga in the center, pats him on the shoulder and speaks. "Franz," he calls him, "tell them that it is a good thing that they have come to this meeting, this important, very important meeting."

"The commissioner says that men who attend big meetings are good men!"

"Tell them that I am bringing greetings to everyone from my government, the government of South Africa."

"The commissioner says that all men must listen to the government."

"Today, I am bringing you bad news and g-o-o-d news."

"The commissioner says that you must listen very carefully, otherwise . . . the commissioner will be very upset."

"Now, before I tell you the bad news, and the good news, I must inform you of the danger that is on the increase in this country, this beautiful country of ours. You must be very careful these days. Things are changing because of people with bad hearts. Tell them, Franz."

"The commissioner says that you must be careful of those among you who walk around with evil hearts to hurt others. Watch them!"

Muronga turns to Kaye and asks, "Do you know what they are talking about? Bad, evil hearts? Where?"

"I have no idea what hearts they are talking about. Let's listen some more, maybe they . . . " Kaye replies softly, his ears cocked to hear more.

"Tell them, Franz, that there are people who have left this country and gone away to far away countries. There they have learned how to shoot and kill people. They are very cunning. They are coming here to kill all the chiefs because they want to possess the land. They say that the white people are bad people. I know that you do not think like that. You like us white people, because we help you," the commissioner says with a benign smile.

"Now listen carefully! You have heard about what happened near Bagani this year. People from the bush fired at the police and there was a lot of trouble there. I am sure you have heard of the people called UPOs. They are people who are very cunning. You cannot shoot them, you cannot arrest them. When the white people shoot at them, water comes out of their guns. If you chain them, the chains go loose at night. They are dangerous people. Be careful of these people. They are not your . . . , our people."

"Very good, Franz, you remember well. This organization called UPO is very dangerous to you. If you hear that they are in your village, report them to the police. As you can see, there are more and more policemen and soldiers here in this country, because of these poeple. Do you understand?"

"The commissioner says that whenever you hear something about these people who appear from the bush and ask all kinds of questions, run to the police station. If you keep quiet, you are one of them and you are breaking the law! You hear?" continues Makaranga in his shouting voice.

Although the men have heard about the clashes between the white policemen and black people who came from the other side of the river to fight with the police, it still does not make sense to them who these people are and what they are doing.

"Who are these people? Do you know?" Kaye asks Muronga in a whispering voice.

"I wish I knew," answers Muronga quietly, avoiding being seen or heard by Makaranga or the commissioner. "Wait, I heard Uncle Ndara saying something about shootings and white people killing black men somewhere near Bagani. He said these people want the white people to leave this land. That is all I heard, and I do not understand the whole thing myself. But this is scary, ehm. . . ?"

"Franz, tell them not to discuss this with anybody after this meeting. Never! With nobody!"

"Now hear this. The matter of the bad people you must never discuss at home. Or else you are in deep trouble. The commissioner has ears everywhere. Don't think that you can gossip and that no one is hearing you. Things have changed these days, do you hear me?"

"Good, Franz, now tell them that the bad news is that all men are required to pay taxes, and those who do not have their tax papers yet must stay for a short while to be fingerprinted in order to get their papers." He raises a sample of such papers for everybody to see. "Things are changing now, and all of us must pay money to the government."

"The commissioner says that everybody must be careful these days. The law says that every man must pay taxes. You must all pay them. This money goes to the government. Those of you without good tax papers will be in trouble, like the commissioner says! Everyone must pay today and if you don't have your papers, come to me after this meeting so that we take your name. This is very important!"

There is a prolonged murmuring among the men. It is clear that it is a sound of disapproval and not of excitement. Rafael, the teacher standing next to Muronga, who has been shaking his head every time Makaranga translated what the commissioner said, says softly to Muronga, "This man is not saying what the commissioner is saying. He is not speaking the truth!"

"What?" inquires Muronga. "What is the commissioner saying? Yes, you are a teacher, you understand *vsvsvsvs*."

"Franz, tell them, please don't complain, the good news is still coming. It is the law and we must obey the law. I am sent by the law to tell you the news. I also pay taxes, more than what you all will have to pay, but I don't squeal, because it is the law!"

"Look now, the commissioner is upset. I told you not to open your mouths, didn't I? You don't speak here unless a finger is pointed at you. Only your ears are wanted here. Do you hear me now? It is the law. There is nothing you can do about it. Do you want to go to prison? Then, listen!"

"Now, the g-o-o-d news! Next month, the government will buy lots of cattle from people like you across the country. Those of you who have cows, oxen, and bulls can sell them to the government and get money to pay your taxes. That's good, isn't it?" He smiles and raises his hands in front of him.

"The commissioner is asking, 'Do you have cattle?' The commissioner says that people who want to sell their cattle to get money to pay their taxes can bring their cattle when the government comes to buy them. From today you must all count your cattle and sell them to the government. You will get good money. Have you heard the good news? The selling of cattle is next month. Have you heard?"

The men look at one another, not knowing what to expect next. But they do not speak.

"The government will also send young men to work in the mines in Transvaal. Those of you who are interested in going to work in South Africa should leave your names today so that we can start making arrangements. Or, you can go to the Tribal Community Bureau at Mukwe, as usual," the commissioner continues.

"Now listen everbody. You young men can go on contract to the mines in Johannesburg. There is lots of work for you there. You can bring home a lot of money, clothes, and everything. Anybody who wants to go there must give me their name after the meeting. Then you will go by 'big bird'," he looks and points to the sky, "to where you will go and work. It is nice there. You will meet other people . . . Shangaans, Pedies, Zulus, Xhosas, Nyasas, and many other people. They all go to work to pay their taxes."

"I know they understand, Franz. Tell them to go now and only those men who want to be fingerprinted or leave their names must stay behind." He nods his head to them, indicating that he has finished speaking.

"The commissioner says the meeting is over. Now you must all go home. The meeting is over. The people who will collect the money from you will come soon. They will go from one village to the other. Your foremen and kraalheads will inform you in time. The men who must be fingerprinted and leave their names must stay with me, under that tree over there. Those of you who have brought presents, chickens and things like that, must not give them to the commissioner, but to me. He says everything must be given to me and I will give it to him when he wakes up. He says he does not want to be disturbed now." With his voice softened now, he repeats, "All the men who brought presents for the commissioner, chickens and things like that, must bring them to me now . . . "

Before they break up, Uncle Ndara, raises his hand high. He has a question. The commissioner spots his hand and gives him a chance to speak. But before Uncle Ndara can open his mouth, Makaranga breaks in. "You are the man who always has something to say. What is your story this time? Remember, the commissioner knows you. I saw your name in his book . . . the big book."

"I just want to know what people who have neither cattle nor physical strength to work in the mines are to do. Where must their tax money come from?"

Makaranga interrupts him. "You see, you are asking irrelevant things. All that matters is that you pay. Don't ask the commissioner where you must get the money from. It is the law. Don't ask such things. You are old enough!" He turns to the commissioner. "He just wanted to thank you for your good words . . . in the name of all the others. He is a good man."

"Very nice . . . he is learning. Tell him that I appreciate his gratitude," replies the commissioner, turning his back on the crowd.

"The commissioner says that he has heard what you said. He cannot help you, it is the law. Go home now. He also says that he knows you!" continues Makaranga, pointing his forefinger at Uncle Ndara.

Before they start walking home, Muronga and Kaye give their names and fingerprints to Makaranga. On their way, they, like most, if not all of the men, are occupied with the thought of raising money to pay the taxes. There are still too many questions that remain unanswered.

One of them, Mbote, remembers what he overheard Makaranga saying just before the meeting started this morning. Makaranga was telling Muhora, one of the teachers who was at the meeting, that the government was going to introduce new tax regulations in the next five years or so. It sounded like one of those regulations that come one way, directly to them and yet they have no voice in such matters. What struck Mbote, though, was that Makaranga, as knowledgeable as he is about new laws, said that in the future people would have to pay taxes for their head of cattle, too.

As Mbote tells the others about what he heard, the young Petrus, who has recently returned from *Thivanda*, interrupts and says, "Yes, I remember, one of my six roommates in our Tsumeb compound told us that some years ago his people, the Namas, were forced by the government to pay taxes for their dogs—their own dogs! And when they refused, no, resisted, rightfully, the government killed them from airplanes. This roommate of mine got so angry every time he told the story of what happened to the Bondelschwarts that he could hardly finish telling it. What you are saying, Mbote, does not sound too far from what other people in this country, South West Africa, have lived through."

The men fall silent again and begin counting their cattle in their heads and wondering what would happen to them in the future if they did not have their cattle. Where will we get milk? How will we plow our fields or pay our debts? Things are so uncertain these days, Muronga thinks, shaking his head in deep meditation. Maybe the only people who are sure about tomorrow are the white

people. They are the ones who come and bring complications. Yes, they are the very ones who come, break to
build and build to break. Today it's this, tomorrow it's
that—and only the devil and maybe the fortune teller
know what's next.

"If I were young again," says old Kakuru, "I would leave
my family next week, go and earn money, and come back
to pay their taxes. On top of that, I could bring some
clothes home to my wife and children. But now, my bones
are cracking. Tough times for us old ones, but how about
you youngbloods? I don't mean you, Mbote. You only
came back yesterday. The others must go now, so that
you can plow the fields. You young men must go and
come back with coins to pay our taxes. We are out of
the running now. We depend on you, as you depended
on us when you were little rabbits."

Muronga and Kaye are challenged by the old man's
words. They want to go and earn money. They have heard
about SWANLA, the South West Africa Native Labor
Association, which recruits African men for work as
contract laborers on white people's farms and in their
mines inside the country and in South Africa. Usually
contract laborers who come back with heavy trunks are
highly respected, especially if they bring thick coats and
hats for their fathers, and long, dark, colorful fabrics for
their mothers. The whole idea energizes the young men.
The sooner they go, the better.

Now that they have given their names, their fingerprints
and everything to Makaranga for the commissioner's
records, Muronga and Kaye only need to go and be
registered as prospective contract laborers at the Tribal
Community Bureau. Then they will have to keep checking
with the Bureau to find out when and where they will
go. They have absolutely no choice in the matter. They
will go where their menial services are needed, on the
farms or in the mines.

After walking in the hot midday sun, the men begin to feel tired, and are silent again. Only when the older men leave the group, one after the other, do Muronga and Kaye decide to pursue a discussion about going to a faraway place to earn money.

"Now that we are alone," says Muronga, "unashamed of what the old men would think about our manhood, we can talk seriously about our next step, . . . you hear me?"

"Yes, my dearest friend," responds Kaye. "I was thinking about that, too. How did you know I was going to say that we should show that we are men, ready to be assets to our people? I think a discussion of this sort is not necessary . . . that's old women's stuff. No. We go to sleep tonight, wake up tomorrow morning . . . and on the road we go to the Tribal Community Bureau office. There we will get registered . . . ready to 'climb the lorry', and then, . . . off we go, to wherever. We come back . . . different, with plenty of money, clothes, Vaseline and everything. All right? Now, don't put your wife to shame, please!"

"Absolutely," agrees Muronga excitedly. "Tomorrow morning, before the sun rises, you come to my hut and together we will go. I will explain everything to *Nyina-Mandaha*. She is such a solid woman. She will understand. I will tell my son, too, even if I have to do it in baby . . . tongue-tutututututu." He laughs aloud.

The two young men have sparks in their eyes. It is as though they have already accomplished everything they set out to do. They shake hands excitedly. "I will see you tomorrow. And we will go together."

"Thank you for being such a good friend, Muronga," Kaye says warmly. "We will be together, from tomorrow." They part, each with a broad smile of contentment. Muronga turns and waves again and again until Kaye disappears on the bushy road.

CHAPTER 4

"*Moro, moro, moro,*" says Kaye brightly. "Are you awake, child's father?"

"*Moro.* You are here already. Very good." Muronga's welcoming voice comes from inside the hut. "Did you sleep well, or did you also have little things to do? This boy does not want to sleep like other babies. He keeps waking us up—he thinks he is big. Anyway, I will be with you in a moment."

He bounces the smiling baby on his knee a couple of times before handing him over to his mother, who is busy with the morning's chores. The child wants to keep playing, and begins to wail.

"Don't cry, my little lion cub," comes Makena's comforting voice. "Everything is going to be all right. Your brave father must go now and do his duty for us . . . for you and me and the old ones in the *kraal.* Say good-bye now."

Muronga, moving about the hut aimlessly, taking stock of all the bits and pieces of the life he and Makena have built together, joins them. Putting his big forefinger into the child's small clutching hand, he looks into his eyes and asks, "What is the matter, old man? Are you angry with us? Don't cry. I will be back soon. I am only doing what I must do, and what you will one day have to do also. When you are grown up . . . hey?" Then, shaking his finger loose, he glances around one last time as if to say good-bye to the hut, their home. Knowing his time has run out, he swiftly caresses the *kafungo*, the bed that has known him and his wife intimately, the place where they have shared their daily experiences, the territory where they have settled their disputes. He sighs audibly, indicating to Makena that it is time for him to go, and slowly walks out of the hut with her at his side carrying their child.

Joining Kaye outside the hut, Muronga begins the ritual greeting. In the greeting, each of the men gives a thorough account of what has happened since the last time they spoke with one another—their lives, their families, their livestock, their land, and their friends—every bit of news must be exchanged, no matter how long it takes, and no matter how little time has passed since their last meeting. Every hurt, every frustration, every uncertainty, every new plan, every hope and every aspiration—everything that is important in life must be shared.

Makena, standing silently nearby, listens to their banter, watching them keenly all the while until, at last, the men seem to have run out of things to say.

"So, you two men are up to some big ideas," she says, smiling graciously. "But wouldn't you like to warm yourselves by a nice fire before you disappear?"

"We are not disappearing for good, we hope. Maybe we will be back before dark," replies Muronga. "But we must be at the office before too many other men get there, so we had better not delay. The sun is getting hot too quickly these days. Woman, tell everybody around here where we have gone. We will see you soon. It is for you that I am going away."

Kaye looks at his friend and his friend's wife as if he wants to give them more time to be alone together. "*Nyina-Mandaha*, it is time for *Wiha-Mandaha* to go away. He cares about you and his boy very dearly. He does not complete a sentence without his tongue carrying your name and that of the big man, Mandaha. Believe me," says Kaye, trying to reassure Makena.

"Why do you say that?" Makena replies, interrupting Kaye. "*Wiha-Mandaha* explained everything to me last night and this morning. I approve of what you men are going to do. Many of the women who have gone before us have had their husbands leave them for a long time, but they managed perfectly well. And the men came back. I would be ashamed of myself if I stood in my husband's way when he wants to work for us. What is a wife for, then? Is she not supposed to approve of what her husband does?" Makena asks, looking at the two men's faces.

Both men are surprised by Makena's heartfelt encouragement, and Muronga smiles boastfully, anticipating that his friend will unleash an avalanche of compliments on his wife.

"*Nyina-Mandaha*, you are saying things that should come from the mouth of someone far older than you. I am overwhelmed by your strength, your courage, your understanding and love. My friend is definitely a blessed man to have you as his other half, and I think it is my duty to tell him, right now, that he has a wonderful wife. Did you hear me, my friend?" asks Kaye, smiling at Muronga.

As gracefully as possible, Muronga prevents Makena from returning the compliments. "Yes, now let's go, Kaye. You are saying what I already know very well. Why do you think Uncle Ndara picked *Nyina-Mandaha* for me from among so many flowers? There are so many women who are good enough for us men, but only one was chosen for me, and I do not wish to have more than one woman, one wife . . . *Nyina-Mandaha.* To be honest, I often think I am not good enough for her."

The two men walk away, leaving Makena standing near the hut. They turn and wave to her a few times and she waves back, watching until they are out of sight.

Muronga thinks, half-smiling, how in Kavango society it is believed that a man's safety is dependent on his wife's upright behavior and any evil that befalls him during his absence is caused by his wife's failure to comport herself properly and remain celibate. When the news of any mishap involving her husband reaches the people in the village and *"ndama,"* as it is called, is suspected, the people blame the wife of the stricken man and she is chastised for her misbehavior, with such chastisement often meaning the end of the marriage. It is also believed that sickness and death are caused by witchcraft possessed by people who wish to do others harm. Thus, if a woman's husband dies and his death was caused by witchcraft, the wife of the deceased and her children are "inherited" by a male member of his maternal family. On the other hand, if a woman's husband dies from *ndama,* then she and her children are driven away from his home. There is no argument about who keeps the children—they belong to their mother. One can always be mistaken about the father, but never about the mother.

It is a long walk to the Tribal Community Bureau— longer than the one to the commissioner's meeting yesterday. Muronga walks behind Kaye on the hard dirt road that leads through the forest. The morning mist thins as the sun heats the day. Thank God there are no old men to delay us now, Muronga thinks. They walk as fast as their strong legs can carry them, watching all the while for any other signs of life along the road. They do not see as many other men on the road as they thought they would, but tire tracks and the smell of diesel smoke indicate that the commissioner must have left early this morning. Missionaries never move about in the small hours of the morning.

Muronga and Kaye have never gone to a faraway place before and all they know of such places is from the stories the other men in the village have told them. Not knowing what to expect, they are rather anxious about the idea of going away.

"I hope we will get everything done today," says Muronga, breaking the silence.

"Me, too," replies Kaye. "I have the feeling that things are going to work out for us, though. I just have this feeling."

"So do I. You know, all of the old people in our village speak very well of both of us. I don't mean to be self-praising—I am simply stating a known fact. Good things happen to people who are in good standing with old people. They definitely have some contact with the skies," Muronga says solemnly.

"Sure. One should always respect the elderly. I strongly believe in that. Since they have wished us the best, I am positive that everything will go well. We shouldn't worry," adds Kaye.

After a long while, Muronga and Kaye arrive at the Mukwe Tribal Community Bureau. There is no office worker there yet, and they have to wait. But it does not matter—as long as he comes sometime. This is African time. It is the action, the coming, that counts—not the amount of time it takes for the action to take place. Muronga and Kaye are used to waiting for a long time. Sometimes they are also waited for. That is life.

Finding themselves a place to stand in the shade of a Stinkwood tree, Kaye says after some time, "The sun is moving up fast in the sky today, don't you think?"

"Yes, it has moved up this high already," answers Muronga, raising his right arm and pointing with his hand to the sun overhead. "I hope that we will not have to spend all day here. I am excited about going to work in the mines, but I don't like the idea of working on a farm, or looking after sheep in *Thivanda.*"

"Oh, I don't like that either. Imagine working in the kitchen with a white woman, a missus who orders you around as if you were a small boy!" interjects Kaye.

"How do you know that is what happens? You haven't worked in a white man's kitchen before, have you?" Muronga asks, sounding surprised.

"No, no, no, but my brother told me. He worked in a kitchen every day for some white people, cooking their food, washing their spoons and cups, cleaning their cats and dogs, and he said that he was not allowed to eat from their plates. He was warned against it, lest they call the police. He had to leave the house after he prepared the food."

"And what did he eat then? And where?" Muronga asks incredulously.

"Well, he went to eat under the tree in the backyard, or in the car house. He stayed there until they called him to wash the dishes. Even the food that he ate was not the same as the food he helped to prepare. They bought him *mealie meal* for his porridge, and they gave him the bones after they had taken the meat off them for their meals. His food was not even considered food by the *baas* and *missus*. They told their children not to touch it. 'It is black people's food; it might kill you!' they would tell their children."

"Oh, I am glad you told me these things. I think we should tell the officer that we only want to go to the mines, not to any farms."

"Yes, Muronga, but we have no choice. We will have to go where we are sent!"

"I know, but I am sure we can ask him, plead with him, nicely. He is our brother after all. I am sure he will understand."

"You do not know how these white men's boys behave. They do not see us as their brothers once they can read those books of theirs. You and I are nothing because we have not gone to school as they have. They think what the commissioner does; and you know what he thinks. He thinks we are trash! It is tough, my friend."

"Well, I am no trash, but maybe they are! Those people, especially those black people, who look down on us, are in the wrong. Can't they see that they are black like you and me, and that they will never be white? And what, after all, is in this pink skin of theirs, anyway?"

"I don't know. Maybe they know something we do not know."

"You see, Kaye, when you start looking down on your own people, your own customs, your own self, then you have lost everything. We are going to work in the mines, not because we are bad people, not because we are unhappy at home, not because we are poor, but because we need money to pay the white man's taxes. That's all. I am Muronga, Mandaha's father, the son of Kapande and Haushiku, from the totem, *Mukanyime*, the lion. And I am not going to change. I am what I am, and shall always be. We have our land, our cattle, our *mahangu*, which gives us the porridge that keeps us alive. We are not hungry yet, thanks to the God of Our Forefathers!"

"Yes, I agree. We are what we are. We are the children of our ancestors."

A moment of silence follows as Muronga and Kaye wonder if it wouldn't be very strange and difficult to work in a white man's kitchen. Men are not ordered around, nor are women, in their society, and everyone knows what his or her duties and responsibilities are. Everything is shared. People do not have so much that they cannot share everything. Muronga and Kaye know right now that when they return home everything they bring back with them will be shared.

Suddenly, they hear noises in the small office. It must be the clerk. Who else could it be? He must have entered through the back door.

"Is that the man who?" asks Kaye.

"I don't know, but I suspect it is. He is the only one who would go by the white man's hour. You see, the office is just opening now—right on time," responds Muronga.

"Shall we go and see him and tell him why we are here?" Kaye asks as he begins to move toward the door. Reaching out, Muronga grabs Kaye by the arm and says, "Wait. Maybe there is someone important with him."

"What do you mean, important? Are we unimportant? Is that what you mean?" asks Kaye, teasingly.

"We are important in our own right. The point is that you and I are not important to the white man. Makaranga is important because he understands and speaks the white man's language. He is the only one who knows both sides. He knows the truth. But who knows if he tells the truth to us or to the white man?" Muronga says, laughing slightly.

"You are right, perfectly right. This man in the office is also important because he keeps the white man's books. All of our names are in those books, you know?"

"Yes, that's what I mean. They look at the papers and can tell what is happening. They know things, . . . new things. They speak *vsvsvsvs*."

"Exactly. We are at a disadvantage, my friend, by not speaking the white man's language. Even today we could be sold and we would not understand what had happened until we were being taken away. It is still as it was in the old days when the Portuguese came to take our people away in exchange for tobacco and gifts. The chiefs simply nodded their heads without understanding what they were agreeing to and took the things they were offered."

"But, if that were to be done today, at least some people would understand and would run away. They would understand that they were being spoken about," Muronga adds.

"True. But you or I, well, we could be sold." Kaye winks and nudges Muronga with his elbow.

Hearing their voices, the clerk comes out to see who is talking outside of his office. He is a tall man who is wearing a blue safari suit with four ballpoint pens in each of the breast pockets. He greets them in a friendly manner.

"Good morning. Did you sleep well? What brought you here today?" he asks them.

Both Muronga and Kaye walk towards him, and reciprocate the greeting politely. "Yes, we slept well. Did you sleep well, also?" they ask him in unison.

"Yes, I slept well, but I have to spend all day here attending to the books in the office."

"I see," says Muronga. "Well, we came to put our names in the books. Can we give you our names today?"

"You sound as though you are ready to sign a contract! Where do you want to go—east or west?"

Both Muronga and Kaye respond together, "East, not west, please."

"That's fine with me. Let's go into the office so that you can be fingerprinted. We will have to do it today because you must 'climb the lorry' this week with all of the other men who have given me their names. You must all leave for Rundu this week. That is where the selection is made. We only send you to the main office and from there you will be sent either east or west."

The clerk enters the office, followed by Muronga and Kaye, who are cautious. The walls of the office are full of pictures of unknown white faces. On the wall behind the desk is a calendar with a big picture of Christ wearing a crown of thorns on his head.

"Come, stand here. What are you afraid of? You people who cannot read are always afraid to enter here. Do you think I eat people?" the clerk asks them as he eyes them curiously.

Muronga and Kaye smile nervously as they take one step forward and stand in front of the desk with their hands behind their backs. They have heard that the way to honor an office is to stand straight, with your hands behind your back.

Then, suddenly, the clerk's behavior becomes strange as he picks up his pen and takes his seat behind the desk. He was friendly outside, but once inside the office, he begins to yell at them like a drill sergeant.

"I speak to only one of you at a time, do you hear me?"

"Yes. . . ," reply the two men, hesitantly.

"Yes, who? I am called *Kamutjangi*, the writer, here in this office! You must say, 'Yes, *Kamutjangi*,' every time I ask you a question, and you speak only when you are spoken to. This is an office, not a sleeping hut, or a tree under which you drink!" While he has been speaking to them, the two men have positioned themselves behind each other. Soon the clerk starts writing in his book. "So, who is the first . . . you?" he demands, as he points his pen at Muronga. "What is your Christian name?"

"Franziskus!"

"Your heathen name?"

"Muronga!"

"Your father's name?"

"Haushiku."

"Your mother's name?"

"Kapande!"

"Your kraalhead?"

"Ndara!"

"Your village headman?"

"Shamashora."

"Your chief?"

"Our only chief, Dimbare!"

"Have you paid taxes before?"

"No, not yet. But I will pay them in the future. That is why . . . "

"Come over here and put your thumb . . . there!" the clerk shouts, as he pulls Muronga a bit roughly by the arm, and then holds his thumb tightly and presses it first against a black ink pad and again on a crisp white form.

"Now, you. What is your Christian name?" continues the clerk in the same harsh voice.

"I do not have a Christian name. I am a heathen!" responds Kaye.

"Yoh, yoh, yoh, you are not good enough for the books. You mean you do not go to church? You don't know this man behind me?" retorts the clerk, pointing to the picture of Christ on the wall behind him.

"No, none of my family knows the church. We are from Angola," replies Kaye.

"Then what are you doing here?" shouts the clerk.

"We have two homes; one here and one in Angola."

"What? Ah, you are wasting my time! What is your heathen name anyway?" continues the clerk.

"Kaye'"

"Your father's name?"

"Shakadya!"

Hearing Kaye's answer, the clerk forgets himself and, relaxing the tone of his voice, he says, "Oh, that is my name, too.   Maybe your father and I were named after the same person. What is your father's totem?"

"He is *Mukanyatji*, the buffalo."

"I see. Do you . . ." begins the clerk. Then remembering himself, he resumes his former harsh demeanor, saying, "You are wasting my time. This is an office! Your mother's name?"

"Mushova . . . "

"Kraalhead?"

"Karupu!"

"Headman?"

"The same; Shamashora!"

"Alright, and the same chief. Come over here. Quickly. I have a lot of work to do! Thumb there . . . !" the clerk shouts, repeating the fingerprinting process.

At last, the registration procedure is over. But not knowing what to expect next, Muronga and Kaye resume their stances in front of the clerk's desk.

"Now, listen you two, very carefully!" continues the clerk. "Today is what day? . . . Wednesday. Go back home with the papers I am giving you and keep them in a safe place. Your names and everything are on these papers, so you must never lose them. On Saturday you must stand alongside the road where the lorries pass and show the papers to the lorry driver. He will take you to Rundu and tell you everything you need to know about where you are going. Do you hear me?"

"Yes, we hear you. We thank you!" the two men reply submissively.

"And don't pretend that you don't know me when you come back with money and goods!" the clerk yells, as Muronga and Kaye begin to inch their way to the door.

"No, no, of course not. Stay well, *Kamutjangi*. We will see you again one day, if we come back alive. Thank you," they reply as they close the office door.

Sighing with relief, they begin the long walk back home, feeling good now that the registration procedure is over. Muronga cannot help feeling happy that he will be with his wife and child until Saturday, but his thoughts, like Kaye's, are of the behavior of the clerk. They do not understand why he changed so suddenly from a friendly man, a brother, to an impatient, strange character when he picked up the pen. Maybe there is power in a pen, Muronga thinks. Feeling inhibited about discussing him, though, lest someone on the road hear them, they exchange very few words until they reach the two roads where they usually part.

"Go well, Muronga. I will see you soon. Give my regards to your people at home!" says Kaye as he extends his hand.

"Go well, Kaye. Stop by tomorrow or the day after, and give my regards to your people at home, as well," responds Muronga as he reaches out and shakes his friend's hand.

"Oh, by the way, I almost forgot!" continues Muronga, still holding his friend's hand firmly. "Uncle Ndara told me that there is a big meeting this afternoon under the Great Tree. It is about the case of Tweya and his wife Mayenga, I mean his former wife, the woman that was taken away from him while he was away working in . . . a . . . far country. It is going to be a big case, Uncle Ndara said, and all the elders are going to be there to make a decision about this poor man's marriage. I would like to go and listen. You can learn great things and great words from a meeting like this."

"Oh, yes, you are right. How could we not go to listen to proceedings of this nature? You did a very good thing by reminding me. I had forgotten about it. You know such a meeting is more important than the commissioner's, because when you hear the elders ask questions and really force people to speak the truth, you learn about yourself and how to be responsible in community. After all, we will do the elders' work one day," responds Kaye, shaking Muronga's hand vigorously.

"Now," interrupts Muronga, "why don't you come with me to my place to get something to eat, and from there we shall go together to the meeting? Otherwise you will have to go a long way and come back again. I live closer to the Great Tree than you, and I have a wife and you don't!" They both laugh and walk in the direction of Muronga's *kraal*.

"*Moro*, I am here. Are you here, *Nyina-Mandaha*?" greets Muronga.

"Yes, I am here," replies Makena from the hut where she has been preparing a meal. "You came back rather quickly. I thought it took a lot of time to be in the office. Did they write down your names?"

"The man in the office wrote down everything about us. There is nothing about us that the book does not know. Kaye is here with me. I asked him to come home with me because there is a meeting under the Great Tree that we also want to go to, and he would be wasting time to go to his place and come back again."

"That's true. Somehow I had the sense to prepare more food. It is a good thing that Kaye came with you. And it is ready now. You two must be tired from walking in the hot sun. It should rain soon and then it will not be so hot when you go to the meeting. Did the man in the office say that you can 'climb the lorry' before the rains are over?"

"He said that we will leave soon. I will tell you about it later. We have to go soon."

After they have finished their lunch, the two men head for the Great Tree. Uncle Ndara had already left to consult with the other elders. On their arrival under the Tree, they find all the elders seated in their chairs by the foot of the Tree. Uncle Ndara is among them, seated next to the thin and aging Shamashora. More and more people arrive, both men and women. All the women sit on the left of the elders and the men on the right, forming a circle.

"Be greeted all of you who are assembled here!" greets the village headman, Shamashora, in a loud voice. "We are assembled here today not to pray for the rains, but to put our heads together about a difficult situation. We thank Our Forefathers that we are getting good rains this year so that we can work our fields well. Today we are lucky that it is not raining, otherwise you would not have come in such large numbers. Unfortunately, we are here today not to celebrate, but to lament together that our community life has been hurt. All of you here, and especially our wise elders by the Great Tree, will help us get to the facts and the truth of the story that has brought us here today and together we will make a good decision."

Muronga feels nervous. The headman sounds more serious than he has ever heard him before. He nudges his friend Kaye's shoulder while the thin, tall old man clears his throat and pulls his worn grey jacket together before continuing his speech.

"As you see very well, I am getting too old to speak too much at a hearing like this. Fortunately, I have my old friend, Ndara, here to help us all go through this. The other elders will ask their questions so that we can know where we are going. Now, the matter before us involves two young people in our midst, Tweya and his wife Mayenga. They are not together now, but in the eyes of the law and our customs, they are still husband and wife."

There is coughing and grumbling from the crowd. One man in the back shakes his head in disapproval of what the headman has said.

"Who is that man, and why is he shaking his head?" asks Kaye quietly.

"I am not sure, but I suspect he is the man who is now married to, or rather living with Tweya's wife," whispers Muronga in Kaye's ear.

"The case," continues Shamashora, "involves Tweya, the man seated here on my right . . . can you stand up so that everybody can see you . . . who married Mayenga. The wedding was duly solemnized and celebrated and everybody was happy. Then Tweya went to work in the mines in a faraway country for a long while. When he returned home, he found his house empty, his wife gone with his child. Now . . . "

"That's not true!" interrupts the man who earlier shook his head. "The woman was half-pregnant when her husband left her. She told me about it and I completed the pregnancy. What would have become of the child if I did not sleep with her to complete the pregnancy? You would see a child without feet, without arms, even without a head now. Is that responsibility on the part of a man who runs away to a foreign land leaving his wife halfway pregnant?" raves the man.

Almost every head in the crowd turns to look at the emotional man. There is general rumbling under the Great Tree as clusters of men and women lean towards one another saying in agreement, "He's right! Imagine—what a child!" while others say in dissenting words, "No, that's just an excuse!"

Suddenly an angry Tweya jumps to his feet, flailing his fists. Charging towards the other man, he is grabbed by his shirt tails by one man and restrained bodily by another man. He shouts,"If this were just between the two of us, you would have no wife or teeth left when I finished with you . . . thief!"

Still standing, the other man shouts back,"Thief? You should thank me for what I have done! You wouldn't have any children if it weren't for me! You ran away. Maybe you knew you couldn't finish the job . . . eh, little boy?" he says tauntingly.

"No, no, no, Fayafaya! What are you saying? Have some respect, please," says an older man at the younger man's side as he holds him firmly by the arm and pulls him down toward the ground. "Everything is in the hands of the law now. That's why all of these big people are here . . . to talk over everything, not to see you fighting like two bulls! Now sit down, my son. Your mother and I are here to stand by you. The law is fair. You know that."

"Sit down, Headman," says one short elder, puffing on his long wooden pipe and indicating to the headman to sit down. "I will tell these people to respect this Tree. Listen carefully all of you gathered here. The reason we are here is because we belong together and we want to work together. If we wanted to fight like animals, we would not have come here. Only people meet like this, to talk with respect for one another. No one is allowed to take the law into their own hands. We all listen and speak when we have to. We are here, as the headman said, for serious matters. Not to show our physical strength. We old ones would not be here if it were for that. But we are here to use our heads."

The people nod their heads in agreement with the elder. There is tranquility again under the Tree. The headman stands up again, pushes his jacket together, glances at the elders around him and begins to speak, "I have nothing more to say. I shall now call upon the other elders."

Uncle Ndara stands up, steps forward and clears his throat, "As I see this case, it will not help us much to waste time fighting among ourselves. The person who is most helpful is the woman in question. Now, I ask the woman who has been referred to as Mayenga to stand up for me, please. I would like to push ahead."

Mayenga stands up and makes a few steps towards Uncle Ndara. "I want you to answer my questions honestly. Will you?"

"Yes, I shall. I have never lied in my life. I swear."

"Good, is your name Mayenga and are you the woman with two husbands?"

"I am Mayenga, but I do not have two husbands. I don't even know if I have a husband, for my husband left me while I was a little bit pregnant. When I knew that I was having something in my stomach, I told Fayafaya about it and he offered to help me get a full pregnancy."

"This means he slept with you."

"Yes. I was only half-pregnant, and I did not want an incomplete child."

"I understand. But didn't I hear that you ran away together as husband and wife?"

"Yes, that was after people knew that he was sleeping with me. I was too ashamed to stay at home in my husband's hut and face the wrath of his family. It was a very bad situation for me. Then I agreed to run away with him and maybe marry him before my husband came back. I was also afraid of my husband . . . , oh, my mother . . . " she begins to cry, covering her face.

"Don't cry, don't cry. You are doing fine. We understand what you are saying. Can you tell us where that child is? You don't look pregnant now."

"The child is with my mother. She is sitting over there. My mother took the child away from me because she was ashamed of what I had done. My parents love my husband very much. But I feel so ashamed that I ran away. I should only have thanked Fayafaya for helping me in my situation and waited for my husband to return. I knew he went away because he cared for me and his, I mean our, families."

"I see. You are saying very good words. You may sit down, thank you. Tweya, the man who married this woman, can you stand up for me, please?"

Tweya stands up and steps towards Uncle Ndara with his hands behind his back. He glances quickly over his shoulder, just to make sure where Fayafaya is sitting.

"You are the man who ran away, ehm?" asks Uncle Ndara sarcastically, with a broad smile on his face that carries his usual sense of humor. The crowd enjoys his small joke and bursts into quiet laughter.

"Yes, I am Mayenga's husband, but I did not run away. I did not know that she was pregnant and I really wanted to go and earn some money for our families and our people. If I had known she was pregnant, I would have waited. How could I?" replies Tweya, shaking his head and shrugging his shoulders.

"Now, since you came back and learned that your wife went off with another man, have you married or wanted to marry another woman?"

"Oh, no, you can ask anybody here. They have not seen me anywhere. I listened to what the old people told me. They said I should not rush into things. And I also thought and believed somehow that my wife would come back to me. We were chosen for each other. What big people have put together, we small ones should respect. I love ... my wife. ... "

"Have you seen the child yet?"

"No, I decided to wait until after this meeting. I would like to see him ... I still think he is my child. I formed him first, and I slept more times with my wife."

"Thank you, Tweya, but don't sit down yet. Maybe the other elders have questions for you. I have satisfied myself."

Another elder, Shangonde, stands up to cross-question Tweya. When he steps forward, most of the people in the crowd are about to burst into laughter. Shangonde is known to be the funniest old man in the village. He is very tall and thin and he likes playing with children wherever and whenever he finds them. The most well-known story about him is that since he has very big feet, and the shoes that his son brought him do not fit, he carries them tied together over his shoulders so that everybody can see that he has shoes even though he cannot wear them.

"Did you say that you did not know that your wife was over the line when you left, but if you had known, you would not have left. . . ?" Shangonde asks.

"Yes, oh, yes, I would not have gone away."

"Now that you know what has happened, and I assume that you were hurt by all this, would you still want your wife back?"

"Yes, by all means. I can understand what my wife did, and in part I feel responsible for what has happened. She was really worried about the child that I did not complete inside of her. She did not want to cheat on me. She cared about me, herself and the child. She is a good woman. I am convinced that after she slept with Fayafaya, he bewitched her. Fayafaya knows a lot of medicine to make women follow him. And his medicine is very strong. I know what he uses. I know from which plants he gets these roots. He took some sand from Mayenga's foot prints, then followed her foot prints and took some of her stool to mix with his roots. He put all of this into a little gourd *calabash* and every morning he would blow into this *ndjungo* and pronounce Mayenga's name while he turned in four different directions. Now, the old people here know that such a ritual could make any woman lose her mind over a man."

"Wait, you seem to know a lot about love medicine. Who told you that this was done by Fayafaya?" asks Shangonde.

"Well, his wife Rumono came to tell me all this. When she heard that I was back, she came to tell me. In fact, because she saw him do it every morning until he ran away with Mayenga she knew where the *ndjungo* was kept. And fortunately, when he went away with my wife, he did not take this container with him. Maybe he did not need it any more. Rumono brought it to me. Here it is. . . . "
He produces a shiny little pear-shaped *calabash* decorated

with beads around the neck. He places it on the ground in the center where everyone can see it.

The wide-eyed crowd mutter in sympathetic unison while Fayafaya's family and friends look ashamed and wish they could sink into the earth. Mayenga's mother, seated in the second row on the left, screams almost hysterically, "Oh, my daughter. I knew she was not acting normal. Oh, my father." She weeps before she is calmed down by her sister.

Everyone's eyes are fixed on Fayafaya. Shangonde, following their gaze, spots him and commands, "Come forward, *Shamakehe.* What do you say for yourself, strong man? You have heard what has been said and showed here. Do you deny any of it? Remember that you are under the Great Tree." The crowd begins to chuckle when they hear the word Shamakehe, a label given to a man who seduces women at the slightest provocation.

"I have heard everything, and I do not deny it. I have done wrong and I will accept whatever the elders decide. Trees do not wrong other trees, but people do. I am sorry about what I have done . . . ," he laments, his chin almost resting on his chest.

When Shangonde goes to sit down, Uncle Ndara, after consulting in a whisper with Shamashora, steps forward. The entire crowd listens very attentively, with those who are seated in the far-most row shifting themselves forward on the ground so as to hear everything that is said.

"Well, where are we now?" starts the respectable Uncle Ndara. "We have all heard the evidence and the man who has brought us here is honorable enough not to deny his felonies. The evidence therefore tells me only one thing, and that is that mistakes have been made, but that there is eagerness on the part of all of the parties concerned to resolve this matter amicably. Our responsibility here is to help reach a decision that is good, not only for the people involved, but for our entire community, and our children. In order to do anything, I think we need to hear again what Mayenga has to say. Child's mother, can you come to the fore, please?"

Mayenga steps forward, not knowing what to expect next. Her appearance commands respect and sympathy from the audience.

"I am sorry to bring you back again, but we need to end this discussion now. We need your cooperation, and your honesty again. We realize that this may be the hardest part of all for you. Now, I will ask you to demonstrate to all these people what you really wish," Uncle Ndara continues, pausing momentarily to go and fetch two short sticks. On his return to the circle, he plants the two sticks in the ground, saying, "The one stick on my right is your husband Tweya, and the other, on my left is the man you went away with, Fayafaya. What I want you to do is, without saying anything, pick only one of these sticks. The one you pick is the man you will go home with today. Your decision will be respected by all of us. We have heard everything now. Do you understand?"

Mayenga nods her head and slowly kicks the stick on her right with her bare foot. It falls flat onto the ground while the other one remains standing. It is clear to everyone that she has chosen to go home with her husband.

"What you are telling us is that you wish to return to your legal husband, Tweya, whose stick you left standing. Is that true?"

Mayenga nods slowly in agreement so that everyone can see. Joyfully, Mayenga's mother and several other elder women burst into high-pitched ululating rhythm.

"Well, then you can sit down," continues Uncle Ndara. "Everything is very clear to us, isn't it? Now it is up to the elders to conclude the case."

Before Uncle Ndara takes his seat, Headman Shamashora signals all the elders to now go behind the Tree to make their decision. The eight elders disappear behind the Tree where they talk alone for a few moments. There is absolute silence under the all-embracing, steadfast Tree.

When they return with smiles on their faces, Shamashora steps forward to speak.

"We have all heard and seen the evidence. The elders have decided to put an end to this story. Unfortunately, people have been hurt and we need to take cognizance of those feelings by way of compensation. Fayafaya, for using medicine to make someone do certain things that she would otherwise not have done, you must compensate both Tweya and Mayenga by paying them five head of cattle. The cattle must be given in a matter of days. We don't want to have another hearing. We also demand that you burn your *ndjungo* right now, so that we can all see it destroyed. It is a very dangerous object. The case would have been different if you had not used medicine. You, Fayafaya, must also pay your own wife, Rumono, two chickens for exposing her to those morning rituals to bewitch Mayenga. She has also been hurt, and it will take her time to forget that."

There is a lot of rumbling and muttering among the crowd. Some agree while others dissent. After listening for a moment, Shamashora continues, "It was difficult for the elders to decide the fate of the child, for in all fairness, both men are part of the child. It is however clear to us that Tweya certainly slept more with Mayenga than Fayafaya did. Therefore Tweya has more claim to have made his wife pregnant than Fayafaya has, although the latter obviously completed the job. Our community life is based on family. Fayafaya has other children while Tweya does not. Therefore the child in this case goes where the mother is going. After all, according to our customs a child always belongs to its mother, because, as we can see, it is sometimes difficult to tell who the father of the child is, but there is never a dispute over who the mother is. Finally, I am asking Mayenga's parents and the elder women to assist in handing over the child to this young couple and in reuniting them tonight. Fayafaya, I want you to take pieces of grass and wood now and burn your *ndjungo*. But first, I want to see you and Tweya shake hands and make peace here."

The two men meet in the center of the assembly and shake hands while they exchange nice words. Their families join them in making peace before they all break up.

"Thank you all very much and the case is closed. Let's all go home in peace, as one family that hurts whenever one of its members hurts," concludes Shamashora.

Everyone goes home reconciled. The general feeling is that what belongs to the past, belongs to the past.

As Muronga and Kaye leave and watch the *ndjungo* burning, they look at each other in dismay. Muronga wonders whether he is doing the right thing by going away, leaving his wife back home for an unknown length of time.

"You look pensive, Muronga. What is wrong, are you not feeling well?" Kaye inquires.

"No, not that. I am thinking about what can happen to one's wife when one goes away, like Tweya did. It is a terrible thing to have happen to you. I am going and leaving *Nyina-Mandaha* here . . . alone."

"Why are you thinking such things? *Nyina-Mandaha* is not alone. She has your child, and everybody in the *kraal* is there for her. And after all, she is the finest woman I know around here. And now that Mandaha is already here, she will not have any reason to . . . , you know."

"Yes, yes, you are right. *Nyina-Mandaha* can never do such a thing. What am I saying? But . . . , she is somebody's child too. These things can happen to anyone . . . "

"*Wiha-Mbushange*, would you like to walk home with me?" Uncle Ndara asks Muronga as he joins them.

"Certainly, we can go together," replies Muronga. Hastily he reaches out for Kaye's hand.

"See you tomorrow at your place then," responds Kaye, giving Muronga a reassuring smile.

"Yes, tomorrow at my place. Go well," Muronga says, turning with Uncle Ndara in the direction of home.

CHAPTER 5

"*Moro, moro, moro!*. How did you all sleep? Is everybody well?" Kaye calls as he approaches the hut. His greeting is something both Muronga and Makena have grown used to. To Makena, it is a reminder that her husband is going away.

"*Moro!* You are here already. Yoh, you are an early bird. How did you sleep?" Muronga calls from where he is standing on the roof of his hut. "How is everyone at home? Did you say good-bye to all your people, then?"

"Yes, I said good-bye. What are you doing up there, my friend?"

"I came up here to fix this cap before we go away. Why don't you come up here and help me put it in straight and then we will be on our way?"

A hand-tooled ladder that Muronga made before the rains leans against the hut. Holding tightly onto the single stalk, Kaye deftly climbs up the shaft to the edge of the grass roof and hoists himself onto it.

"Hey, this is a good ladder. It looks new! What happened to the old one you made when I made mine?"

"Oh, that one I made fire with. I found this beautiful *Mushosho* tree when I went to fetch the cattle not many days ago. It was such a beautiful piece. I took the bark off and made ropes out of it. The tree's branches were perfectly spaced for climbing on, as you can see."

Now standing on the edge of the roof, Kaye whistles loudly to express his appreciation of the view from the top of the hut.

"Whew, I would spend all my time up here just looking at the world, if I were you. Is this why you decided to build your hut here?"

"No, I found that out later," Muronga says as he finishes placing the grass-bundle cap over the hole in the roof. "I spotted you coming when you were way over there," Muronga replies, wiping his hand on his trousers and pointing in the direction of the river. "You can see everything from up here—the river, the *kraals*, the cattle grazing, and everybody coming and going." For a moment they look out over the quiet pastoral scene. The heavy morning mist is lifting as the warming sun rises gently into the sky.

"Now, Kaye, lend me a hand. Push the cap down while I hold it firmly. very good, it's in right. Thank you."

"I cannot get over this view . . . Look at all these huts!" Kaye continues, sitting down on the edge of the roof. "Can I see my hut from here?"

"Wait, wait, let me show you what you are looking at," Muronga responds, poising himself next to his friend. "There is Uncle Ndara's hut, the big one, there, then Mama Rwenge's, then my parents'. The little one is my unmarried sister's. By the gate is my other uncle's hut. Now look, if you count one, two, three and you skip one, two, three, and you count again one, two, three and you keep looking further ahead, you will see your hut on the extreme right. Can you see it?"

"Hmm, yes, it is quite close. I didn't realize that we lived that close to one another." The two men sit contentedly for a while, enjoying the smell of the fragrant air that wafts over them. The scent of blossoming fruit trees, drying beef and wild game meat, and the smell of wet grass and dirt create a heady aroma.

"This is nice. Maybe I should climb onto my roof sometime and see if we can see and talk to each other," Kaye jokes.

"A good idea! Then Mandaha can see you, too. Sometimes I sit up here with my little boy and we look at all the moving things below. He likes looking at all these great huts. One day he is going to build the tallest hut around here."

"And where is *Nyina-Mandaha* when you come crawling up here with her baby?"

"Ha, ha, ha, I wait till she is gone to draw water. She would kill me dead if she knew. And please, you are my friend. You don't say a word of this to her if you want to see the next rains, you hear?" Muronga says to Kaye in a half-threatening, half-joking manner.

"Let's go down now. We need to get going soon. And maybe the boy is waking up. I want to say good-bye to him, but only if he is awake."

The two men descend quickly. Kaye politely waits outside as Muronga enters the hut for the last time for a long while. Makena is inside tidying up while Mandaha lies quietly asleep on the *kafungo*. Muronga looks wistfully at Makena for a moment. Sitting down on the kafungo, he takes a long last look around the hut, as if to take stock of everything in it. He then stands up, and putting his weight on his right leg, gives the wall a push with his right shoulder. He wants to make sure that the hut is standing firm, and that it will provide shelter for his wife and child while he is away. Then, sitting down again on the *kafungo* where Makena now sits, he puts his hand on his wife's inner thigh and, sighing audibly, says to her, "Hmm, woman, you know that this is mine. Keep these legs for me until I return. I will think of them all the time . . . especially every night. When I come back, strong, this *kafungo* will see a different me. I will rock it with you again. And the result will be another small one, maybe Mandaha's little sister this time." He laughs, patting his wife's thighs.

"Hush now, stop saying things like that," murmurs Makena shyly. "You know Kaye is here already. You cannot keep him waiting. And after all, Mandaha is still small. I shall wait for you. I do not know any other man. And I will think about you, too—every night. Keep yourself for me, too."

"Yes," he says. He has too much to say but can't find a way to say it all. "Well, I must go now and wait for the lorry by the car road. The man at the office told us to stand alongside the road early this afternoon. That is when the Shakawe lorries come. So, come with me now and say good-bye to Kaye. He is a great friend. I am sure he will look after me, as I will look after him."

"You and Kaye will be fine. The God of Our Forefathers will be with you, wherever you are."

Leaving the baby sleeping on the *kafungo*, they join Kaye outside. The two men chat briefly while Makena looks on. It is by listening to them that she is able to understand them. They need a lot of courage for their undertaking; she can sense it from the uncertainty that taints their discussion about their future.

"We have been through this parting before, have we not?" asks Kaye.

"Yes, we have, but this time we are leaving for good. We are not coming back today," replies Muronga.

"I wish you were coming back today," Makena says, laughing. "No, no, I am only joking. To me, you are always here, even if you go far away to other countries. Go well. Work well. We will all wait for you. I am sure your people said the same to you, Kaye."

"Oh, yes, they did," Kaye reassures her. The two of them continue their conversation, while Muronga quietly slips away to say good-bye to Uncle Ndara, Mama Rwenge, and the others. "In fact, they asked me to tell you that when the rains come, you must let my father know when your *ndjambi* will be. He will send two spans of oxen and some people to help plow your fields and harvest the crops."

"That is wonderful. I shall surely tell him. It will be a pleasure to feed them, and nice to work in your people's fields, too," Makena says gratefully.

Muronga returns. "Uncle Ndara and everybody bid us good voyage. Now we must go, Kaye," he says. "We must not miss the lorries."

"Yes, let's go. *Nyina-Mandaha*, stay well. We will send you news from time to time."

They say good-bye to Makena once again. Walking swiftly, they are soon swallowed up by the verdant forest and arrive at the roadside before the sun passes zenith.

The sun hangs in the sky directly overhead. It is so hot even the birds seem indolent, perched in the Stinkwood trees that wall in the narrow road.

"There has been no car on this road for the past two days, at least," says Muronga after sniffing the ground in the path in order to detect the odor of the last car that moved on it. "They haven't come yet. We can wait under that big tree over there," Muronga suggests. "We should be able to hear the droning of the lorries from afar."

"Yes, I guess we will just have to stand with the papers in our hands. Otherwise the lorries will not stop."

"That is true, Kaye. Maybe we should put the papers on the ends of two long sticks. Then, when the lorries come, we can raise them in the air. It will be easier for the lorry drivers to see the papers if they are right in front of them."

"Oh, good idea! Let's do it right away." They step into the dark forest to find sticks. Emerging, they split one end of each stick to hold the documents. "Now no one can miss the papers flying above the road, and get the message, least of all the Shakawe drivers, who are used to this experience," comments Kaye.

Then, they find two large rocks and place them in the shade. With their heads resting on the rocks, the two men stretch out flat on the ground, their sticks and papers at their sides. They wait, and wait, and wait.

Every time the wind whistles through the trees they hold their breath, sure it is the droning of the lorries. To the lullabye of the birds hidden in the trees, they grow drowsy.

"There!" shouts Kaye, jumping to his feet.

"There, what?" Muronga jumps up too, shaking himself awake. "Are the lorries here yet?"

"No, I was dreaming," Kaye mumbles. "I was dreaming that we were late . . . we didn't raise the papers in time . . . Oh, what an awful dream'."

"I am glad it was only a dream." Muronga says, still a bit dazed. "But I don't think we should sleep anymore."

Kaye is listening intently. "There, I can hear the lorries now. Can you hear them, Muronga?"

"Wait. Keep quiet!" Muronga holds his breath. "Yes, there they are," he says, holding his breath again. "There is definitely something coming . . . a car . . . I hear *vroom-vroom-vroom!*"

Grabbing their sticks, the two men begin waving them in the air. A few moments later an Albion lorry emerges from the forest underbrush like a charging elephant. Grey, kicking up dust, and trampling everything in its path, the huge elephant-like lorry disturbs the small creatures of the tranquil forest, as its sides brush against the small trees beside the road. After the usual three quick gear changes, the lorry comes to an abrupt standstill. The lorry driver has seen the two men with their sticks and papers waving in the air. Shaking and heaving, as if out of breath, the mechanical elephant suddenly trumpets loudly. Within a few moments, two more lorries appear, one following the other, and pull up behind the first one. Then, as if connected trunk to tail, a small blue Ford sedan and another lorry appear and stop, the last lorry bringing up the rear. The baby elephant blue sedan carries one white man. *Watji*, as he is called, is the watcher, the supervisor of the black lorry drivers. Like a baby elephant's position in the herd, his position in the convoy is strategic—it guarantees protection from both ends and ensures constant observation. Always dressed in a multi-pocket khaki safari suit and wearing sunglasses, the *Watji* is responsible for seeing that the black lorry drivers do their jobs properly and punctually. In Botswana . . . in Africa . . . this is the way things are done.

The driver of the first lorry climbs down from his seat in the driver's cab.

"*Le ya kae, koRundu?*" he asks them, motioning to give him their papers. He is speaking Setswana, and although Muronga and Kaye do not understand it, they deduce that he must be asking them if they are going to Rundu. With their hands properly behind their backs, they nod and reply, "Rundu, yes, Rundu."

The driver looks at their papers and at them, and handing back their papers, he says, in Setswana, but using more sign language, "Okay, get in. Here, let me open the back gate for you. Get in and sit there . . . on the middle bench."

Muronga and Kaye sit down next to each other on the middle bench. The men in the packed lorry come from different parts of South West Africa and speak many different languages. Most of them are well-dressed and have big trunks next to them. Next to Kaye sits a fat, elderly man wearing dark sunglasses and a large cowboy hat with two long ostrich feathers, one on each side. He smells like the white people who come to tribal meetings and he speaks a language that is completely foreign to Muronga and Kaye. At one point he asks Kaye something in a strange-sounding language, *Sfanakalo*. One old man whom the lorry picked up after Muronga and Kaye, sees that the two young men do not understand *Sfanakalo*, so he translates for them. "This man is asking you, 'Where do you come from? Are you going to work in the mines? Do you understand Oshiwambo?' He is asking because he says there is no one else in this lorry who understands Oshiwambo. It is his language, but he has neither heard nor spoken it for sixteen months now. He does not know how his family is right now. They are in Ovamboland. He came to Kavango so that he could have the opportunity to work in the mines." Muronga and Kaye can only stare at each other as the man talks enthusiastically to them, wishing they could understand him themselves.

The sandy road to Rundu is long. The lorries stop at every Catholic mission along the way to pick up mail bags. As the sun goes down, the lorries pull into the camp at Shamvura, and all the men prepare to spend the night there. The *magayisa*, the men who are returning home after completing their contracts, display the wealth they have accumulated while working in the mines. Muronga and Kaye watch with interest as the *magayisa* play their radios, phonographs, flutes, and guitars. Some of them sleep under good blankets, and some even under sheets. For those less fortunate, like Muronga and Kaye, there is a hut where they can get mats and blankets for the night.

Muronga and Kaye put their mats next to one another on the ground. After the strain of watching others displaying their goods ostentatiously, they are exhausted and try to sleep.

"Muronga, are you tired?" asks Kaye.

"Me? Why?" responds Muronga.

"I mean . . . did you see enough. . . ?"

"Yes, I am exhausted from looking at so many people. I wonder how I would behave if I had so many things, clothes, money, and so forth. These people seem to be so different from us. They behave so differently—like excited children, or drunken adults."

"What do you mean? Do you think they are happier than we are?"

"Heh, heh . . . happier? That happiness is on the surface. Deep down inside I am sure they are not happy. Their lives are buried under those heavy boxes. Did you see the way they looked at us? As if we were deprived?"

"Yes. I can only hope that they will share all those things with their people back home."

"I hope so, too. I would feel very unhappy if I possessed so much while my people had almost nothing. But what makes me really sad is that some of these 'possession-havers' behave like white people. It is as if they don't see you as a person—they only need you to help them, to do a task. Do you remember how that short man asked us to help him unfold his new blanket? He didn't need help. He only wanted us to see his beautiful blanket. And he didn't even thank us."

"I know. He is not like a real person. Do you think the same thing will happen to us? Or were these people just not well brought up?"

"Only if we let it. We must remember why we are going away. We are sleeping outside in the cold like this because we need money to pay the white man's taxes. We are going not only for ourselves, but for all of our uncles, brothers, wives, and fathers—for everyone we have left behind. What we earn, belongs to the rest of them. That is why we are going."

"Yes, you are right, Muronga," says Kaye. "Let us sleep now. We leave very early tomorrow morning. Think of it, tomorrow at this time we will be in Rundu. In the big place."

CHAPTER 6

The rains left the road between Shakawe and Rundu in very bad shape. Awakened before dawn, Muronga, Kaye, and the other men boarded the lorries just as the day was beginning to break. Even half asleep, each man knew his place in his lorry—the same place on the hard bench to which he had been assigned the previous day. Bouncing gently and rocking slightly to and fro, the lorries lulled the men back into an uncomfortable sleep, which was disturbed only by their occasional slewing on the muddy road, slamming the drowsy men into one another as they slid haphazardly on the benches. At first, some of the *magayisa* tried to escape the discomfort of the ride by singing songs learned in the mines, but they were quickly silenced by the protests of those trying to sleep. Stopping every now and then to pick up men with the right credentials and to drop off those returning home, the lorries are almost full by early afternoon.

"Oh, my buttocks are sore from sitting still the whole day," says Kaye, rubbing his rump.

"My backside is screaming with pain, too," responds Muronga. "I did expect this, though. It is part of the whole business."

"Well, I only hope that our tails will not have fallen off by the time we reach this Rundu of theirs," replies Kaye, somewhat dismally. Turning off the road to the right, the lorries make a final stop at Shambyu, the Roman Catholic mission nearest Rundu to the east. "Do you have any idea where we are, Muronga?" asks Kaye.

"No, I haven't. But it looks exactly like our mission, Andara. The buildings, the roads, everything is the same," replies Muronga, sounding somewhat surprised, as he joins his friend in watching the scenery from the opening in the back end of the lorry.

After the last brown mailbag has been thrown into the lorry, the final stretch of the long trip begins. The road is a bit better here because there are more cars to use it, so it must be taken better care of. Muronga and Kaye overhear an elderly man opposite them explaining to his friend that they are almost at the end of the road. He says, "This road leads to Rundu, the main town in the region, where most of the white people live. Originally called Runtu, and meaning 'too many people squeezed together', Rundu is the source of all things foreign to the Kavango people; all things 'white'. In the beginning, the white missionaries came to civilize the heathens and save their souls. They came, that is, to pave the way for the white man's new system of trade, finance, and justice— all the ingredients needed to support a 'healthy' civil service. Rundu," he continues, "is the source of new ideas, new technologies, and the many new structures needed to house them—hospitals, stores, and offices where workers sift stacks of paper. But Rundu is also a breeding ground for much that is evil—it is a place where the survival of the fittest is the order of the day. So the white people made laws to control the evil, and jails for disciplining wrong doers." Some of the things he says Muronga and Kaye do not understand but they have often heard of the place Rundu.

Like them, virtually everyone in eastern Kavango knows the story of a man named Makombwe, a criminal, who was sent to Rundu to be punished for a crime he had committed. In accordance with the new white man's law, the chief of the haMbukushu was required to send Makombwe to the commissioner's court in Rundu for sentencing. Although no one really knows what happened to Makombwe while he was in the white man's custody, it is sure that no one else ever suffered the way Makombwe did in the Rundu jail. So misbehaving children are often warned that they must behave well, lest they see what Makombwe saw in Rundu.

Bang! Bang! Bang! Everyone in the lorry is startled by the banging sound on the metal side panel of the lorry.

Kaye's eyes spring wide open. "What was that, Muronga? What is happening? Are we in trouble?"

"I don't know. It isn't hail, because it isn't raining. Is it someone throwing rocks?" responds Muronga, looking in every direction through the side of the Lorry. "Oh, my mother. Do you see that man, one of the *magayisa* in the back?" Muronga asks Kaye. "You see, he has been hurt. There is blood on his face, look, look quickly!"

"Yes, I see. But what is happening? How did he get hurt?"

"Maybe someone hiding in the bush was throwing rocks. You remember, boys do that all the time. Sometimes they do it for fun, but other times they have done it because they are angry at the people who travel on these lorries and throw things out at the people on the road."

"Yes, I saw some boys throwing rocks not very long ago. I confronted them and one of them showed me where he was hit by an empty tin that was thrown from a lorry by the *magayisa*. But maybe we should not talk about this here, now."

"Yes, you are right, Kaye. Some of the *magayisa* might be angry if they hear us talking like this. I hope we arrive in Rundu soon. My whole body aches," Muronga says as he rubs his sore muscles.

The sun is turning red in the west as the lorries circle around the main compound in Rundu and drive through its main entrance. The arriving lorries are greeted by the singing of the men who are waiting to be sent away to begin their contract labor. Answering their songs, the men in the lorries greet their fellow men as the drivers stop in the middle of the compound.

"So this is Rundu," says Kaye, hopping out of the lorry, with Muronga right behind him. Wide-eyed, the men look around at their surroundings. To one side there are a couple of large buildings—no doubt one of them is the main office. The other one looks like a place where the men eat. It has tables, benches, pots and smells of food. On the other side there are six *rondavels*, or imitation huts, situated next to one another in a half-moon shape, their entrances facing toward the center of the compound. Opposite the main entrance, there is another large building, which looks like an assembly area, where announcements are made, and behind it there is a high free-standing wall. Shady trees fill the rest of the compound, which is itself encircled by a high concrete wall.

"Yes, this must be it," says Muronga, his voice betraying his mixed emotions.

They fall silent again, each one drowned in his own thoughts and anxiety. Presently, a short, fat white man, accompanied by two black baton-wielding guards and another black man, comes out of the office and approaches the men. Since they look very official, the new men automatically assume that announcements are imminent. Thus, without being told to do so, they all gather around. Everyone wants to hear what is going to happen next.

Addressing the black interpreter in *ʋsʋsʋsʋs*, the white officer says, while motioning with his arms and hands, "Tell them that everyone from here to here is going to sleep in *rondavels* A, B, and C, and everyone else will go to *rondavels* D, E, and F."

Turning to the men, the black interpreter says in a very loud voice, "Listen to me, everyone! You must all listen very carefully! From the tall, barefooted man there, . . . yes, you there . . . , to this man with the torn undershirt, here. You must go to the three *rondavels* there. You are going to sleep there." He points at three of the *rondavels* while he speaks to the men. "The rest of you must come with me and I will show you where you are going to sleep. And listen . . . you only sleep where you are shown to sleep. Only six men will sleep in each hut."

As the interpreter finishes, the white officer says, "Now tell them that there is food for them in the eating place over there. They will get plates and spoons there, and they must not steal these utensils. They belong to the government. Tomorrow morning at nine o'clock, when the bell rings, they must all assemble in the building there."

The interpreter begins again, "After we show you where to sleep, you go to that place over there where you see the smoke. You will get plates and spoons there, and also food to eat. Tomorrow morning, when you hear a bell ring, you must run there as fast as you can. Then you will be told what to do next. And listen. The plates and spoons that you will be given are not yours to keep. You must not steal them, otherwise you will be in big trouble. They belong to the government. Do you hear me, all of you?"

Even though the interpreter has been speaking in Rukwangali, the men have been able to understand, since the various local languages are fairly similar. All of the men nod their heads and reply with a resounding, "Yes."

Muronga and Kaye have been assigned to *rondavel* C. With a mixture of mild trepidation and amusement, the men approach the circular concrete-walled, thatched structures. At the entrance they pick up mats and blankets. The mats they place in rows on the cold concrete floor, with the blankets folded at the head of each mat. Muronga and Kaye's mats are next to each other again. To be next to each other is one of the things they always wish for.

Then the bell rings, and the men, like cattle herded to a waterhole, assemble at the eating place. They are first given metal plates and spoons, and then a large serving of *mealie meal* porridge covered with gravy. They eat quickly, without talking. As darkness descends, they finish their meal and go directly to the *rondavels*.

Muronga and Kaye lie quietly side by side, having grown closer to each other in the days since this undertaking began. They are now fellow-achievers and fellow-sufferers. Whispering, so as not to be heard, they speak of the day's activities and of their impressions.

"Shooh, it's hot in here! Are you hot, too, Kaye?" Muronga inquires.

"Yes, I am cooking under this blanket. I wonder who has slept under it before? I mean, think of the many people who have covered their bodies with it. It feels used," replies Kaye.

"Mine too. In fact, all of the blankets and mats have been used many times before. I wish I had my own blanket, instead. It is warm . . . it is mine . . . and it has my own smell on it. My father gave it to me when *Nyina-Mandaha* and I separated, when she was big with Mandaha."

"I am grateful, though, that we have these mats and blankets. Otherwise we would be sleeping in the sand like last night, or worse yet, on this hard floor."

"That's true. We must always be thankful for good things. Like the food we were served tonight from those huge three-legged pots. It was not bad, after not eating anything for more than a day. I wonder what will be in store for us tomorrow."

"I wonder, too. I don't understand everything these interpreters say. They are funny people, I think. They just shout and scream. Can't they talk normally, like you and me and the other men in this room?"

"No, they can't. They have to shout to show the white man that they are different from the people they translate for. They cannot be themselves when they translate. Probably they are themselves when they are in their homes with their families, but not when they are with the white man."

"Yoh, that must be very strenuous!"

"Yes, well, that is how it goes. Either you are with your own people, or you are the white man's instrument, and you jump on your own people while the white man stands comfortably in the background."

"Again tomorrow we will see and experience many things. It is going to be a hard day."

"A hard week, you mean. Not just a day. We are going to be here for a whole week. While you were fetching your food, I overheard two men saying that all of the men who have been here for a week already, and who will be going east, will be leaving on the lorries tomorrow morning."

"It is, perhaps, good that way. Then we will be able to see more of Rundu. And we may even meet some of our own men who are returning home."

"Yes, that's true. My friend, we had better go to sleep now. We must not be sleepy tomorrow. Sleep well, Kaye."

"You, too, Muronga. Let's hope that tomorrow will be a good day, better than today."

A beautiful Monday morning dawns. Almost everyone in the *rondavel* has been awakened by the sunlight filtering into the hut. They lie on their mats silently, not moving, in order to hear every sound outside.

"Ding! Ding! Ding!" comes the sound of the bell finally. All of the men leap from their beds.

"There we go'" exclaims Muronga, already on his feet. "How did you sleep, Kaye? All right?"

"Yes, under the circumstances. And you?" replies Kaye, equally alive.

"Ah, not very well, I am afraid. It was so noisy outside. There were autos vroom-vrooming all night long. There must have been at least ten of them. I would just like to know what these people do and why they have to drive around at night. The lights from their cars were shining right in my eyes."

The other men are folding up their bedding, so Muronga and Kaye follow suit. There is no harm in learning new habits and adapting to new situations. The six men leave the *rondavel* together and head towards the big building where they have been instructed to go first thing in the morning. As they cross the compound after their breakfast, they see some of the men who have been in the compound longer, playing *wera*, a traditional African game, in the sunshine while others watch, waiting for their turns to play. It looks as if it may be one of the only ways to spend leisure time in the compound. The rest of their time will no doubt be spent on carrying out orders, fetching food, eating and sleeping.

Muronga and Kaye walk fast so as to be there on time. All of the new men, the *manyowani*, assemble in the large open-walled, building. Two white officers, the black interpreter, and the two black guards are already inside waiting for them. The two white men are seated behind a long table while the three black men stand nearby.

When everyone is inside, the same rotund white officer who met them yesterday says to one of the guards, "Guard, blow your whistle, so that these people know that they must keep quiet and pay attention to me!"

The guard blows his whistle, and raising his round-headed wooden scepter, or kerrie, in the air, shouts, "Silence! The boss wants to speak."

There is absolute silence. The white man pounds his pipe on the table and says, "Ehm, what is your name again, interpreter?"

The other white officer responds, "His name is Blackie."

"Oh, yes, thank you very much," replies the first officer, turning to his colleague. Then, with a patronizing smile, he winks and nods to the other officer, saying under his breath, "He is a real blackie, this man!" Then, turning his attention once again to the interpreter, he commands, "Listen, Blackie. Tell these people that we are going to collect their papers now . . . from all of them . . . so that we can write down their names. Tell them that all of the Christians, those men with Christian names, must form a line on my right hand side, and the heathens must form a line on my left hand side. They must each hold their papers in their right hands. Tell them what I have said in your language."

"Now, listen carefully, everyone!" begins the interpreter. "You are going to form two lines, and in this way. The Christians will form one line, beginning here, on the right hand side of the master, and the heathens will form another line, here, on his left hand side. Now, start separating yourselves, . . . quickly! Hold your papers in your right hands. Everyone. Do you hear me? And don't talk! This is not the place for you to be talking. You have talked enough already and you will be able to talk more when you go back home, but not here. Do you all hear me?"

The men form two lines as instructed. Muronga and Kaye sadly part for the first time since leaving home together. The two guards approach the table, and walking down each line, collect the papers. Then stacking them in two separate piles—one stack from the men with Christian names, the other from those with heathen names—they place the papers at the two ends of the table.

"Okay, Blackie, now tell them to leave the room," says the white officer. "They must wait outside until we call them back. We need to compile the lists of their names. And tell them not to forget that when they return they must stand in the same positions they are in now."

"The master says that you must go out and stand in the sunshine until you are called back," instructs the interpreter. "You must know your places. When you come back you must stand exactly where you are right now, otherwise you will be in trouble. Look around and make sure you know your places." He gives them some time to study their places. "Now go . . . quickly! Don't talk and don't get out of line!"

The men leave the room in silence, keeping in their lines as if tied to one another with an invisible rope. In the beautiful African sunshine, they wait anxiously to be recalled. The usual communication that would exist in such a situation has been broken by the white man's decree. Like all of the other men, Muronga and Kaye can only communicate with each other across the new barrier through eye contact—they dare not speak to one another.

After an hour or so has passed, the whistle sounds. Everyone understands what it means. They walk rapidly back into the room—but carefully, so as not to lose their sacred positions.

"Stand upright in your places now:" shouts the interpreter. "Is everyone in the right position?"

"Yes!" the men shout back in unison.

"Blackie, tell them that we have thirty-six men here; twenty-five Christians and eleven pagans. Tell them that the doctor is coming from the hospital this morning to see how healthy they are. They must all be checked, so show them where to go. Okay?"

"There are too many of you, the master says. From here you must follow the two security guards to the place where the doctor is going to listen to your bodies. You must be healthy in order to go on contract. If you have T.B. you must go home; you have drunk too much beer. Now, stay in your same lines . . . don't mix together. Okay. Follow the two men there!" shouts the interpreter again, pointing to the two black guards.

Single file, the men follow the two guards behind the tall free-standing wall. First, they are told to take their clothes off and hang them over the wall. Then, they are told to form a large circle and run around naked, which they do while the fully clothed guards watch. This is what they will do when the doctor comes, they are told. The doctor must see their private parts in order to ascertain their state of health.

After a while, a white doctor, wearing a stethoscope around his neck, arrives. He talks to the guards for a few moments. Suddenly one of them shouts, "Stand in your lines and spread your legs wide apart. Run slowly in a circle so that the doctor can look at you." The guard knows all the steps of the exercise. He tells the men, step-by-step, what to do, while the doctor walks back and forth, eyeing them intently, as if he is inspecting a guard of honor.

"Now stand still in your lines. Don't move!" bellows the guard.

The men do as they are told. Repeating the few phrases of Rukwangali he has learned, the doctor inspects each of the men individually. He thumps each man's chest and listens with his stethoscope, then looks at each one's penis while saying, "Breathe in, cough loudly, laugh—now jump up and down, lift one leg up, the other leg—now squat just like you do when you shit in the bush."

This procedure takes up the whole morning. When it is over, the men dress and go to have their lunch. They are free for the rest of the day, and for the next two. The next time they meet will be on Thursday, when they will be told their final destinations.

On Tuesday and Wednesday Muronga, Kaye, and the rest of the *manyowani* spend their time walking around the compound, fetching wood, playing *wera* and sleeping. During these two days they also get to see a little bit more of Rundu. Muronga and Kaye are amazed to see so much that is new to them. They are astonished to see so many people going into and out of many offices and shops. They are fascinated by all of the cars that come in different shapes and colors, all moving in different directions. They have never seen so many objects in motion before! At first, they both count every car they see. One, two, three, four, five and many. Eventually they are forced to give up the excercise. There are simply too many of them to count. When darkness comes, they watch as some strange objects begin to glow like hard fire. They have been told that the light comes from the wires they see strung from dry trees. They enjoy drinking the water that comes like little rivers out of metal pipes, unlike their water at home, which is drawn in buckets from the mighty Kavango River. Rundu is too big a place for them. There are too many people walking in all directions not talking to each other. It makes them tired to see all this.

It is almost dawn, "Hey, Kaye," Muronga whispers. "Today is Thursday. Wake up. You remember, don't you, that we will not be allowed to be together, maybe for the rest of the day?"

In a very soft voice, Kaye responds, "I know. Is anybody else awake?"

"I am not sure, but the man over there was coughing hard a while ago. I hope he does not have T.B."

"I was half awake already. I was thinking about all the things we have seen so far. It feels as if my head is too small to remember everything."

"Yes. There is too much to see here. When we go home one day we will have lots of stories to tell."

Soon there are more men talking softly in the room. The morning is growing older as the night decays. "Ding! Ding! Ding!" goes the bell again. The men do their morning chores swiftly before assembling in the dividing place. The two lines are established almost automatically this time, long before the two white officers and their black lackeys come. When they arrive, the black semi-officers greet the men. The white officers do not bother with the ritual—they are there to give orders, not to acknowledge that black men are people. They greet only fellow whites.

The white officers take their seats at the table while the black guards stand, almost at attention. The senior white officer opens his large book with his fat hands as a deathly silence is maintained by the other men in the room.

"So, today is the day you have all been waiting for," begins the white officer. "Okay, so now you must listen very carefully." Addressing the interpreter, he says, "Tell them, Blackie. Tell them in your funny language what I have just said."

"The master says that you must listen to his words very carefully. Today is the day when you find out where you will be going."

"My assistant here, Master Ramsbottom, will read off all your names," continues the white officer. "Some of you will be going on WENELA contracts to work in the mines in South Africa, and will not be leaving until next week. Another group will board the SWANLA bus to Grootfontein tomorrow. Some of those leaving tomorrow on SWANLA contracts are going to work on farms as shepherds and kitchen boys; the rest will be going to CDM to work in the diamond mines. Now, listen carefully."

Again, roughly interpreting what the white officer has said, the interpreter says, "Your names will now be read by the other master, and you will be told where you will be going. Some of you will be going to work in the gold mines, some in the diamond mines, and some to work as shepherds or kitchen boys. You are not allowed to ask questions or refuse. You go where you are sent, or else back home!"

When he has finished speaking, the tall, skinny white officer, Master Ramsbottom, stands up and says in a high squeeky voice, "All right, listen carefully. I cannot read your difficult names easily, especially your funny heathen names. Anyway, the first fifteen names I read are the names of the people who will leave next Monday for South Africa. Okay?"

"The master is now going to read the names of those men who will be going east, to South Africa. They must go and stand under the tree over there."

"Johannes Kaveto, Thomas Wetu, George Thawo, Florian Munkanda, Gregorius Kalyangu, Franziskus Muronga, Jona Kudumo, Ndango, the son of Kantana ... "

As their names are read, the men go one by one and stand under the designated tree, until the officer finishes, and fifteen men are there. Muronga wonders if he heard correctly that his friend Kaye is not in his group. He glances at Kaye. He is on the verge of saying something, but refrains. "The following people are leaving tomorrow for Grootfontein to work as·shepherds, kitchen boys, and so forth," continues Master Ramsbottom.

"Those men whose names are called next will go west to Grootfontein to work on the farms. You go and stand by the wall over there," the interpreter translates.

"Sitentu Mungongi, Fabianus Sirema, Otto Shitembi, Gerhard Katjire, Kuyakenge Herehere, Paulus Sikondom-boro, Pius Pangandjira, Mukena Mbadimbayitawa, Tangeni Mwenyasirongo . . . " Twenty-five names are called out and he continues, "The following ten people are the ones going to CDM in Oranjemund. They stay right here. They are also leaving tomorrow."

"Those of you whose names have not been read yet must remain here in this building. You will also be leaving by bus tomorrow. You will be going to work in the diamond mines in Oranjemund."

When the interpreter has finished, Master Ramsbottom reads the names. "Josef Neromba, Heikki Sintango, Kaye the son of Shakadya, Longinus Shidjukwe, Franz Nyangana, Edward Sirongo . . . "

Finally, at the signal from the senior white officer, the black interpreter tells the men they can now take a break. In the afternoon, the men will be issued their new papers. They may now mix, but they must know their proper groups when they return this afternoon.

Muronga and Kaye are sad that they must part tomorrow, but glad that neither of them is going to be going to the farms to be a kitchen boy. They are both going to work in the mines, though not the same ones, to do men's work. Muronga is going east to South Africa, and Kaye west to Oranjemund, South West Africa.

In the afternoon each man is fingerprinted and given the appropriate papers. Muronga and Kaye cannot make head nor tail of the contracts they have "signed" and now have to carry, and neither can most of the other men. That doesn't matter; they will guard the sacred papers carefully. But what does matter is that they now know where they are going, and, luckily, neither of them is going to be a *missus'* boy.

The following day, Friday, Kaye's group prepares to leave by bus for Grootfontein. Muronga is very sad, thinking of the lonely weekend he will spend in the compound without Kaye. It would have been better if he, too, were leaving the compound. He would not have so many memories of the time they had spent together.

Before Kaye boards the bus, the two men grasp one another with both hands. Shaking hands warmly, they gaze silently at one another for a moment or two. To Muronga, the bus is like another huge monster that comes to swallow his friend. It reminds him of the story of a monster that swallowed people and saved them from a cruel storm.

"Stay well, and go well, Muronga. Thank you for your friendship . . . thank you for everything."

"Go well, and work well, my friend. The God of Our Forefathers bless you and keep you. We will see one another again one day."

The two friends let go of each other's hands reluctantly. Parting at last, they walk steadfastly in opposite directions, Kaye towards the bus, and Muronga towards the *rondavels*. Every now and then they turn to wave and smile at each other. Kaye, now in line with the other men, waits his turn to board the bus. Soon he and the other men in his group are seated aboard the bus and, wasting no time, it slowly pulls out of the compound. Muronga, from a distance now, watches and waves, unsure if Kaye can see him, until the bus disappears behind the high wall surrounding the compound. Alone for the first time since beginning his adventure, Muronga walks slowly to the *rondavels*, wondering what will happen to him and his friend in the days, in the months to come. Looking down at the ground, he says to himself, if I had had the choice—no, if I had had the freedom to choose—I would have chosen to be with Kaye, to go with him, east or west. But now, I must go east and he, west! Where will I ever find another friend like Kaye?

PART II:
GOING THE DISTANCE

CHAPTER 7

At dawn the lorries enter the compound in Shakawe. The vehicles begin to slow down as they approach the huge metal gates at the entrance, waking the drowsy men who gradually become aware of the fact that they have arrived at their destination. Stretching and shaking themselves, yawning and rubbing their eyes, one by one the men turn to look out of the side and back openings in the lorry. After making a circular turn around the open center of the compound, the lorries come to a gentle halt. The drivers immediately leave their cabs and enthusiastically stride to the back ends of the lorries, where they unlatch the backdoors. They are glad to be home.

"So, this is Shakawe in Bechuanaland—across the border," Muronga murmurs to himself. "I am now in a different land." He alights from the lorry with the other men into the bright morning sunlight. Glancing first in one direction and then in the other he quickly takes in his surroundings. The sun rising in the east casts a reddish glow over the Kavango River, but it remains hidden behind a high wall of Milkbushes that enclose the compound as the concrete wall surrounded the compound in Rundu. Save for the wall, this compound looks the same as the

one in Rundu. Only one thing is different—this compound
is cleaner, neater, tidier.

God of My Forefathers, this is it! I have arrived in this
country I have heard so much about. So many of my
relatives are here. If only I knew where to find them,
Muronga says to himself excitedly and with a sense of
pride. At the same time he realizes that more uncertainty
lies ahead. The lorry trip is behind him, but what lies
ahead can only be described as fantastic. Men who have
come this way before have told stories about huge magical
birds that fly at the command of one super-powerful and
all-possessing white man whose Christian name is The,
and whose heathen name is Government. He is almost
as powerful as the God of Muronga's Forefathers or the
God, the father of those people like himself, who turn
white and become children again when they are baptized.
The Government possesses the power to make laws, to
seize people's land, demand their dues, and chastise those
who do not obey commandments. When Mr. The
Government arrived in the land, he claimed the wealth
of the soil for himself. Then he created something he called
"money", which is now exchanged among the people, and
whereby he controls their lives. In fact, he seems to control
everything, including this flock of mysterious birds that
swoop down out of the sky like hungry hawks searching
for prey. On the ground, they wait impatiently for the
men from the Shakawe compound to come to them,
whereupon these huge monsters swallow the men whole
and alive and carry them in their bellies to an unknown
place where they are vomited upon the ground, only to
be swallowed again by noisy, lorry-like machines that
crawl like giant zig-zagging millipedes through the
grasslands of southern Africa, where they are deposited
in the mines. Muronga finds the thought of such creatures
both fascinating and unbelievable. Surely the stories he
has heard about them are true, just like Pater Dickmann's
story about the man who was swallowed by the giant

fish must be true. Muronga cannot wait to experience all of this for himself! If only his family back home could see him now!

Coming out of his musing, Muronga sees a smart-looking uniformed black policeman striding confidently towards the group of men. He is dressed in crisp, well-pressed khaki knee-length shorts and a matching jacket with shiny brass buttons adorning the shoulders and front. From his left shoulder hangs gold rope, which is, in turn, attached to a wide, well-polished brown leather belt. From his belt hang a whistle, handcuffs, and a baton on one side, and a small white notepad on the other. He looks impressive, but his air is friendly; his manner is not at all like that of the white officers or black guards in Rundu. Before the policeman can reach the group of men he is met by the lorry driver, who shakes hands with him and they exchange smiles, banter and official papers. As the lorry driver parts company with the policeman, he waves slightly. At the same time the policeman beckons to the men to join him. The men approach quickly, silently, with their hands behind their backs, and stand to attention in front of the policeman, who greets them with a gentle smile. Bewildered, only a few of the twenty-five men dare to smile back.

"*Dumelang!*" he says, still smiling. The men glance cautiously at one another, but do not return his greeting. "Oh, you do not understand Setswana!" He repeats his greeting in Sfanakalo. When a few of the men respond, the others begin to understand that he is welcoming them. But this is also not satisfactory. Pausing for a moment he bites the tip of his pen and taps a well-polished shoe on the ground.

"Hmm, I wonder . . . let me see," he murmurs. "Do you understand Thimbukushu?" he asks in Sfanakalo, looking at one of the men who responded to his greeting.

"I can understand Sfanakalo and Thimbukushu, so maybe I can translate for you. But I do not know Setswana," responds the man.

"Very good. What is your name? Please come here, then, and ask the other men to listen carefully. It is important that you all understand what I am about to say, so if you do not, feel free to ask me questions. You must also know that from now on everything will be said to you in Sfanakalo. It is the law, and that's how you will learn the language."

The interpreter translates what the policeman has said into very simple Thimbukushu, since not all of the men understand it well. It is enough if they get the gist of the message.

"On behalf of the Botswana Government," continues the policeman, "I warmly welcome you all to Shakawe, in the Republic of Botswana. You have permission to stay here in the compound today, but you are not allowed to visit the village. It is against the law in Botswana. Later this afternoon you will board an airplane and be flown to Maun, a large city in Botswana. From there you will travel by train to Francistown, and then on to the mines in South Africa. You will hear a bell ring twice while you are here. The first time it rings, you must all assemble here and you will be given some lunch. The second time you hear the bell, you must assemble here again. At that time you will be taken to the airport. When you hear the bell, come quickly, without delay. You must always be on time. Do you understand? Do you have any questions?

There are no questions. The men are hungry for more information about what they will soon experience, but how do you ask questons about what you don't know, have never experienced, and do not have the foggiest idea about? In any case, you simply do not ask your mother what she will cook tomorrow, you wait graciously for the food, eat it, and then ask your questions. The future will have its own rules. You do not ask today what you will do to the bridge tomorrow—you will either cross it, or burn it, when you get to it.

Before the men disperse, the policeman instructs them to go to their assigned *rondavels* and stay there until the lunch bell rings. Muronga walks slowly toward one of the *rondavels*. This is the first time that he has really thought about his friend, Kaye, since they were separated in Rundu. To his surprise, Muronga is not as lonely as he thought he would be.

I wonder where in this world Kaye is, muses Muronga, his head bowed, his gaze fixed on the ground. If only there were no trees on earth, I might be able to see him. He looks to the west. Suddenly hearing an unfamiliar sound coming from somewhere off in the distance, he looks up and scans the horizon with a discerning eye. Hm . . . just the birds. Oh, my mother, some of these river birds really sound like people! Muronga, who is not yet accustomed to hearing so many different languages, is relieved at seeing the noisy creatures and resumes his meditation. I wonder what languages Kaye is listening to there in the west?

Once inside the *rondavel* with the other men, Muronga lies down on a mat and tries to relax after the long night ride, but he is very restless. He tosses and turns on the mat. He sits up for a while. Finally, unable to sit still any longer, he gets up and begins to pace the room quietly, not wishing to disturb the other men. Every time he hears a sound in the compound he looks up expectantly, wondering what will happen next. After a while he stops by the doorway of the *rondavel* and stares blankly at the grounds of the compound. The sun is now nearly overhead and its brilliance bleaches the azure sky to a pale shade of blue. As his gaze settles on the metal gates of the entrance, Muronga catches sight of something flickering in the air above one of the gates. Curious, yet unconscious of his movements, he sets out from the *rondavel* and crosses the open area of the compound. In a trance, he walks without faltering and without being noticed by any of the half dozen brown-uniformed policemen. As he nears the entrance, Muronga is gradually able to make out a large rectangular piece of blue fabric which almost matches the color of the sky. It is suspended from the top of a tall metal pole, and flutters in the breeze, high in the sky. Now within a few feet of the pole, Muronga sees that the cloth has a design on it—it has one solid black stripe running from one edge to the other, with two thinner white stripes on either side. Struck by its appearance, but unaware of its significance, Muronga intuitively perceives its importance. I wonder why this piece of cloth has been put up there in the air to be torn by the wind? he says to himself. It must mean something.

In the shade of a small Baobab tree, Muronga sinks down onto his haunches to think. He is unconscious of the fact that he has left the *rondavel*, breaking the rules of the compound. He is only aware how tranquil and free this place seems. His mind wanders. He thinks of everything and nothing. The shape and color of the Baobab tree remind him of his son Mandaha when he was newborn— so brown and wrinkled, with a crop of thick curly black hair on top of his small head. He remembers the last time he held his son and caressed his wife. With a smile he closes his eyes and thinks about the last time he rocked his *kafungo* with her. His mind wanders further back into the past to the first time he saw his future wife, and still further back to his adolescence. He remembers how eagerly he used to listen to the stories his elders told about 'climbing the lorry'. Having heard these stories told and retold so many times over the years, he feels that each place is familiar and that he has passed this way before.

Opening his eyes at last, Muronga lets his head drop back and he stares up into the branches of the Baobab tree. There, perched right overhead, rests a large snake, which has coiled itself around a branch to sleep in the midmorning sun. Without thinking, Muronga instinctively jumps to his feet, grabbing a stick from the ground at the same time, and pivots on one foot so as to be away from the base of the tree if the snake should suddenly awaken and decide to strike. Muronga's traditions dictate that once a snake has been seen it must be killed, because most snakes are dangerous. But what is more, he now knows that snakes are also evil. Didn't Pater Dickmann teach him that at the beginning of time, an unusual snake came walking on two legs, traded oranges with a woman, and corrupted her with a desire for knowledge and never-ending life? And didn't he also teach Muronga that because the woman accepted the snake's promises, all unbaptized people go under the ground when they die, and they burn forever in a big fire? How any woman could believe that simply by eating an ordinary orange she would become wise, and would never die, is beyond Muronga's comprehension. Certainly no woman in his village would go near a snake dressed in missionary's clothing, to listen to its stories, let alone trust it!

Muronga watches the snake for a while. He can see that it is not moving and that it does not appear to pose any threat to him. He only hopes that the snake is not a bad omen for him and his family's immediate future. Maybe this is an unusual snake, so I shall not kill it, he contemplates further.

"*O dirang fa?*" comes a voice from behind Muronga. The policeman speaks sharply to Muronga, who only hears the sounds of the words. Startled by the voice, Muronga whirls around, forgetting the snake entirely. Facing him is one of the brown-uniformed Tswana policemen. Where he came from and for how long he has been standing there, Muronga is not at all sure. Muronga, suddenly conscious of having left the *rondavel* and gone against the rules, stares back at the policeman, eyes wide open and unable to speak a single word. "Are you one of the men who arrived today?" asks the policeman in Setswana. Muronga, not understanding one word of what the policeman is saying, can only continue to stare back in fearful silence. The policeman can see by Muronga's reaction that he has not understood his question. "Do you understand Sfanakalo, then?" he asks. Muronga, finally recognizing a few words, shakes his head, now smiling slightly. "And Thimbukushu? You are from South West, are you not?" queries the policeman.

"I am a muMbukushu. I speak Thimbukushu," replies Muronga at last, with a sigh of relief.

The policeman continues kindly but sternly in broken Thimbukushu, "Well, you are not allowed to be here, you see. You were told to stay in your *rondavel* until you are called. Do you understand? You must go there now, immediately. Otherwise, if the corporal catches you here, you will be in deep trouble. Do you understand?"

"Yes . . . yes . . . I am going now," replies Muronga, shaking his head vigorously. The policeman's eyes follow him as he turns quickly away and walks briskly back to the *rondavel*.

Finally the bell rings for the midday meal. Unlike the compound in Rundu, here the men walk at an easy pace to the building where the food is served. They are not given any harsh commands, but are served politely. They take their plates of food and gather in small groups under the trees in the center of the compound.

Muronga follows the other men from his *rondavel* and joins the meal line. There are many more men than arrived with Muronga earlier in the day, and he can see by their clothes that they are *magayisa* on their way home from the mines. Unexpectedly, a couple of them further up the line begin to speak in Thimbukushu. Muronga's ears immediately prick up at the familiar sounds. He cannot make out what they are saying, but he keeps his eyes glued to them, and follows them, once he has received his plate of *mealie meal pap*. He settles himself close enough to hear what they are saying, but far enough away to be considered polite.

"This food is not very good," says one of the men to the other, while taking a taste of his food.

"You are right. But remember, we have already paid for this food. The mine manager told us that before we left. If we buy any food in the village, we are only paying twice for what we eat," responds the other man.

"Yes, that's true. All the same, I am glad that woman in the market took me to her home and gave me a good meal."

"Hmm . . . and if I hadn't come and found you just when I did, she would have taken advantage of the fact that you have spent the past two years in the mines without touching a woman, and she would have demanded all of your money! These women in Shakawe know what to do with sex-starved *magayisa*! That is why the Government only allows *magayisa* to go into the village—they have the money to spend in the market and on women—not the *manyowani*, who have nothing. Do you know how many men have arrived home empty-handed, having squandered all their money here in Shakawe? Do you want to do that?"

"No, no, no. Of course not! It was just nice to talk to a woman again, but I already feel as if my wife has seen me there. I am glad you came to fetch me in time. That woman was really . . . eh . . . It has been a long time, you know?"

"Well, it will not be long now. Our wives have been waiting a long time, too . . . we hope." The two men look at each other with sidelong glances and begin to chuckle. Muronga and a few of the other men who have also been listening start to laugh along with them.

The food consumed, the men disperse to their respective *rondavels*. Muronga stretches out on his mat once again, this time falling fast asleep. The next sound he hears is the bell ringing, signaling to the men that the last leg of the trip is about to begin.

CHAPTER 8

The lorry trip to the Shakawe airport is a short one, but to the anxious men it seems long. Their hearts are pounding in their chests, though they try to act calm and indifferent. They are all excited by the thought of seeing these big birds they have heard so much about. Finally the lorry reaches the airport, which is nothing more than a small building surrounded by flat, empty, hard-packed dirt. Many times larger than the building, and looming over it as if ready to pick it up in its beak, stands the bird. Deathly still, wings outstretched, with a featherless body of gray metal and an orange tail, the bird glistens brightly. It does not look like any bird Muronga has seen before. It is terrifying and beautiful.

The lorry circles around under the belly of the big bird and stops near a long, metal stairs that reaches up into the side of the creature. The men are instructed to get out of the lorry by a uniformed white man who comes over to them and begins speaking to them in Sfanakalo. After he greets them coldly, he explains that they will soon be climbing up the stairs into the airplane and, once inside, each man will be assigned a chair that he must stay in for as long as the airplane is in the air. Muronga listens attentively, not wanting to miss a single word, but all the while he keeps one eye glued to the bird's closed beak, half afraid that the monster may come to life and devour him on the spot. He is relieved to find out that they will not be entering the creature through its mouth, lest they risk being torn to shreds by its sharp beak. Once the speech is over, the officer turns toward the stairs and begins climbing, instructing the men to form a line and follow him one by one. When they reach the top of the stairs another uniformed white man takes them individually to their chairs. Muronga, seated towards the back of the aircraft, is strapped into the seat with a large belt by the officer. He cannot remember ever hearing about such belts, and for a moment he wonders if they are necessary because this bird can also fly upside down. This thought is frightening, but what other explanation can there be?

From his seat at the back of the aircraft, Muronga can now see the inside of the big bird's stomach. It does not look like anything he has ever seen before. It is about as wide as a lorry, but much longer, and it looks like a tunnel. Each chair resembles a king's throne. All the chairs are very soft and comfortable, in contrast to the hard wooden benches of the lorry, and they are placed side by side facing forward in many rows. This strange bird also has small windows in the sides of its stomach, and Muronga wonders if ordinary birds have such holes in them as well under their feathers.

At last all of the men are secured in their seats and the huge bird begins to groan noisily. Muronga can feel the bird moving now. It walks slowly at first, then it begins to run, its head down at first and then raised into the air. Without flapping its wings very much, it lurches into the air, and Muronga grabs onto the arms of his chair with all his might, digging his fingers into the soft cushioning. The bird groans so loudly that it hurts Muronga's ears, and he would like to cover them with his hands, but he is afraid to let go of his grip on the chair, lest the beast make a sudden move, and he fall out of his seat. He is not sure the belt will hold him. It seems to be climbing higher and higher into the sky, and Muronga begins to feel dizzy. It is a terrible feeling to be up in the sky like this! Soon his stomach feels as if it is being turned upside down and inside out. He hears someone retching in front of him. Muronga can no longer hold onto the arms of the chair—he is definitely going to vomit, and he looks anxiously at one of the officers, hoping to attract his attention. The officer sees him and rushes over to him with a paper bag, just in the nick of time. A number of other men are apparently experiencing the same thing. Muronga has never felt so awful before in his life.

A bell chimes.

Oh . . . my mother! What is going on now? wonders Muronga, feeling nauseous again.

One of the officers comes and stands in the pathway that runs down the length of the aircraft, cutting through the rows of chairs.

"Men . . . ehm, the toilet . . . ," he begins hesitantly, pointing to his fly and pretending to unzip it, and then squatting. "Ehm . . . , the shit room," he continues, "is in the tail of this flying machine." With both arms outstretched in front of him, he points to the back of the airplane. Then with one finger raised in the air, he finishes his talk by saying, "And listen, only one man can go at a time. Do you all understand? O.K.? Thank you!" The men nod their heads, indicating that they have understood.

The mere thought of getting out of his seat and walking a few yards to the back of the big bird is enough to start Muronga's stomach churning and he vomits again. The officer comes over to him, and without saying a word, takes the half-filled paper bag from him, and gives him a new one in its place. Exhausted, Muronga sinks listlessly into his seat, his eyes closed, his hands gripping the arms of his chair. He would like to sleep but cannot relax. His mind wanders. How, he wonders, can such a beastly machine have been created? And who, other than the white man, could have conceived of such a fantastic monster? Muronga is both impressed and terrified by it. How does it work? He cannot even imagine. He would understand if the bird were very light and could be carried on the wind like a leaf, or if it were small like the real birds that live in the trees around the village, but this thing is neither lightweight nor small! I wonder how I would explain this creature to my son Mandaha? he thinks. Maybe by the time Mandaha is old enough to ask about such things, I will have the answers to his questions.

The airplane suddenly begins bouncing. Muronga's eyes pop open again. His stomach leaps into his throat again, and he swallows hard to hold it down. After a few moments, the airplane stops bouncing and begins to descend. Muronga takes deep breaths and holds them while continuing to swallow hard. At last the big bird seems to be nearing the ground. With a thud, the creature's feet hit the hard-packed earth. The bird runs some distance, slowing its pace all the while until finally it is walking and then stands still. Muronga begins to breathe normally again and his stomach settles down somewhat. Soon one of the officers comes and stands in the pathway and shows the men how to unfasten their belts. Then, walking down the pathway, he assists those who are having difficulty rising out of their seats. As he passes each row, the men file out into the pathway and walk to the door at the front. All of the men walk unsteadily, but a few, close to collapsing, lean on others for support. Muronga staggers out of the beast and down the stairs with the other men. He is thankful to have survived this experience and to be back on dear Mother Earth again.

To Muronga's surprise, the sky overhead is black, and the ground is lit by the same oddly shaped fire-holding objects that he first saw in Rundu. A short distance away he can see the now familiar lorries. An officer appears, who instructs them to get into the lorries. Muronga is so accustomed to this routine by now that he is hardly aware that his ears are blocked and he can barely hear anything. He is so tired after the big bird that he can think only of how good it will feel to lie on a mat in a *rondavel* and sleep for a long time. Like weary sheep, the men herd to the lorries, climb into them, and settle onto the hard wooden benches. In the darkness of night, the lorries speed away, finally slowing down at the entrance of yet another compound. Even in the dark, the drowsy men can see that it is laid out like the ones in Rundu and Shakawe. Straining their eyes to see the *rondavels*, they look hungrily at them while waiting impatiently for their assignments. Soon they are dismissed and without delay hurriedly trot off to their beds. There is no discussion; each man simply lies down on a mat and drifts off into deep sleep.

"Manyowani . . . manyowani!" Sunlight streams into the *rondavel* as the men are awakened by the crisp voice of one of the compound's officers. *"Manyowani!"* he shouts.

Thus rudely awakened, the men hastily roll up their mats and, wiping their hands over their faces and clothes, gather outside the *rondavels* in the center of the compound. An officer joins them and directs them to an open shelter, a corrugated metal roof held up by several cement pillars. The half-awake men are instructed to form a line, get their food, sit on the cement blocks scattered throughout the area under the roof, and eat all of the food they are given, because they will not be eating again before evening.

Muronga is given a plate of *mealie meal pap*, a chunk of something that looks like dark, dry, very stiff baked porridge, and a cup of thick whitish liquid. The drink, *marewu*, has a pleasant flavor, both tart and sweet. It is the only thing that makes the dry, fist-sized lump of bread edible. The *mealie meal pap* goes down easily. Muronga is ravenous after losing most of yesterday's food to the bird. It wasn't a bird at all, Muronga thinks, digesting his food. It is a flying machine, an 'airplane' as the people here call it.

Their hunger somewhat dissipated, the men become more lively and alert. Once they have finished eating, an officer addresses the group in Sfanakalo and tells the men to go now to that building over there, as he indicates the particular building by pointing at it. No translator is needed, as the men whisper to one another the gist of the message. They all rise from their seats and do as they have been told.

The medical center is staffed by several Afrikaans-speaking white male doctors, a number of black male nurses, and an equal number of black orderlies. The medical testing begins in the same way it did in the compound in Rundu—the men are commanded to run in a circle, jump up and down, breathe deeply, squat, stand with one leg up in the air, and so on. Then they are given an eye exam which consists of three tests. In order to ascertain which of their eyes is stronger, each man is asked to look through a cardboard tube at a small spot on the wall. The eye that the man chooses to use is obviously the stronger one. To determine whether each man's eyesight is adequate, the doctor stands some distance away from the men and drops a small piece of money on the floor and then asks each man to retrieve it. Anyone who cannot see the coin and pick it up has poor eyesight. Finally, to check each man's reflexes, the white dootor talks with each man and, while doing so, makes a sudden move with his arm, as if to strike the man. If the man attempts to protect himself, his eyesight and reflexes are considered to be good. The final exam is to test their endurance. They are required to lie down flat on their backs on the ground and hold weights in the air for some time.

These last four tests are necessary to determine each man's ability to see and carefully dig out the gold deposits from inside the narrow, dark mine shafts while maintaining uncomfortable positions for long periods of time.

But the final part of the medical examination is the worst part. After forming a line again, the men file past a nurse who instructs them to take off their shirts, whereupon she hastily grabs them by one arm and rubs a pungent liquid on the flesh near the shoulder. Within moments of leaving her cold hands, they are at the mercy of a doctor wielding a big instrument with a long needle. Trembling with fear, each man steps forward courageously to have the menacing instrument jammed ruthlessly into his tensed body. Six or seven men are given injections using the same carelessly cleaned instruments before they are discarded. An orderly waits nearby to assist the doctor and to help any of the men who become faint from this ordeal. Finally it is over. The men are escorted back to their *rondavels* where they are told to stay and sleep until further notice. Like all of the other men, Muronga is already feeling the soreness in his arm, and the muscles in his body begin to tighten up. His body feels very heavy and he starts to feel feverish. He quickly falls into a deep sleep, even though it is only midday.

As dusk begins to fall the men are awakened and instructed to get into the lorries. Almost mechanically, they follow orders. They are deposited at the main railway station in Francistown. Feverish and weak, the men wait as patiently as possible on the railway platform. Finally, one of the officers from the compound informs them that they will now be assigned to different trains that will take them to their respective mines. The men listen attentively for their names to be called off his list and follow his instructions. Muronga goes with his group to where one of the huge mechanical millipedes sits waiting, oozing white smoke and making loud, squeaking noises. He is feeling too sick to notice much about his surroundings and desires only to be back in the *rondavel* where he can lie down and rest undisturbed. But within moments, the men are being escorted to their compartments aboard the train. Muronga is given a compartment with three other men, only one of whom he recognizes as having been with him in the compound in Shakawe. Each man takes a bunk and tries to get comfortable lying on his side, so as to protect the arm with the injection. As the train begins to snort and sputter, moving grudgingly out of the railway station, Muronga dozes off and dreams of big birds swallowing long needle-brandishing doctors and vomiting them up into huge pots filled with *mealie meal pap*.

CHAPTER 9

Strange sounds and shafts of light filter into the compartment where the men lie sleeping. Aroused one by one, they shift themselves in their berths and shake their sore limbs. The sounds, a peculiar accompaniment, penetrate Muronga's dreams. Makena and Mandaha drift through his mind, but the words they speak do not belong to them. The voices he hears are those of strangers. Slowly Muronga realizes where he is, and the images shake loose from the sounds. Sitting up in his berth, he continues to think of his family, the village, and how far he is from them. It seems as though he has been away for a very long time already, and yet, it has not been so long compared to what lies ahead. Momentarily closing his eyes again, Muronga brings back the images of Makena and Mandaha, and he realizes how much he is missing them now.

The millipede lurches, and Muronga rubs his eyes as if to erase the images, then wipes the rest of his face with his hands. He proceeds to run his open palms over his clothes, trying to tidy himself as he looks across the compartment at the two disheveled men opposite him. He has not washed himself nor changed his clothes in the ten days since he left the village, and he can only assume that it has been at least as long since the other men have done so. Being used to bathing frequently in the Kavango River, Muronga feels very uncomfortable with his own uncleanliness.

He tries to distract his thoughts by looking out the small window of the compartment. The sunlight is not yet very bright, so it must be early in the morning. Small bushy trees fly past the window as the train speeds along its way. The landscape has become flat, dull, and rocky where once it was green and lush. Tswana women, dressed in brilliant dresses with water pails balanced on their heads, stop to cheer as the giant millipede rushes past them.

Soon houses can be seen dotting the landscape—a definite sign that a town is nearby. The millipede begins to slow its pace slightly. Suddenly the door of the compartment flies open and an odd-looking man dressed in a khaki-colored uniform pushes his head in the door. Muronga can hardly believe his eyes—this man is neither black nor white! His hair is almost the color of Muronga's, but lighter. But his skin is . . . well, almost black, and yet, it is . . . hmm, almost white! Muronga cannot even begin to guess where this person could come from, but it appears that he is an older man who has been around for some time.

The man shouts in *vsvsvsvs*. Tino, another man who joined Muronga's group in Shakawe, speaks Thimbukushu too. He also understands many other languages, including *vsvsvsvs*. He has been through this experience before. He tells Muronga about this funny-looking man, "This man works here. He says that we must get up now, all of us. We are in his country now. We must follow his instructions carefully. When we are outside we must follow him through the black gate. We must not go near the white gate. It is strictly forbidden. That gate is only for white people . . . the *baas*. If we even go near it we will be in big trouble. Now, come with me, quickly. Let's follow him!"

The four men in the compartment jump down from their berths and stand to attention, listening to every word the strange man speaks. They do not understand one word of what he has said, but they follow him, assuming that this is what he has instructed them to do. Muronga and the other men from his compartment are joined in the corridor by half a dozen other men, and when the train stops, they hop off and march quickly behind the porter. Other people are getting off the train, and Muronga is awed. Both white and black people are very well-dressed and Muronga cannot help wondering, as he passes through the black gate, if he must go through this gate because he is not so well kept. He feels somewhat ashamed as he looks down at his wrinkled, soiled clothes and then at these other neatly attired people.

The porter leads the group of men to a small office where they are lined up in front of a neatly uniformed white officer who, like the ones in the Rundu compound, is flanked by two gruff black lackeys. Muronga and two of the other men in the group are told by the white officer that they have been assigned to one of the gold mines in the Transvaal. He, like the porter, speaks this strange *vsvsvsvs* language, which none of the men understands, but it is enough for them to know and remember the name Doornfontein. The station master then goes on to instruct them, using words and sign language, to wait on the platform outside until they are called to board the bus that will take them to the mine.

Muronga and his two comrades go to a reddish-brown brick shelter to wait. Sitting on a wooden bench there, they can observe the train station and watch all of the people coming and going. Another train pulls into the station, huffing and puffing as it screeches to a halt, belching steam in every direction. Men and women mill on the grey concrete platforms. The white people walk about leisurely, reading their newspapers, smoking their cigarettes, and speaking *vsvsvsvs* to one another. The black people, by contrast—or rather those who are obviously laborers—are constantly being ordered here and there to carry suitcases or heave freight onto the trains. A train whistle can be heard blowing in the distance, first once, long and piercing the air, then two more times, shorter and louder as the train nears the station.

So much is going on around him that Muronga hardly knows where to look next. It is all exciting, yet bewildering. I wonder if I look any different than when I left my village, he thinks, now that I have flown high up in the sky in the airplane and then ridden on the *stimela*, the train. Surely I must look different after such adventures! If only my family could see me now!

Muronga's attention is once again riveted to the scene in front of him. He is fascinated by these giant millipedes, but does not understand how their many legs can be so well hidden from view, nor can he understand why they seem to follow these long shiny pieces of metal. Have they been trained to run between them? Is that how they know where to go? But why? So many questions fill Muronga's mind, but the answers evade him. Language is a big problem. Smiling shyly and shaking his head to and fro gently, Muronga glances at the other two men on the bench. They smile back and nod as if to say that they, too, are not sure what to make of all this.

Soon, another one of these odd-looking, not-exactly-black, not-exactly-white men dressed in an ill-fitting khaki uniform approaches them slowly. He is below the concrete platform in the area where the millipedes wait. With a stack of papers in one hand and a pen in the other, the man masterfully flips through the white sheets, bending down now and then to check the metal rails, all the while muttering in *vsvsvsvs*. The shunter walks skillfully on the rusty brown and shiny dark grey rails so as not to pick up too much of the tar that coats the black wooden railroad ties.

What if a millipede were to come along at this moment? Muronga thinks to himself. Would this curious man not be killed? How can anyone walk so expertly on these pieces of thin metal? Muronga is both frightened and fascinated by the man's behavior, when suddenly it all makes sense to him. Didn't Pater Dickmann tell the story of how the son of God, Jesus Christ, once walked on water? And was Muronga not told when he was baptized that he would turn white? Well, this man is almost white, and he can walk without fear in the path of the millipede! Surely this man and the other man who came into the compartment are very devout Christians! That explains why they are neither all black nor all white, Muronga concludes happily.

The shunter sees the three men staring at him wide-eyed and, putting on an air of importance as he checks his papers and shakes a loose coupling, he mutters loudly, *"Here God, die goed is los . . . demmet!"*

Hearing the words "God" and "damn it" Muronga is assured that his suspicion about the man being a Christian is correct. He has heard Pater Dickmann say these words many times before.

At last, one of the black lackeys from the office motions to the men. They follow him through the office to where the bus is waiting. It is already half full of men who look much as Muronga and his companions do. The three of them look at one another briefly as they search for seats. Finally the two others sit together in one seat while Muronga sits in another seat with yet another stranger. The seats on the bus are more comfortable than the benches in the lorry. To Muronga, the bus is something like a cross between a lorry and a train. It moves like a lorry, on wheels, but otherwise the interior looks more like that of a train. As the bus driver revs up the engine and pulls onto the black-tarred road, Muronga watches the vehicle glide smoothly along. The ride is more pleasant than any of those Muronga took by lorry.

The time spent on the bus passes quickly. The landscape grows more and more barren until there is not much more than a few trees sprinkled over the dry earth. Soon it changes, though, as small uniform brick houses begin to appear; obviously there is a town up ahead on the road. Women carrying bundles and babies stop to wave and the children jump about excitedly as the bus flies past them on the smooth pavement. The town is swarming with people who appear to be doing all sorts of things, including selling merchandise along the roadside. Gravel roads intersect the paved road and the sound of pebbles spattering against the underside of the bus can be heard until the town is well out of sight.

Again the terrain is barren for some distance and then signs of civilization begin to appear again. But this time the houses are very big and elegant with large stretches of finely trimmed grass surrounding them on all sides. Muronga sees only white people here, and now that he thinks about it, he doesn't remember having seen one white face in the other township. This town is very clean and not at all crowded, unlike the other one, he thinks. All of the roads appear to be tarred and people are only seen walking when they have their dogs with them on leashes. Muronga finds it curious to see dogs wearing collars and such things. Soon this town is also out of sight.

After passing through this town, a huge pink structure appears on the horizon. As the bus draws nearer to it, its shape becomes more defined. It is a massive compound similar to the others, but it appears to be several times larger. Broken bottles and large jagged pieces of glass glisten in the midday sun atop the ten-foot-high wall that surrounds the compound. Two five-foot solid metal gates block the entrance and are guarded by two mean looking policemen. Only the roofs of the barracks can be seen above the glistening, jeweled wall.

The bus stops in front of the main gates. The driver leads the men to a building just outside the wall, where their papers are checked again. Then each man is given overalls, a hard hat and headlight, socks and gumboots, pads for his knees and buttocks, a book of meal tickets, and a plastic wrist band which, by its color and number, indicates the man's status and his job.

Tomorrow, they learn, they will begin to go to the mine school. There they will learn Sfanakalo, and they will also learn how to handle the mine equipment. The rules and regulations, policies and procedures of the mine will be explained to them. They are also told that they must attend the school and that they will now be taken inside the compound on a tour.

A tall, robust policeman is waiting inside the gates for the men. He is strikingly friendly as he leads the men to the barracks and indicates to them that they are to leave their new clothes and equipment there in the barracks. The group of men follows the policeman from the barracks to the communal washrooms, and then to the kitchen where they are each given a tin plate, a mug and a spoon. They are told in Sfanakalo that every morning they must bring one page from their meal ticket book with them and for each meal they must bring these utensils. Finally, the policeman reminds them about going to school tomorrow and says someone will fetch them in the morning. The men are then dismissed and they make their way back to the barracks where they deposit their new possessions.

In his room in the barracks, Muronga throws himself heavily onto his bed and gazes around the room thinking to himself, Ah, . . . at long last! After so many days, and so much traveling, I have finally arrived. Thanks be to the God of My Forefathers and to the departed souls of my ancestors! Guide and protect me and my family back home from evil, and especially protect me from any harm that may befall me as a result of following the white man's orders. Help me and my brothers as we go about digging the rocks to make the white man smile. When I have finished my days here, return me safely to my home, where I will live in happiness with my family.

PART III:
BETWEEN ROCK
AND GOLD—RESISTANCE

CHAPTER 10

Friday morning . . . yes . . . it is Friday morning, thinks
Muronga, counting the days backwards since he left his
village. School begins today, he thinks somewhat
anxiously, still motionless on his bed in the barracks.
Friday morning. But it feels like a Monday morning.
Monday, the day when work begins. This is like the
beginning of a new life, he reflects, I have never been
to school before. I wonder how I will look sitting on a
school bench, being taught new things, clever things, he
muses, rolling over onto his side, now fully awake. I always
wanted to go to school, and this may be the only
opportunity I will ever have. But am I not too old for
this kind of thing? Wouldn't my wife and the others at
home laugh to see me going off to school everyday at
my age! Yes, it is good that I am far away from home.
School is for the young ones. For those who can afford
to be beaten on their hands and buttocks.

"*Lo manyowani, lo manyowani . . . !*" The voice of a veteran
compound security guard can be heard through the grey
metal door. Hearing the guard approaching, the eight men
in Muronga's room hop out of their beds and try to look

alert. This time they don't need to make up their beds. Each man's bed is his own for the length of his contract.

The guard kicks the metal door open and thrusts himself into the room. "You are up. Very good! These are the kind of men we need in the mine. I mean, . . . the kind of men the mine needs. Awake, strong, and ready to work. *Nina vukile kahle, madoda*?" continues the guard in his pompous manner. While Muronga and the other men get the gist of the guard's message, they wish they could understand this new language, Sfanakalo. Certainly the old man is talking about the mine school where they will be going today. Gesturing, he tells them that they must first wash themselves and then go to have their breakfast. With his jaw set and his fists clenched, he demonstrates to them that it is important for them to eat well so that they will be strong during the day. After he has finished his speech he goes to the next room to repeat the same story. He seems to enjoy this part of his work very much. As soon as he has left, Muronga and his roommates rush to the washrooms.

As they are coming out of the washrooms, they see other men lining up at the eating place. Hurrying back to the barracks, they grab their tin utensils and run back to join the line. For breakfast they are given a thick, dark, odd-looking bread dipped in apricot jam, two huge ladlefuls of *mealie meal pap*, and black coffee. As the men file by, the headboy in the kitchen tells them to eat quickly, wash their dishes, and that they must take all their clothes and equipment with them. They are told not to delay because their instructors are waiting in their classrooms. The men stand while eating their breakfast, and when they have finished, wash their dishes under the taps in the *pondok*, a metal roofed shelter. As instructed, they then return to their rooms, deposit their utensils, collect their clothes and equipment, and wait outside their doors until they are shown where to go next.

Two uniformed guards stride swiftly toward the groups of men and brusquely herd them into classrooms outside the compound near the office. Each classroom is equipped with rows of long, hard wooden benches and a huge chalkboard in the front of the room. To the right of the chalkboard is an overhead projector with various supplies for its use. Between the chalkboard and the benches is an open area where the instructor stands to demonstrate his lessons and quiz his pupils on what he has taught them.

Muronga and the other men are counted off by one of the guards and sent to their respective classrooms. They sit down on the benches and, without greeting them, the instructor begins the lesson. He is a young, well-dressed, confident black man who wears spectacles and carries six ballpoint pens in his pockets.

"*Madoda*," he says slowly in Sfanakalo. "I am your instructor. I am not a teacher. Only white people are teachers. You must call me instructor. Now listen. The first thing you will learn here is Sfanakalo, the language we use in the mine. Every man has to learn this language. You will learn it very quickly. So, watch and listen carefully. I am going to tell you the names of the pieces of equipment you will be using in the mines, and then the names of the parts of the body." He points at each piece of equipment and repeats its name three times.

"*Ena lo sgcoko.*"	(This is a hard hat.)
"*Ena lo layit.*"	(This is a light.)
"*Ena lo gogels.*"	(These are goggles.)
"*Ena lo ovarol.*"	(These are overalls.)
"*Ena lo madolo.*"	(These are kneepads.)
"*Ena lo skatulo . . .*"	(These are shoes.)

"And now the names of the parts of the body. Listen carefully and see what I am touching. Do you understand?" "*Ewe,*" the men reply eagerly.

"*Ena lo mzimba.*"	(This is a body.)
"*Ena lo skop.*"	(This is a head.)
"*Ena lo mehlo.*"	(These are eyes.)
"*Ena lo mlomo.*"	(This is a mouth.)
"*Ena lo sandla.*"	(These are hands.)
"*Ena lo mqolo.*"	(This is a back.)
"*Ena lo mpundu.*"	(These are buttocks.)

Stopping for a moment to catch his breath, the instructor clears his throat before continuing. Slightly embarrassed, he puts his hand on his genitals and says,

"*Ena lo mtondo.*"	(This is a penis.)
"*Ena lo masende.*"	(These are balls.)
"*Ena lo mlenze.*"	(These are legs.)
"*Ena lo nyawu . . .*"	(These are feet.)

After repeating each word in the list three times, the instructor begins again by touching each object and saying its name. He motions for the learners to join in and soon the men have mastered most of the new words. It really doesn't take long to learn this new language. The instructor continues by teaching the men a few expressions, and by the time they break for lunch, they understand most of the talk in the kitchen. Muronga is excited by this whole process and relieved to be able finally to understand some of what is being said to him.

The afternoon is spent learning short phrases, so that by the end of the day, the men will have a good grasp of the language. Before the end of the session, the instructor pulls out a cream-colored cotton bag filled with money of various denominations, from one cent to the biggest paper notes.

"*Ena lo mali.*   (This is money)

"We know that," shout the men, almost annoyed.

"Yes, but I must teach you all these things."

He raises a piece of bronze money in his hand, throws it up and says, "This is *pikinini* money. It is a cent. You cannot buy anything with this alone. You need bigger money, like this, and this, and this, and this. This is a *tickey*, this is a sixpence, this is a shilling, this is half a crown, this is five shillings, this is one *rand*, and this is a pound."

It is clear from the look on the men's faces that they know all about money. Even Muronga, who has not worked much with cash before, knows what to use money for. It does not take long to know how to live. All he wants to do is to get his first payment so that he can buy things for his family.

He has already been to the store in the compound to look at the various goods that they have there. He already saw the trunk that he wants to fill with clothes for his people. In the store, he heard the cashier telling those men who were shopping, "This costs one shilling, this costs two pounds . . . ," and so on. There is one dark blue fabric that he wants to buy for Mama Rwenge and a few nice clothes for his wife and son. When the instructor continues talking about money, he thinks about how he will count his first money and how he will keep it safely under his bed until he is able to go on his first buying trip to the store. He is excited.

I will have my own money in my hands. I hope it will be a lot. Then I will count it, one, two, three, four . . . Muronga thinks to himself. Yes. I will buy many clothes for my people. But I must also save some of it to take home to pay the taxes. That's why I came here. Suddenly, the bell rings and the class comes to an end.

As Muronga walks back to the barracks in the evening, and during the evening meal, he repeats the words and phrases he has learned. Learning the names for his new clothing and tools delights Muronga and makes him feel somewhat proud of himself. He imagines how he will look in his new attire, and how he will skillfully drill and crush the rocks. With these images floating in his mind, he drifts off to sleep.

All Saturday is spent in much the same way so by Saturday night the men can communicate quite well in Sfanakalo. When they do not know a word in Sfanakalo, they throw in words from their own languages. That is what Sfanakalo is—a mixture of all the miners' languages.

Sunday is a day of rest. There is no school, only relaxing, eating, practicing their lessons, and attending a church service in the evening. The men were told on Saturday that a white Afrikaans-speaking preacher would be coming to conduct the service, and it was compulsory for them to attend. Going to church is not difficult for Muronga, so he doesn't mind. He is used to going to church to hear Pater Dickmann's stories. After all, being in church unites him with his wife, Makena, beside whom he knelt until his knees hurt.

In the evening, the gate security guards come to the barracks and escort the men to a small church just outside the compound. When the men are seated on the hard wooden benches, the guards retire to the back of the church and stand by the doors until the church service is over. Once everyone is in their place, the white minister, the *dominee*, and his black interpreter enter from the right side of the church. Unlike Pater Dickmann, he is very plainly dressed. He wears a black suit and shoes, and a white shirt and white necktie. He does not make the sign of the cross as Pater Dickmann does, but greets the men in a patronizing manner and then says, "Let us close our eyes and pray.

"Our heavenly Father, we thank You for your providence. Thank You for this country and for its wealth that You have blessed us with, Your children. We thank You for Your Word which You have put in our mouths. And we thank You, Lord, for giving us a responsible government. Lord, we know that those who govern us have been placed there by You. You have determined everything, Oh Lord, and we, as Your people, have no power to change Your will on earth. Make us know and understand Your divine will. You have made us as we are, different from one another, and one day we will be with You in Heaven, where we will all rejoice to be with You. Bless the workers in this mine, Lord, and give them strength to work hard, and in so doing, glorify Your Holy Name. In Your Name we pray. A M E N.'

While the minister is praying in Afrikaans and the interpreter translates every line, most of the men in the church find it difficult to keep their eyes closed. With his arms outstretched, and his eyes closed tightly, the minister energetically beseeches God to listen to him. His body trembling and his voice frequently rising to a crescendo, he is so engrossed in praying that, to the startled men, it seems he could soar up to heaven by the power of his own will. Muronga tries hard to concentrate but cannot help stealing a quick look every now and then. He has never seen anybody pray like this before! When the "Amen" is finally spoken, the men open their eyes and glance at one another, smiling slightly, surprised by what they have just witnessed. They can only wonder what will happen next!

With perspiration beading his forehead, the minister pauses to recompose himself. He takes several deep breaths, and then, smiling broadly again at the men in front of him, beckons his Sfanakalo interpreter to join him. Then, addressing the men, he says, "We are now going to listen to the ever-powerful Word of the Almighty God as it stands in the New Testament. We read tonight a few verses from Chapter Thirteen of the Apostle Paul's Letter to the Romans." The interpreter translates every word into *Sfanakalo*, so that the men will understand thoroughly what is being said. He is used to this exercise and does it very well, and is, therefore, trusted by the white ministers and the compound manager. The minister then signals the interpreter to read in Sfanakalo a text that has become standard in the mine services. He reads,

> "Let every person be subject to the governing authorities.
> For there is no authority except from God, and those that exist have been instituted by God.
> Therefore he who resists the authorities resists what God has appointed, and those who resist will incur judgement.
> For rulers are not a terror to good conduct, but to bad. Would you have no fear of him who is in authority? Then do what is good, and you will receive his approval, for he is God's servant for your good. But if you do wrong, be afraid, for he does not bear the sword in vain, he is the servant of God to execute his wrath on the wrong-doer. Therefore one must be subject, not only to avoid God's wrath but also for the sake of conscience. For the same reason you also pay taxes, for the authorities are ministers of God, attending to this very thing. Pay all of them their dues, taxes to whom taxes are due, revenue to whom revenue is due, respect to whom respect is due, honor to whom honor is due."

Muronga listens attentively to the words of the minister and is reminded of the church back home, Pater Dickmann, and his family. He has heard this kind of harangue before and now, as then, feels more uncomfortable with what he is hearing. Should I be obedient to the people who have the law, the "authorities"? he asks himself. And to which authorities? To the white people and their laws, or to the chief and headman in my village back home? If the authorities are the white people, and they have been given this authority by God, then which God has given them this power? Does it come from the church God—the God of money and guns—or from the God of My Forefathers—the stern but fair God?

Muronga contemplates these questions as the interpreter finishes the reading and as the minister begins the sermon.

"My dear workers, you are very welcome in our humble church. In this church we share with one another the Word of God. We have just heard God telling us why we are here in this world. He says we are here to honor Him. But because God is not within our reach, we have to honor His representatives—the government. The government governs our land and keeps us safe. And how do we show that we honor God? The Word of God says that we show that we honor God by listening to and being obedient to the government. That means we pay our taxes and obey the managers in the mine. They are there by the will of God. We who are responsible for you, and have authority over you, have been placed here by God. If you do not obey the laws of the authorities, you insult God, and the door to heaven will then be closed to you. God pays every person who does not oppose the authorities. God will be watching you all the time while you are here to see whether or not you are obedient to Him. If you are not obedient to Him by being obedient to the authorities, he will judge you and punish you. That is how God works."

This last sentence, as it is translated into Sfanakalo, hits the men hard, and they look at one another fearfully. Has a curse been put on us? they wonder.

The preacher is happy. He believes his message has had an impact on these black men. He finds black people unpredictable, so he invokes the word of God to tame them and stop them from rebelling in the mines. He is an Afrikaner. He knows too well how his people were oppressed by the British people until they rebelled. No, he thinks, black people must not be given an opportunity to oppose the white authorities. There are too many of them to deal with, and their labor is vital to provide us white people with food, clothes, shelter and security. For that reason alone, it is necessary to watch each one of them carefully during the services and during informal encounters, to keep the Management Board of the mine informed.

When the service is over, the minister and his interpreter leave the church first and disappear without waiting for the men to come out. Muronga is struck by this. He remembers how Pater Dickmann would stand outside the church by the door and greet people as they were leaving. This way he could get to know his converts, and they him. As Muronga strolls out of the church with the other men he thinks how different this church service was from the ones he attended back home. There men and women were not allowed to sit side by side, but here there are no women at all, not even outside the compound. Muronga wonders where the daughters of this country have gone.

Later that evening, Muronga and his roommates are back in their room relaxing. Now that they know some Sfanakalo, they can talk to one another. At first, only two of the men exchange names, but soon all eight men are introducing themselves to one another. They exchange information about their countries, their villages, and their families. That night, Muronga sleeps more soundly than he has since leaving his home. At last he has some friends.

When they get up the following morning, Muronga and his roommates greet one another, and though they will probably be together the whole day, they wish one another a happy day. Dressed proudly in their new bright yellow uniforms this time, all eight men go to breakfast together, chatting like old friends. Breakfast consists of the same dark bread, *mealie meal pap* with milk and sugar, and rather bitter black coffee. On a bench under one of the large *pondoks*, Muronga sits down to eat his breakfast. Next to him is his roommate, Musoke, from Malawi. This is not the first time Musoke has worked in a South African mine. He explains to Muronga that he used a different name before, because otherwise he would not have been allowed to return to work in South Africa so soon.

"Where did you say you come from?" inquires Muronga.

"From Malawi, or Nyassaland. We call it Malawi now. When I worked in the other mine, I was called 'Munyasa', meaning someone who comes from Nyassaland."

"Where is that? Is it very far away?" asks Muronga.

"Yes, very far away. But..."

"Do you have a wife and children?"

"Yes, and that's why I am here. I must earn money to support my family. One of my three children must go to school. Otherwise the government will punish me."

"Oh," replies a surprised Muronga. "You must have a cruel government if it forces you to send your children to school. In my country we are forced to pay taxes, not go to school."

"I know. But you see, we are an independent nation. We have our own government. We no longer have white governors and commissioners. Our own brothers and sisters run the government. So, you see, it is very important for us to send our children to school. Do you know a man, a black man, named Kamuzu Banda?"

"Kamu what? Who is that? Is he the commissioner?"

"Kamuzu Banda. He is our President, the President of Malawi. He is a very clever man—cleverer even than all the white people. He is the most important man in our country."

"He is black, you said?"

"Yes, he is. Just like you and me. But he is very clever and educated, so white people fear him. He is a white black man. They say he has read more books than the white people."

Muronga wonders how it is possible that a black man can be feared by white people. Does he have a lot of money and possessions, or lots of cattle? But before he can ask any more questions, the men realize that it is already time to go to the classroom.

On their way, Muronga would like to resume the conversation with Musoke, but there are too many other men who join them and greet them. Musoke begins talking in a different language to someone who is not from their room. Muronga suspects that they are both from Malawi and perhaps from the same town or village. He is engrossed in his thoughts, however, and walks all the way to the classroom without talking to anyone. He is still thinking about what Musoke told him a moment ago. Imagine— a black man who is feared by white people! A black man who is above a commissioner!.

When the men have taken their seats in the classroom, the instructor begins to test what they have learned so far. He asks each man to stand up, introduce himself and say a few words about himself, count to ten, ask his neighbor a few questions, and so on, in Sfanakalo. The men do very well and the instructor is pleased.

"Good, you have learned your lessons well and you understand well. Now, everyone follow me to the mine. If you have any questions, ask me now. In the mine, no one speaks. You listen very carefully. Now come with me!" For the first time beyond the compound walls, they follow enthusiastically, anxious to see the inside of the mine.

Huge amounts of yellowish sand are visible in the distance. Pointed at their tops, the regularly spaced sand hills have become misshapen from the force of the wind and rain. A fine powdery dust hangs in the air, blocking the sun's rays. It seems to coat everything in sight, including the few scrubby trees and bushes that dot the barren land. As the men draw closer to the mine, they see scaffolding rising out of the ground and several small prefabricated buildings. Nothing that Muronga sees reminds him of anything back home.

The men walk in perfect unison, and the sound of their black rubber boots kicking up gravel, creates a rhythm that reflects their excitement. Muronga again wishes his wife and child could see him now wearing his new yellow uniform.

The rhythm is so strong it turns into a song. "Hey, hey, *Wiha-Mandaha!*" he sing-talks softly to the rhythm of the rubber boots. "Mandaha, hey, Mandaha, hey. See me now, hey, this your father, hey! This your husband, hey, hey!"

They arrive at the mine shaft at the entrance to the mine. Muronga interrupts his exercise abruptly to look at the huge shaft in front of him.

"This is where we enter the mine," explains the instructor. "Don't be afraid . . . it's all right. The place where you will work is underground. A moving box called a lift will take us there. It's nice to ride in the lift, so let's go. Come with me."

Muronga does not know what the instructor is talking about. What is this thing that takes us underground? he wonders. It cannot be like an airplane that goes up in the sky—not underground like a mouse.

A bell rings. The instructor quickly moves forward toward the hole in the ground. The men follow him down several stairs to a platform. They wait for a moment; then a strange box appears from below. The instructor slides open a large door and the fifteen men follow him into the box and he then slams the door shut. The bell rings again and the box lurches and sinks rapidly. Muronga, standing next to the instructor, steadies himself. With his eyes closed and his hand on his chest, he says to himself, Oh, my mother, where am I? I am not a mouse. Why must I go so deep underground? Muronga slowly opens his eyes again. He can see nothing but the inside of the box, and wishes he did not have to go through this awful experience.

The box bounces and comes to a sudden halt. The men can feel that they are being suspended by a rope. Reaching up to touch his hat, the instructor shouts, "Turn the little knobs on your hardhats so that the lamps will go on so you can see in the mine." After the big door is pushed open, the men follow the instructor out into the pitch-dark tunnel. "This is where you men will work," he says. "Your job will be to drill these rocks and break them up. They will be picked up by a car that is made for that. The sand you see here you will shovel on to the next man, until it is taken out of the mine and deposited outside in those big heaps you saw. Inside the mine it is dangerous, because these rocks can fall on you. It doesn't happen very often, but you must know how to do your work."

As the instructor continues explaining, Muronga looks around, using the light of his face lamp to see. It is nice how this light shines where you want to see, he thinks. Feeling the heat underground, Muronga wonders how close he is to Satan's place and whether Pater Dickmann will tell him that he will have to be born again—again. He hears noises further down the hole that sound strange. While he is anxious to get out of the hole quickly, he is altogether pleased with himself for being inside the mine at last. Musoke, who has been standing next to Muronga, looks a little less scared than the others. As he watches Muronga nervously looking about, he gently nudges him, to reassure him that everything is all right. "Don't be afraid, Muronga," he whispers, "it will be over soon. You will like it here once you get used to it. It's a man's place. I was scared, too."

The time the men spend in the darkness underground seems like a lifetime to Muronga. The longer they stay there and move around in the insides of the mine, the more frightened Muronga becomes. But at the same time he consoles himself. This is a man's experience, he thinks. I am here, inside the mine, like other men from my village have been. Now I am here myself. But I hope I will see the sun again soon.

Finally, they are saved by the bell. It is midday already. Lunchtime. The instructor calls them together. "Now you have seen the mine," he says in a loud voice so as not to be drowned out by the drilling noises nearby. "The next time you come here, you will come to work. Your *chiefboss* will tell you everything about your work. I do not know what kind of work all of you will do here, but there will definitely be someone to teach you everything. The clothes that you have on now are the clothes that you will wear all the time when you are down here in the mine. It is important for you to wear these clothes to protect yourselves, so don't forget." Muronga listens carefully. He touches his hardhat with the palm of his hand to make sure that it is firmly on his head.

Again the strange box appears and the men get into it. The door is pulled closed behind them and the box begins to rise quickly. As they rise to the surface, their fear diminishes. Muronga gives a sigh of relief as the box stops moving and the men emerge into the daylight. He looks around, just to make sure he is not still inside the machine. Hmm, I was in the mine . . . inside the mine . . . , Muronga thinks almost aloud.

Throughout lunch, the men talk about nothing but their experiences in the morning. Most of them have no words in their own languages to explain the elevator and the other things when they try to explain their trip to the mine. They call the elevator a jumper or a big egg. They realize that now that they have overcome their initial fear, being in the mine was exciting. They are glad they have gone there and returned safely. Now, at least, they know it is safe to go down there.

The rest of the afternoon passes quickly as the men relax in their barracks. Now that Muronga has some new friends and is so busy learning new things, he realizes, oddly enough, he is not missing his home and family as much as expected. But he constantly wishes that they could see him now, in his new yellow uniform, talking a strange language, and crawling around underground like a termite.

Soon after their sunset dinner, the men hear a siren, which reminds them that the instructor tells them earlier that they must assemble in the large *pondok* behind the kitchen when they hear the whistle. "Tonight you will learn the rules and procedures of the compound," the instructor tells them.

Under the *pondok*, the white compound manager, flanked by two black guards and the interpreter, is seated at a large table. Muronga says to himself, "Just like the compound in Rundu." He is half-dreaming that he is with his friend Kaye. When he realizes that he is talking to himself, he walks faster. Here, though, the white compound manager does not speak; his black lackeys do all the talking for him. But his presence helps the instructors get the attention of the workers.

"Sit down on the ground and listen, *Madoda*," commands one of the guards.

Taking their places quietly, the men listen attentively to their instructor, who explains the compound's rules and disciplinary code.

"Here in the compound, we have *lo mteto*, the law," he begins in a loud voice. "The first law is that you respect the compound manager. He makes the law. The second one is that you respect the *nduna*, the black man who is the manager's assistant. The third law is that you respect the *sibonda*, who is the caretaker in your room. The fourth one is that you do not urinate anywhere except in the latrines."

The men smile. The instructor smiles back, then continues. "The fifth law is that you are not allowed to fight in the compound. If someone quarrels with you, report him to the *sibonda*, who will take up the matter. The sixth law is that stealing and drinking alcohol are big crimes here."

The men smile again. "This is serious," the instructor interrupts their smile. "The penalty for breaking any of these laws is the cancellation of your contract and immediate dismissal. You go home!"

The men begin to murmur among themselves, but one of the guards strides towards them and tells them not to speak. At the end of the session each man's name is called by the instructor who tells them where to report the next morning. Some of the men are told to go to the processing plants, but Muronga is told to report directly to his white supervisor, who will meet him at the entrance to the mine. Ah, straight to the mine! How wonderful.

I am glad I saw the mine already, Muronga thinks as he walks back to the barracks, dreaming of the work he will do the next day.

The following day Muronga reports to his supervisor. With a group of other men, he follows the supervisor into the mine where they are taught their respective jobs. Muronga is assigned the job of a *malayisha*, shoveling broken rocks from the tunnel into steel cars on rails. Disappointed that he was not assigned to be a blaster, he nonetheless tackles his work with enthusiasm.

At the end of his first month, Muronga, like all the other men, gets his first pay check. They are all paid in hard cash. Muronga only realizes that it is payday when his roommate tells him that it is the last day of the month and that he must go with him to the pay office.

"Do you have your ticket book here, Muronga?" his roommate asks.

"Yes, I do. Here it is," he replies. "Why?"

"You see, when you have no more paper to tear out of your book, you know that the month is over. That means that you can go and get your money. Come with me."

Muronga and his roommate arrive at the pay office which is already packed with men. The way the men's names are called out reminds him of his experienes in Rundu. His name is called out. He goes to the desk where he is handed a brown envelope with paper money only. He takes it gracefully and puts the envelope in his pocket.

Back in his room, he counts his money carefully, over and over again. He counts four stacks of one pound notes five times. He decides to do some shopping.

In the store, he buys a big metal trunk, a skirt for his wife, a pair of shorts for Mandaha, a large piece of dark blue fabric and a blanket. When he finishes, he packs everything into the trunk and walks home with some change in his pockets.

Is this really me, he thinks to himself. Who thought that I would ever carry a huge trunk like this with clothes in it, clothes that I have bought myself? I wonder what people will say when I arrive home with goods and money.

That night, Muronga sleeps soundly with a great sense of accomplishment.

CHAPTER 11

For four months Muronga has been working in the mine. He has adjusted to the routine and is quite content with his new identity as a mine worker. He has very few opportunities to leave the compound and little free time, so the compound has become almost his entire world.

At first, he was eager to learn everything he possibly could about his work and his new environment. Because of his youthful physique and good health, Muronga was assigned to work as a lowly shoveler. After the *machineboys* have blasted the rocks off the working face at the new end of the tunnel with dynamite, the choppers break up the larger chunks, and the line of shovelers pass the gravel shovelful by shovelful back to the loaders at the trolley car on its narrow iron rails. To Muronga and all of the other men, the work soon becomes routine, so much so that one day Muronga decides to ask his supervisor if there are any other jobs he can learn.

"*Chiefboss,*" Muronga exclaims, careful not to break the rhythm of his shoveling. "Everything you have taught me here I know how to do. I would like to learn something new—like learning to drive that trolley car."

"What? Are you crazy?" the short fat white supervisor shouts. "You are a shoveler! That's all you were meant to do. You cannot drive that thing, ever. It's dangerous, so only boys who can read and write a little bit can drive it. Not you . . . it's not for baboons like you. Now get to work! I am busy!" The supervisor shoves Muronga aside with the butt of his flashlight and stalks self-importantly down the tunnel toward the face.

Taken aback, Muronga swallows hard as the men begin to sing, "*Tshotsholoza, tshotsholoza,*" the chant they often sing to help them keep a rhythm and feel less tired and more united in their battle with the rocks.

At first, Muronga did not mind taking orders from his white superiors, since he had thought that he would one day become a supervisor himself. But he soon found out that only whites could get promoted or become supervisors. Blacks can only follow orders, the whites believe.

And this man, this supervisor even seems to take pleasure in treating us like children—or even like animals, Muronga thinks while shoveling. He seems to think that a black man like me does not breathe, think or feel what a white man does. He thinks we are here simply to do the work, the heavy manual work, and be at his command—to do his bidding. We must keep working. We are not here to live a life or to be real men, he thinks further. The metal handle of the shovel gets hotter and hotter and hurts the inside of his hands. But he doesn't dare stop. "Time is money," the supervisor screams at them whenever he sees the muscles in their bodies relaxing. Muronga has come to dread the supervisor's harsh, insulting tone.

Gradually Muronga becomes aware that there is a big difference between what is called discipline and what is actually abuse. He has always known and appreciated discipline. He is not afraid of hard work, but this work isn't so much hard as it is demeaning—deliberately demeaning. And the orders, the commands, and the insults are not discipline, but abuse. As time passes, he finds it harder and harder to accept his situation. How can one man treat another with such contempt? Didn't Pater Dickmann say God expects people to love one another as they love themselves and treat one another as they themselves would like to be treated? Perhaps, though, the supervisor has a different God from Pater Dickmann's. Muronga often wonders about this, and remembers what Pater Dickmann said about the devil, who lives underground and uses a huge fork to prod and torment his slaves. To Muronga, this is the only logical explanation for the supervisor's behavior. Certainly he couldn't wish to be treated as he treats others! Whites are more "white" than they are human, and their black guards are more dangerous than brotherly. Surely their souls must be troubled, and they must be suffering, for it is only a dead heart that does not feel pain when pain is inflicted on another, Muronga surmises.

If it weren't for the white man's laws, I would have fought that little white pig long ago, Muronga seethes. I am taller and stronger than he is. He wouldn't stand a chance of defending himself against me if he didn't have that gun, Muronga thinks to himself.

Fortunately, by this time Muronga has only a year left on his contract. He counts the days until he will be back home with his family and friends. At first he was so busy learning and experiencing new things that he did not think about them much. But now that he has been away from his wife for a long time, he misses her very much, especially at night when he tosses and turns in his warm bed, imagining that she is with him on their *kafungo*. It is fortunate that there are no women in the compound— that way there is little temptation. He also thinks often of his little son, Mandaha, who must be growing bigger every day. How Muronga would play with him and teach him things if he were there with him now! And then there is Kaye. Even though he has some new friends, Muronga misses Kaye and tries to imagine what his life must be like, wherever he is. No doubt he is also being ordered around by white supervisors who think they are too good to be human, and no doubt he, too, is able to tolerate such treatment only because he knows that he is working for a reason. Earning money for his family and for the taxes allows Muronga to persevere, to endure the pain of separation and degradation.

But that is true for all the men working in the mine. They must find comfort in each other's company. Muronga's new companions are two old hands, Nyangana and Ndango, from Kavango, who both speak Muronga's language. They know all about the compound and the mine, since they have already finished their original sixteen-month contracts and will soon finish their three-month extensions.

Sunday afternoons are usually very pleasant and relaxed in the compound. As was the case in the Rundu compound, men play *wera*, checkers, and other board games. Gloveless boxing and gumboot dancing are also very popular with the men. The winners of the boxing competitions are usually chosen to be guards and watchmen.

Walking quickly through the compound, the three comrades stop to watch a group of men rehearsing a gumboot dance. Fascinated, they watch and listen to the men slapping their worn palms against their knee-high black rubber boots.

"This is great! I have never seen people performing like this. What do you call this? Is it hard to learn? Can anyone do it?" Muronga asks excitedly, trying to imitate the men's movements.

"Sure, all you need is a pair of rubber boots to learn gumboot dancing. You have a pair of those boots, so you are all set. Every man learns the dance some time while he is here. It is like Sfanakalo. It goes with the territory," says Ndango, with a broad smile, remembering how he too had been mesmerized the first time he saw the dance, many moons ago.

After watching the activities for a short while, the three men move on through the compound. Since the sun is shining in such a way as to remind them of the beautiful African sun that shines lovingly on the trees that grow alongside the mighty Kavango River, they impulsively decide to take a long walk outside the compound to explore the surroundings. Luckily, the gateguard happens to be fast asleep as they go through the gate, so there are no questions about where they are going.

Once outside, they pass uniformed mine workers—some about to begin their day's work, others weary from the night's labor. Skilled crews work even on Sunday. Soon leaving the main path, Nyangana and Ndango silently lead Muronga towards the largest sand mound.

"See, Muronga," Ndango says. "This is what becomes of your work. All the ground you have scooped out has helped to build these great mountains."

"From up there you can see everything," Nyangana explains, pointing to the top of the yellowish pile. Hard packed from exposure to many rains, the mound is easy to climb. It is not very steep and soon the men reach the flat top. Looking down from their perch they again see uniformed workers passing from the compound at their right to the mine off to the left. The high wall of the compound hides all but the roofs of the barracks. They can see the mine heads, too, with the huge, slow turning wheel that raises the lift from the depths. Further away, straight ahead, lies an open area with some unusual structures built on it. Some men dressed in shorts and shirts can be seen running back and forth along its length.

"What are those men doing down there?" Muronga asks inquisitively.

"Oh, they are playing soccer," Ndango answers. But he can see that Muronga does not understand what he is talking about. "They are playing a game. By kicking that ball around they try to score points for their team. Like we play *ndandari* in the village, remember? Instead of throwing the long wooden spear to strike the *ndandari* before it reaches the men on the opposite line, they kick a ball with their feet. They chase and kick it through the poles of the men on the opposing side. Then they win," Ndango explains further.

Seeing that Muronga is interested in this subject, Nyangana goes on, "The part you see there where the roof is, is for when it rains or when the sun is too hot. Sometimes I go there to watch the players. The next time I am going I will invite you to come with me if you like."

"That will be nice," Muronga replies. "I would like to see them play. It sounds interesting. But don't they kick each other in the legs if they run around like that?"

Just as Ndango is about to reply to Muronga's question, a number of bright green and pink birds flies overhead. Instinctively Muronga follows them with his eyes. They look like the river birds that live along the Kavango River. "Oh, look! They are going to the stream over there," Muronga says excitedly. "Can we go for a swim in it? I would like to have cold water around my body again to remind myself of our great river."

"Sure, why not? Let's go!" Loping easily down the sand mound, they hurry to the edge of the stream. As they approach the stream, Muronga sings a swim song that they used to sing in their young days. His two comrades join him singing, *"Kuvera yira ngororo, tjulya!"*

At the stream they peel off their clothes. Naked, the three friends plunge into the cool, clear water and swim about.

"Doesn't this remind you of when we were boys?" Muronga shouts, swimming with his head just above the water.

"Oh, yes," responds Nyangana as he floats on his back. "Remember how all the young boys and girls used to play water tag together?"

"Ha! How could I forget?" Ndango bellows, paddling around in the rushing waters. "Little did I know that one of those naked little girls would one day be my wife!"

Muronga thinks back nostalgically. "I remember when the mother of my child was a shy, slender, flat-chested girl, who I always used to tag like ... this!" Tapping Ndango on the shoulder, Muronga races away through the water, yelling back, "You have it!"

Like children again, the three men race back and forth through the water taking turns tagging each other. Ndango finally ends the game by climbing out of the water. He strides towards the rocks, with Muronga and Nyangana close behind. Resting for a few moments and drying off, they pick up their clothes and get dressed.

"We came this way. Can we take a different way when we go back to the compound?" Ndango asks. "Let's see where this other path leads. It doesn't lead to the compound. Shall we follow it and see?"

"Oh, yes," Nyangana agrees. "Maybe we can see more around this place. I heard there is a store somewhere along this path that has more goods than the store in the compound. Let's go there."

With Nyangana in the lead they walk on the path one behind the other. Seeing the store on the other side of the mine, they decide to make a brief stop there to see if there is anything there that they can't find in the store inside the compound. The shop is usually called "the white man's shop," because it is the place where the white mine workers buy their daily necessities.

Looking through the glass doors outside the shop, Muronga and his "homeboys" can see black men working busily inside the store, so they assume that the store is not exclusively for whites, as they had heard. However, as they approach the entrance, two khaki-uniformed black guards with *kerries* on their hips followed by their white supervisor, who wields a gun on his hip, suddenly burst through the doors.

"What do you want here?" they ask brutally in Sfanakalo, waving their *kerries* in the air, ready to strike.

Ndango silently confers with his two friends about how he should respond. After a moment's hesitation, he replies, "What do you mean, what do we want here?"

The taller of the two black guards immediately turns on Ndango even more threateningly. "Don't argue with me! Don't you know that this shop is not open to people like you?" He glances at the white supervisor standing in the door a short distance behind him. "Are you all fools, or what? Go away immediately, or you will be arrested! Go back to the compound at once!"

Taking a few steps backwards, the three friends look at one another. "What is going on here?" asks Muronga somewhat fearfully. "What have we done?"

"We have done nothing," Nyangana mutters. "We are black—that is our sin. That's all, my brother."

"But these two men are also black—or do my eyes not see the difference between black and white anymore?"

"Yes, they are black, too, but they are different blacks," replies Ndango. "They are the white man's blacks. They protect the whites. They are no longer black like we are

. . . they are dead inside. They are no longer for us, but against us. And they are dangerous . . . even more dangerous than the white man himself, you see."

"Stop cursing me, you stupid fool!" bellows the abusive guard.

The other guard, who until now has only looked threatening, glances at the white supervisor and then says in a low tone, "Wait, Skhulu. Let them go without too much trouble. They didn't enter the shop and—well, after all, the master won't do anything if we tell him we chased them away. They are our people, you know."

"Don't try to stop me from doing my work!" the taller guard retorts. "These people pay no attention to the laws here. They must be disciplined . . . now! I am a policeman here. My job is to uphold the law! If you cannot do that, then you are a coward!"

"I am not a coward!"

"You are a coward!"

"How dare you say that to me! You are the coward!" Anger and bitterness are now audible in the voice of the kinder guard.

"Ha! Me? A coward? I will report you to the master, and then we will see who is standing here with me tomorrow!"

The argument is now one between the two guards. Muronga and his friends are stunned. They do not know what to say or do. Meanwhile, the guards' argument has attracted the attention of their white supervisor. He moves toward the group of black men, and the argument is suddenly over. The friendlier guard has changed his tone and now says, "Go away from here! You do not belong here. You are forbidden to enter this place. If you do not leave immediately, you will be arrested. Now, get out of here!"

Muronga and his friends turn and walk away. Angry and puzzled, the three men walk toward the compound, silent, but now and then glancing back to see what the two guards and their master are doing.

Once inside the high concrete wall of the compound, Nyangana is met by a new man from his barracks, and the two of them discuss some matter pertaining to their room. Muronga and Ndango push the loose sand about with their feet while waiting for their friend to finish. It is late afternoon, nearly dusk, and the sun casts soft yellowish-red rays which sparkle when they are caught by the broken glass atop the concrete wall.

Many thoughts swarm through Muronga's head as he gazes at the glittering glass. "I wonder why that glass is up there?" he muses. He is surprised when Ndango answers his question.

"They are there because the white man thinks that we blacks will try to jump up and climb over the wall to escape."

"Escape from what?" Muronga is incredulous.

"Escape from here. A white man would die if he had to live here."

Muronga is silent for a moment. "Would he be able to jump or climb that high?"

"I don't know. But the white man thinks we are different. We climb trees, so—"

"So what? We do not climb trees to escape from anything. Trees are wood. We use trees to build and maintain our homes. We use them for everything."

The conversation drifts off with each man sighing in frustration. Muronga is more aware than ever that he simply does not understand how these white people think. Meditatively, he stands with his hands in his pockets,

wondering how things got this way, when his eye is caught
by a moving object. One of the doors of the barracks closest
to him has been gently eased open by the pleasant
Transvaal breeze that blows over the compound. There,
inside the room, Muronga sees two men who are both
naked from the waist down sitting on a bed and touching
each other in a manner that is unusual for two men. Or,
at least, that is what Muronga thinks he sees. Unsure
whether the setting sun is playing tricks on his eyes, he
quietly bends over and, with his hands on his knees, he
squints his eyes to see more clearly. It appears that an
older man is applying vaseline jelly to the inner thighs
of a younger man, who sits passively on the bed. The
two men are apparently unaware that they are being
watched.

"What is the matter, Muronga?" asks Nyangana, who
has finally rejoined his comrades.

"Nothing . . . ehm . . . just looking," Muronga replies,
looking ashamed and disgusted.

Nyangana, looking toward the barracks, can also see
the two men. The younger man is, by this time, lying
on his back with the older man on top of him. "Ah, I
see. Yes, of course. You must be shocked if this is the
first time you have seen this sort of thing," Nyangana
says sympathetically. "I myself was certainly shocked, too,
when I first saw that."

"But what is this? Men . . . together?"

"You see, Muronga, many of these men have been here
a very long time and they are sexually starved," explains
Ndango. "That is what they call *matanyuna* here. There
are no women here, so men turn to other men. They sleep
with each other as if they were sleeping with their wives,
you see."

"Ah, *matanyuna!* I have heard about it. The priest at home
said that it happenened in Sodom and Gomorrah; in some

white peoples' country. But . . . but . . . what if one of them becomes pregnant?" Muronga asks.

"No, it doesn't happen that way. I don't know why not, but it has never happened. They do it between the legs, like you just saw," explains Ndango.

Muronga is dismayed. How can a man do such a thing with another man? he wonders.

"But these are men, real men, like we are. And they are friends who stand by each other while they are here in the mine. When they return home, they remain good friends . . . family friends, although they do not tell their wives about what has happened between them. This is what I have heard from different people."

"I have heard that, too," interrupts Ndango. "I have also heard that when they leave here, they do not sleep with each other any more. They go back to their wives and children. But while they are here in the mine they are more than just friends or brothers. They take care of each other. Perhaps it is like what we have with our wives."

"I don't understand it at all," says Muronga, feeling guilty. "All I can say is that two men doing that must be different from us. I mean, if there is the kind of warmth, understanding, love and caring that exists between them as there is between me and my wife, then I understand. But . . . "

"It is sad," sighs Nyangana. "The white man thinks we will do more work if we are kept away from women, especially our own women. So we are locked up like animals in this place."

With a wry smile Ndango says, "Like oxen. We are nothing but beasts of burden to the white man."

"Certainly not men at all, with needs and feelings like the white man. We are just workers, here to do a job, but not here to live like men. This is just one of the miseries we endure in the mines. There are many other things, . . . many things . . . " Nyangana's voice trails off as the dinner bell sounds. The three men, suddenly realizing that they should not have lingered so long, begin walking towards their barracks.

"Other things? Like what?" asks Muronga inquisitively.

"Do you remember that fat white man we just saw near the gate? Do you know who he is and what he does?" demands Ndango.

"No, I don't," replies Muronga.

"He comes to the compound every few days to collect the garbage for his pigs, and he brings bags filled with bottles of medicine and a kind of tobacco they call *dagga*. He tells people that the medicine will make them strong and rich."

"Yes, and then some men buy his bottles and get drunk, or they smoke *dagga* until they become mad. When the blacks buy these things the white man calls them stupid, superstitious drunkards. But who sells those things? The white man! Who pays? The black man! With the money we get here! Ah, I get angry when I start talking about these people. One day this white man will taste a bit of his own medicine!" states Nyangana loudly and bitterly.

"But what makes me even angrier," Ndango goes on, "is the story of my elder brother. He worked here many years ago. He dug every hole in this mine! Then he and his white boss got T.B. The law says that anyone who gets this lung disease must be sent home immediately, with lots of money as compensation. But the white man is clever. He is sneaky, *skelm!* The white supervisor got lots and lots of money. So much, in fact, that they had to give him checks, because the money was too much for him to carry in his hands. But my brother got almost nothing. First they made my brother sick, then they sent him home with almost nothing." The three friends have walked across the compound and are now standing outside Muronga's room. "Ever since that happened, I have been attending the meetings."

"Meetings? What kind of meetings?" inquires Muronga, enthralled.

"No . . . I cannot tell you now," says Ndango. "It is dangerous . . . and besides, we will miss our dinner if we don't hurry."

A few minutes later, after picking up his utensils, Muronga arrives at the *pondok*. In a moment, the others have joined him, and the three comrades go through the food line, get their daily rations, and sit down on concrete blocks to eat.

For most of the meal the men are silent, but finally, as they are finishing, Ndango leans towards Muronga and whispers, "I know you want to know more about our meetings, but it is dangerous to talk about them. We will have to meet secretly. Come to my room tomorrow night after dinner. But, do not tell anyone where you are going."

At work the next day, Muronga keeps thinking about Sunday's events. Ndango was very emotional when he spoke about his brother. If he had been a woman, he probably would have cried, but being a man means never shedding a tear. Still, Muronga cannot dispel his growing feelings of frustration, anger, and bitterness. Deep in thought, he works steadily on until he realizes that the other five men in his line have stopped to take an illegal break while their white supervisor is out of sight. Exhausted, Muronga bends over and breathes deeply, wiping his face on his sleeve and readjusting his hat. He and the other men are still in this position when their boss unexpectedly returns. Muronga, being the first one in the line, is found with his tools on the ground and his hands empty.

"Jesus Christ, what do you think you are doing, eh, eh, you *poephol*?" screams the supervisor. "You are standing here like someone who has money in the bank, eh? Do I have to kick your backside before you will do your work, eh? And you stand there staring at me like I am your dirty mother, eh? Stop looking at me, you *kaffir*, and do your work! Here . . . a nice kick should wake you up! The next time I find you standing here like a king, I will burn your backside! Now, hurry up, *tshetshisa*, quickly! Pick up your tools and get to work!"

Caught off guard, Muronga is neither able to cover up his offense nor dodge the kick to his shins. He can only stare silently at the white man, and try to maintain his balance. Enraged, Muronga, without thinking, poises to defend himself. For a moment the two men are ready to strike, until Muronga's wisdom prevails, and he controls his anger. His jaw firmly set and his eyes aflame with rage, he picks up his tools and joins the other men. They saw everything that happened, and although they cannot say anything to Muronga, their eyes and their movements express their care and sympathy.

Snorting and spitting, the supervisor arrogantly strides past the line of men on his way out again. As he leaves, he notices an older man, fast asleep in a dark corner of the mine shaft. Striding, he shakes him violently and slaps him in the face.

"*Haai, haai, ini lo*?" the old man cries out, not knowing what is going on. Bewildered, he jumps up and looks around, blinking. Seeing the white man standing over him and glaring viciously, he apologizes profusely and joins the work line.

The supervisor leaves again and stays away for a fairly long while, but this time no one dares to rest for even the briefest moment. The men do not talk about what has happened. Nor do they sing, "*Tshotsholoza, tshotsholoza.*" Their comrades' humiliation makes them irate, but it unifies them too, and for the rest of the day they take out their anger on the stubborn rocks.

At dusk, Muronga walks back to the compound alone, not wanting to share his misery with anyone just yet. He finds a low rock near the office outside the compound. Sitting down on it with his arms crossed, his head hung low, he remembers the supervisor's harsh voice, the cruel words, the tyrannical manner. He touches his shin with his hand and can feel the swelling. Ashamed at having been shouted at and kicked by another man—and a younger man at that!—Muronga is glad at least that his wife and family did not witness his humiliation. Never in his entire life has he felt so helpless, so defenseless, so completely subjugated. There must be something we can do to defend ourselves, he thinks. But what, or how? We are always suffering at the white man's hands— working for him, paying his taxes, and being separated from our people for such long periods.

After dinner Muronga heads for Ndango's room. He is very curious about the meetings he heard about yesterday. He knocks at the door. There is no answer. He knocks again.

"Who is it?" comes Ndango's voice from behind the door.

"It is me, Muronga. I am here."

"Come in. The door is open. We have been waiting for you." Muronga enters cautiously, not knowing what to expect. There is another man in the room with Ndango. Both of them welcome Muronga with warm handshakes and friendly smiles.

"This is a good friend of ours," begins Ndango. "His name is Nakare. He is a muMbukushu like you and me and he has worked here in the mine even longer than I have. I asked him to come tonight and tell you about our meetings because, being our leader, he knows more about them than anyone else. But before he begins, I have to tell you that what you hear tonight in this room you must swallow in your heart. No one must hear it. And if we find that you cannot keep quiet, you will find yourself in big trouble and we will say that we do not know you. Do you understand? Only true men know these things."

Muronga listens attentively and nods his understanding while his eyes bounce back and forth between the two men sitting next to him. "Yes, of course," he replies. "I will not open my mouth to anyone. I know how to keep secrets. In fact, I had a very unpleasant experience earlier today, and up until now, I haven't told anyone about it," says Muronga carefully.

"Oh? what happened?" the other two men ask in unison.

Reluctantly Muronga answers softly, "I was kicked in the shins by my supervisor." Ndango and Nakare look at one another and nod.

"Yes, it is always the same. You see, Muronga, this is exactly what we talk about at our meetings. Anyway . . . Nakare will explain everything," comments Ndango.

Clasping his hands together and positioning himself firmly on the bed, Nakare coughs loudly to clear his throat. "Brothers, this is a very serious matter. I cannot begin to tell you all the details about how we started having our meetings, nor can I divulge our plans for the future. But I will tell you many things that I think you will find interesting. Ndango has already told you a lot. You yourself have just told us that you were kicked today by a white man—a white man, that is, who has two legs, two arms, and so on, exactly like you and me. Every day in the mine we are treated inhumanly by the white man. We are not allowed to do our work without a lousy white man ordering us around.

"But this is only one example of our suffering. The story of Ndango's brother is another example. And then there is the story of my friend, Kangura. When I came here for the first time, I met Kangura and we soon became great friends. He taught me a lot and helped many of the other men, too. He became like a father to us. Everyone knew him and respected him. But because he was so highly respected by all the blacks, his white supervisors began to fear him. And do you know what finally happened? They killed him. They sent *tsotsis*, thugs, to kill him. We know who is responsible for his death, but there is nothing we can do about it. My friend is dead and I still cannot accept this fact."

Nakare, caught up in his story, pauses for a moment. "And do you know why we are here? The white people are taking our land away from us and then imposing taxes on it that we must pay. We must leave our homes and families and come all the way here, for what? We must come here to work and earn money so that we can pay the white man's taxes—taxes on our land—the land that the white man is taking away from us! When we work in the mines we are paid much less than the whites. We have no freedom here. We are not allowed to choose our work, leave the compound, or go home when we want to. We cannot argue with our supervisors, and even if we are capable, we cannot get promoted. Aren't we people, like any other people in this world, who know what we want and how to get it? Why should we need a white man's permission to breathe . . . permission to breathe God's air?" Nakare stops for a few moments to let his words sink in.

"Many people—no, most—of the people in our land and elsewhere in Africa have suffered at the hands of the whites. But now, in places like Malawi, Zambia, and Tanzania, there are black people just like you and me who are governing themselves. They are not listening to the white people anymore. They are not being kicked in

the shins anymore! Instead, they kick the whites who do
not want to listen—to them! Those blacks are free. But
they had to fight for their freedom. We, and our country,
South West Africa, can also be free if we are willing to
fight the white man. It is our land, not the white man's
land."

Muronga has taken in every word that Nakare has
spoken. At the mention of blacks governing themselves,
Muronga recalls what his friend Musoke told him about
blacks who are feared by whites. As Nakare finishes his
talk he and Ndango watch Muronga. A subtle nod to one
another expresses their agreement and Ndango interjects,
"Maybe we need not say anything more right now."

"Yes, I agree. But let me say one more and very important
thing," adds Nakare. " . . . That is that this is not the
first meeting at which these things have been said," he
continues, pausing to see the reaction on the other men's
faces.

"As I said, I found other people here having these kinds
of meetings. They are our brothers, although we do not
know them. They began these meetings because they
wanted to do something about our country. There were
many who used to meet as we are meeting now who
went away to I don't know where. From there they have
been helped by other people, black people to go back
to our country and fight to get our land back from the
white people who are taking it away from us. You may
have heard of the fighting that is beginning to happen
in our land, between the so-called strange people from
the bush and the white policemen. Those are our people
returning with strength. They go back under the name
of the United People's Organization. We also call ourselves
the United People's Organization. That is why you must
be very careful with what you say, Muronga. Do you
understand?"

Muronga's eyes open wide, as if he is waking up for the first time. This is what the commissioner was talking about, he muses, half frightened, half excited. This could be very dangerous for me. The commissioner said that those UPO people just wanted to kill whites. He didn't say they wanted to liberate anybody or get our land back. How can you free anybody by killing? I wish Kaye or Uncle Ndara were here. This is too much for me. I came here to work and earn money, not to hear these destructive words . . . But, then, why should I believe what the commissioner has said? Muronga thinks, confused.

Before Nakare sits down, he looks at Muronga's pensive face. Knowing that he has many questions running through his mind, but that the time to answer them will come later, Nakare says to Muronga in a softer voice, "Muronga, if you are interested, you may come to our meetings. You look like the right kind of man to join us. Our next meeting is Saturday night, in my room. I will tell the other men about you so they can help you learn as we go along. But right now, I must go. It is getting late and I have to be up early in the morning and be a *baasboy* at the gate. And Muronga, remember . . . " He raises his forefinger to his mouth, "Shh . . . "

After Nakare has left the room, Ndango and Muronga talk on for a little while. "So, now, what do you say, Muronga?" asks Ndango.

"What can I say? I am . . . "

"You are not afraid, are you?"

"Oh, no. I am impressed. But there are so many questions that I want to ask. How did you start all of this? And how can we fight the white man? You know he has guns that spit fire and can kill even at a distance! How can we win?"

"Don't worry about all of that now. Come on Saturday night and you will hear more. But remember, it is very dangerous for you to know these things, so keep it to yourself. And now, you had better go before my roommates come back. They don't know about all of this."

Muronga leaves Ndango's room with his head filled with questions. Cautiously, he walks back to his room, feeling already that he is engaging in dangerous acts. In his own room, he finds his roommates asleep. Relieved at not having to answer any questions himself, he sinks into his bed and begins dreaming of a white man who is running away from two black security guards who are hitting him with their hats . . .

On Saturday evening, Muronga rushes through his supper and takes a few moments back in his room to get ready before heading for Ndango's room. His thoughts are of the past few days and of the many things that have happened during that short period of time. Before he left the village to come to the mine, he never would have imagined working for someone who had assaulted him, let alone someone who had never bothered to apologize. He had found it extremely difficult to pretend that nothing had happened between him and his boss to put them at loggerheads, or that the white man was in the right and that he, Muronga, was not offended by his boss's behavior. With such thoughts on his mind, Muronga reaches Ndango's room where the two men had agreed to meet so that they could go together to the meeting.

"So, you are here. Very good. The business is about to begin," says Ndango with a smile.

"Yes. Am I on time?" asks Muronga.

"Yes, you are. Wait for me there. I am just tightening my shoes," Ndango says. "Okay, I am ready. Let's go. We must not keep the others waiting. The meetings are kept short so that the whites do not become suspicious. If they ever found out about them, we would all be dead."

Changing the subject, Muronga hesitantly inquires, "Ehm . . . isn't Nakare a *baasboy*? I mean . . . "

"Yes, I know what you mean. He is a *baasboy* . . . but a different kind of one. He is a good man. He is with us. His blood flows in the right direction. And we need people like him who can read, write and speak *vsvsvsvs*. They know the white man. They know his laws and tricks. And, yes, there is this, too. He protects the white man during the day, but he protects us during the night . . . and as you know, it is the night that is more dangerous. Hopefully there will come a day when we will no longer fear or trust people because of what they wear, but will judge people by what they do to make life better for everyone."

"Yes, I agree with you," concurs Muronga. "I hope that day comes soon so that my son, Mandaha, can see it."

"That is our reason for having these meetings. We are talking about the future. It will take a lot of hard work to make that day arrive. We will need good men who are willing to make sacrifices now to bring about a better future—for themselves and for their children. I think you are just such a man and I am glad that you want to join us."

"And I am glad that you want me to join you," says Muronga, flattered. "But tell me, is there anything you want me to do right now?"

"No, not yet. There will be time for that later. We must not talk about these things anymore now. You never know, the wind can carry our words far from here. Now, let's hurry a bit, eh?" says Ndango.

In Nakare's room, they find about twenty men gathered, some sitting on the floor and others sitting on the beds.

All of them either smile and wave or nod their heads when Ndango comes in, but otherwise they talk quietly to one another. The two men find an empty space on the floor near Nyangana. His face and a few others are familiar to Muronga, but most of the others are not.

As soon as Ndango and Muronga are seated, Ndango whispers in Muronga's ear, "All of the men you see in this room are our true brothers. They all come from our country, South West Africa."

"Are they all from Kavango?" Muronga whispers back.

"No, not only from Kavango; from the whole country. Although we belong to various ethnic and tribal groups, we share one land. The white man has tried to take our land away from us. He has tried to keep us apart so that we will have less strength to defeat him. The men in this room, Ovambos, Hereros, Kavangos—everyone—feels that by uniting, by coming together in meetings like this, we will soon have the power to say to the commissioners, 'Get out and leave us alone!'"

Muronga is impressed by what he has heard and excited by the idea of uniting with these men to save their country. He looks again at the faces in the room and is reminded of tribal meetings back home in his village. Curious about the men in the room, he gazes at each one for a few moments. These people look different. I can tell that they are not from my tribe, he concludes. This one here is definitely too fat to be from my tribe, unless he has been here too long, eating the white people's food and getting bigger and bigger. He certainly would not be good at working in the fields, Muronga thinks to himself. The other man next to him is also too short to come from my tribe. Nakare and Ndango are unmistakably my people, I can tell. They are tall, dark, thin and strong, like me. He continues to look about the room, taking it all in, and feels the importance and seriousness of this meeting weighing on him. He is happy to be present in this room tonight. I never thought I would be among so many people, all of whom are not known to the people in my village. What does this mean? he wonders.

Caught up in his thoughts, he is oblivious of the man who has come and sat down beside him. His gaze finally comes to rest on the elderly man's high-topped, laced leather shoes. They were too pointed so the man made holes in them so that his little toes could stick out at the sides. Uncle Ndara has shoes like that, Muronga thinks, wistfully. Smiling, but disguising his smile with a cough, he remembers how Uncle Ndara used to fix his shoes "so his toes could breathe," he used to say when children teased him. I wish Uncle Ndara, or at least Kaye were here with me, Muronga thinks.

Nakare, who has been standing near the door, finally steps to the front of the room and begins to speak, but this time he speaks Sfanakalo, unlike during their earlier meeting with Ndango when he spoke Thimbukushu.

"Be greeted, my brothers. I am happy to see you here tonight. And to those of you who are here for the first time, a special welcome. As you all know, every man in this room is from South West Africa. We come from many different ethnic and tribal groups and speak different languages, but we are brothers all the same. We share the same frustrations, concerns and hopes for the future of South West Africa. That is why we have organized these meetings. The white man is trying to increase his power in our land and over our people. He is taking our land away from us and trying to enslave us. It is our land that is being stolen from us. It is ours, and we must know that. Then we must say, 'How will we get it back from the whites?' When each one of us returns to our country when our contracts are finished, we must not forget what we have learned at these meetings and while we have worked in the mine. We must know what the white people are doing to us. We must not believe what they tell us.

We must not believe them when they tell us that we are less than they are—that we are inferior to them. We are not. And when we go home we must tell our people that they are equal to the whites. It is our responsibility to fight for what is rightfully ours."

As Nakare speaks, Muronga listens attentively.

"Do you understand everything Nakare is saying, Muronga?" asks Ndango.

"Yes, I do. But I don't understand why he is not speaking Thimbukushu here. There are no white people here. These other men are not from our tribe, are they? They are foreigners. I thought we were talking about getting our land back. Do we want to share it with total strangers?" Muronga asks in a concerned whisper.

"I understand what you are saying, and I agree. But you see, Nakare is not only for us. He is for everybody, the whole country . . . ," Ndango answers.

"That means he can be against us."

"Oh, no. Never. He is a very knowledgable man. He has learned many deep things. He talks about the whole land, about the whole people. You see, to him a tribe is too small. One group cannot stand against the big guns of the white people. This organization is about uniting people to be stronger, you see," Ndango explains quickly in a soft voice. "I can tell you more later. But believe me, Nakare will never be against us."

"I see. I understand what you are saying. I remember Uncle Ndara's story of two brothers who could break a stick if they tackled it together, but could not when they did so alone."

Ndango and Muronga's dialogue is broken by Nakare who suddenly stares at them and indicates to them that he needs their attention, too.

"Yes, yes, you are right! It is our land!" interrupts one very short man in the room who has been half asleep most of the time. All the other men smile slightly when they see him almost jumping to his feet to speak in a loud excited voice.

"But how can we do this? First, we must encourage our brothers to join our organization, The United People's Organization. We must invite them to come to our meetings. We must come together and stand together— united. We must help one another, give each other ideas, and support one another while we are here in South Africa. Our friends in this country, black people like you and me, are doing it. Then, when we go back home, we must help our people to understand why we must resist the authority of the white man. We must make our people understand why they are poor and why they are paying taxes. Why, that is, they are paying taxes to white people on their own land! We must get organized!"

"Now! Let's start now. We have the opportunity here, now!" come the words of an elderly man in the corner of the room, who hits his fist against the wall. The other men look at him.

"Let me finish first. We all have to think about this. We must join with one another and demand our land back! We must be united— Hereros, Kavangos, Ovambos, all the peoples in our land! We are the only ones who can rescue ourselves and our people from the bondage of slavery that exists both here in the mines and at home. Remember, divided we are doomed, united we will win! This is all I have to say for tonight. Our brother, Nyangana, will share his thoughts with us next time, and after that, someone else will have an opportunity until everyone has had a turn. The next meeting will be a week from tonight. Now, remember . . . keep everything you have heard tonight in your chests."

The meeting is officially over, but since the men must leave the way they came—only one or two at a time lest someone suspects something—they stay in Nakare's room for a while and talk softly amongst themselves. Muronga meets a man from Ondangwa in Ovamboland named Natangwe who has been one of the organizers in the mine. Natangwe tells Muronga about his nasty white boss and that in the beginning there were very few men who attended these meetings, but now the group keeps getting larger and larger. He further explains to Muronga that he will be finishing his contract in five days and then he plans to go home and begin doing what Nakare suggested tonight.

Muronga and Nyangana eventually leave together and part company near their rooms. Muronga slowly enters his now darkened room and gets into his bed without disturbing his roommates. Before falling asleep he thinks about the meeting. He recalls what Ndango told him before the meeting, what Nakare said during it, and what Natangwe told him afterwards. He was excited to hear about all of it and thinks about the day when he, too, will be going home. He is anxious to become the master of his own life again and to help his people to become free again. God of Our Forefathers, he prays silently, protect me and my brothers and take us safely home to our people who are suffering. Help us to have the courage and strength to become one people—united and free. With these thoughts he falls asleep.

CHAPTER 12

On Monday, Muronga greets his supervisor with more confidence than ever before. The meeting on Saturday night made him realize that he is not alone. While he scoops up gravel with his shovel, he remembers Nakare's speech. "We must be united. We are the only ones who can rescue ourselves and our people from slavery. Divided we are doomed, united we will win." The words pound like drums in Muronga's ears. Repeating them over and over helps him to do his work without feeling the soreness in his body.

If only I could read and write some words, Muronga thinks. Then I would know what these white people are saying. But now they hide their words from me. I cannot tell this white man that I, too, am a man—not a boy. I have a wife and child of my own. I am a man like any other, and one day I—we—will be strong enough to strike back when we are struck. All we can do now is duck the blows. This time I ducked, but what about the next time? What will I do then?

Muronga can hardly wait for the big Saturday night meeting. This will be another time of big words, he thinks.

Words about life . . . the life of my people. The people I need, and who need me.

On Friday at suppertime, Muronga and Nyangana meet in the food *pondok*. They stand together devouring their dinner of *mealie meal pap* and big pieces of well-done stewed beef. Although they are both looking forward to the meeting, they avoid talking about it. Instead they talk about anything that comes into their heads.

"Muronga, didn't you say your uncle taught you to interpret dreams?" Nyangana asks.

"Well, yes . . . sort of," Muronga replies, looking quizzically at Nyangana. "Why?"

"After that nice swim the other day, I have not been able to stop thinking of home. I keep thinking about the river, the trees, the fish, and everybody I know. Then, last night I dreamt that my wife and I were swimming together—naked." He gives an embarrassed laugh. "What do you think such a dream means?"

"Hmm. When you dream about swimming, it means that you will have to swim through some difficult days," Muronga says with a smile. "Surely you have heard this before. And it also shows that your wife has a very strong spirit to be able to visit you here. She is a very strong person, just like my wife. These women are great people," Muronga says with a smile.

"Yes, well, I only hope I am not going to have many big problems. Anyway, aren't we too far away from home? I thought dreams meant nothing in the white man's land."

The two men continue their conversation until Nyangana, lowering his voice, whispers to Muronga, "Don't look now, someone is watching us. Wait a moment, then turn around and look. Right behind you. I don't know who he is. Maybe you do. He looks like one of the *manyowani* to me. You can tell by his clothes. He's wearing new clothes, like the clothes we wore when we first arrived."

Muronga slowly turns around and quickly looks at the young man, then turns back to Nyangana. "I don't know him, but I saw him here yesterday. He was right behind me, and he stood nearby then, too. He looked like he wanted to say something to me, but he didn't. I don't think we have anything to fear from him. I am sure he is new here."

"Yes, I think you are right. He looks too new to be one of those people Nakare warned us about. Remember? The ones who get paid to tell the white man what we say and do."

Having finished eating their dinner and washing their plates, they prepare to leave the *pondok*. "My friend, I am very tired," Nyangana says with a yawn. "I will see you tomorrow. Go and sleep well."

"Thank you. You sleep well too," Muronga replies, with a wave as he turns towards his barracks.

From across the *pondok* Nyangana adds in a loud voice, "Muronga, don't forget! Tomorrow!"

"No, I won't. How can I forget? I will be there!"

Stepping out from beneath the shelter of the *pondok*, Muronga wearily heads in the direction of his room when, from out of the dusk, a figure comes running towards him. The young man who was seen earlier in the *pondok* races towards Muronga, speaking impetuously.

"Are you Muronga? Muronga from my village?"

"Who are you? Where do you know me from?" Muronga asks, somewhat alarmed and surprised.

"I am your brother . . . from Kake . . . your village . . . kraalhead Shakandandu! My father is Rumapa. My name is Diyeve. Do you remember me now? I was watching you because I know you. You are my brother! I just arrived four days ago. People at home told me about you. They did not know where you were. Are you fine?" the young man blurts out.

"Yes, I am fine," Muronga replies with equal excitement. "I remember you now. I know you very well. It is only that I did not expect to see anyone like you here. How are you, my brother?" Muronga asks a bit emotionally. The two men embrace for some time before letting go of each other. Muronga cannot believe his eyes and stares back at the familiar face for a moment before speaking. "Come to my room and tell me about what is happening at home. I am so happy to see you, Diyeve. But how did you recognize me after so much time has passed?"

"Oh, I saw you yesterday for the first time, but you look so different. I wasn't sure it was you I saw and I was too afraid to ask you your name. You don't look like you are from my village."

Muronga chuckles. "How can I look so different? I am the same."

"No, you are not the same. You know many things now, and many people, too. Look at me. No, we are not the same. And you are a big man now. I thought I recognized you first when I heard you speaking our language. Then when your friend called you by your name . . . our people's name . . . I knew it was you," Diyeve explains as they enter Muronga's room.

"I see," Muronga replies with a nod of his head, as he leads his guest to his bed. "Here, sit down."

"Even your bed is different," comments Diyeve, more calmly now, as he settles himelf comfortably on the bed. "It has more on it than mine. The way you walk is different . . . not like us, the new ones. And you speak Sfanakalo very well, too. Maybe one day you can teach me some of what you know."

"Yes, I have learned a lot. I have also bought many goods here. Under this bed I have a big trunk with many clothes in it for my people. This is one of the reasons I came here. We will get more money and buy more goods while we are here. But there will be plenty of time for that. We will be together for a long time. But now, tell me, how are our people at home? And my wife and child?" Muronga asks, anxiously.

"Everyone was fine by the time I left about three weeks ago. Before I left I saw practically everyone in our village. And everyone talks about you. Your wife, *Nyina-Mandaha* is healthy. I always see her carrying the child on her back. Your sister Kahambo has also been blessed with a baby, a girl. Judging from the way your niece cries on her mother's back, it is clear there is a powerful woman in that little body. She is a perpetuator of your family."

"When did she give birth? How wonderful to have a child of my own sister! I wish I were able to see the baby now."

"I am sure they would like to see you, too. Your wife is still the great woman that you know and left behind. In my *kraal* there are now three babies. The village is growing fast, not to mention the baby cattle. Since the time you left, there have come one, two, three, four, five . . . too many calves."

"And the rains? When I left, the grass was beginning to come up and the red rain insects were coming out, too. I knew that there were going to be good rains."

"Yes, we had plenty of rain this year. You mean you left before the rains came? Yoh, you have been away a long time. No wonder everybody misses you."

"Tell me more. Give me the news. Has anyone died since I left?"

"Now that you have asked, I can tell you that the old man Karupu is no longer with us. He died a very painful death."

"What happened?"

"As you know, he liked hunting. One day he went hunting with his dogs."

"And then, how did he die?"

"This time he didn't kill a hare, as he usually did. He killed a python."

"A what? A python?" he repeats courteously to show his interest. "A big one?"

"Yes, a very big one. He found it lying still after it had swallowed a whole goat. That's when he cut its throat with his famous knife. He then carried it on his shoulders. Little did he know that the slimy thing was not totally dead yet. As you know pythons don't die quickly. As he was carrying it home, it suddenly coiled itself around him. He fell to the ground. The animal got hold of his neck. The dogs didn't help him because they were too afraid of the huge snake. In no time it forced all the air out of him. By the time people arrived on the scene, the monster had already pressed him dead. Oh, it was terrible. Maybe I should not tell the whole story. It is too frightening. He was buried a few days before I climbed the lorry."

"Please, don't tell me any more of this story," adds Muronga while clenching his teeth and grimacing.

"Otherwise, everyone else is fine," continues Diyeve. "At least at the time I left they were. I don't know what has happened since then. Oh, I almost forgot to mention something."

"What is it? Bad news again?"

"No, there was a meeting with the commissioner, just before I left. Many people are coming here these days, or going to *Thivanda* because of the new laws. All the big people went to the meeting to hear about the taxes, taxes, taxes. I went, too, because my uncle wanted me to go with him. Your Uncle Ndara was there, too. He spoke very great words to the commissioner. Your uncle told me about you, but he did not know where you were. Whenever I went to fetch the cattle, I met him as he was going to the fields. I am sure you know that he is one of those wise men who took black cows to Chief Disho who gave us such good rains. This year our people will harvest plenty of *mahangu*."

"Now you are telling me good news, news that I want to hear very much. Very good. Let the God of Our Forefathers be praised. I am so happy you came here with news like this. It is very nice to find a homeboy when you are so far away from home. How happy our people will be to hear that we are together here! Did you hear about my friend Kaye, too?"

"Yes, I did. Where is he? You climbed the lorry together, didn't you?"

"Yes, we left home together. But he went to the west to work in the mines there. I don't know exactly where. We were separated in Rundu. I hope he is fine."

The two homeboys talk for a long time. They are both pleased with each other's good health. Their conversation is interrupted when Muronga's two roommates return to go to bed.

"Diyeve, let me walk you to your room. I want to see where you sleep, so that we can visit each other often. There are many things here in the compound that I can tell you about.   Tomorrow evening I will not be in my room. There is a meeting. I am going to another room to see my friend who is working here and who has been here a long time. We can talk again on Sunday."

"Where are you going? Can I come with you?"

"No, no. You cannot . . . not yet. Maybe later, but not now. I will tell you all about it sometime, so don't worry. You are still new here."

It takes Muronga awhile to fall asleep this night, unlike other nights when he is too exhausted to keep awake. The conversation with Diyeve makes him think of nothing but his family back home—his wife, his son, Uncle Ndara, Mama Rwenge, his father and mother, the cattle and the green fields yet to be harvested. Finally sleep comes and his soul visits his village.

"*Moro, moro*, I have arrived, I am here!" he says in his dream, upon his arrival. "Come and help me with my goods. Where is my son Mandaha? Is this my boy? He is so big!"

"Yes, Mandaha is a big boy," answers his wife Makena who has been reunited with him by the elders. The elders were the first to shake hands with Muronga. They then poured some *Mono* oil onto Muronga and Makena's hands and foreheads in a brief ceremony. Uncle Ndara told them, "You are joined again as husband and wife after a long time of separation. With this oil on your hands, touch your child and be reunited."

"This morning, Mandaha was singing a song and he was singing about you in his song. I was wondering why the boy was doing that," Makena says, laughing. "He was very small when you climbed the lorry. But he talks of you as if he knew you. He is so active, he wears me out. Now that you are here, you can keep him busy. He likes playing with men and bigger boys. He thinks he is as big as they are."

"Yes, that's my boy. He is so big! Look, his head can reach above my knees. Come, my boy, come let's play. Dada is here. Do you remember me?"

"Mandaha was ill for some time. Uncle Ndara had to fetch Shamashora to drive away the spirits that were visiting him in his sleep'" explains Makena.

"And how is he now? How long ago was this? Are you sure he is fine now? I have brought some white man's medicine with me, too. It is very good for children. It burns the bad feelings out of their stomachs."

"No, he is fine now, as you can tell. He never stops moving. He is so happy to see you. Children know their parents by their smell even if they have not seen them before. The spirits are very strong in children. They are pure and still clean because they haven't offended the ancestors yet. Mandaha likes to go to the fields with me. And he does not cry as much as the other children do. It is only some nights that he gets restless. Then he cries and cries and cries. I put my breast in his mouth until he eventually falls asleep."

Everyone in the *kraal* comes to greet Muronga. They all exclaim how different he looks. The women bless him on his hands and face, while the men who come to greet him shake his hands warmly. Everyone is excited to see him. Then his father opens the trunk that he has brought home and Muronga starts to divide the clothes from inside the trunk among the people seated around him. Everyone gets something. A new black hat and a heavy beige coat symbolically go to his father. Another similar coat, a blue-striped blanket and a large grey hat are given to Uncle Ndara. Another dark blanket and a new three-legged pot go to his mother. Mama Rwenge gets a large brown woolen blanket, a large piece of dark blue fabric and bangles. Makena gets two dresses, one dark blue and the other red, a hat rag and a few blouses. She also gets a few articles for her own parents and a pair of overalls and a bag of sweets for Mandaha. Muronga hands a large rectangular head cloth to his sister, a pair of pants to his paternal uncle and many small items to each member of the family. He gives all the money in a big brown envelope to Uncle Ndara who, with Muronga's father knows further what to do with it.

"Who wants to help me here?" asks Mama Rwenge.

"With what?" asks *Nyina-Muronga.*

"With these new things. I cannot use these items that *Wiha-Mandaha* has brought me. They all smell like these white people who come to stay in the camps. I will vomit if I use this blanket tonight. I need someone to use them for me for sometime, until they get rid of the *munuko ghothikuwa.* You young people do not mind this 'white' smell, do you?"

"You are right, Mama Rwenge," interrupts *Nyina-Muronga.* "I was thinking of that, too. The smell of these new things is too much for me."

"We can use them for you," says Ngombe, a young woman in the back. "I have my sister and other friends who can also help make the things older. I can go and fetch them now," she continues in an excited tone. Ngombe lives in the *kraal* adjacent to Muronga's. She, her sister, and their husbands are known to be very good at taking the *munuko ghothikuwa* out of new clothes. This is why she came to the reunion.

"Oh, no, you can take everything with you," says Mama Rwenge. "I am sure *Nyina-Muronga* feels the same. We trust you. You can take the things and return them when they look and smell good. We are so happy that you came." She bursts into a loud ululation, while the others look at Muronga with great admiration.

"You have worked well, *Wiha-Mandaha.* I am very proud of you. Look, you have clothed everyone in our families.

Even Mandaha looks like the little white boys who we always see running around in the camps," Makena says to her husband when they are alone in their hut. "But what you brought home with you is not what is most important to us. What is more important to me and Mandaha is that you returned to us safely. Your son, as you can see, is very happy to see you. If he could speak for himself, he would tell you that. Just pick him up and feel how big he has grown while you were away! He is even beginning to walk like you—fast and straight. He is going to be as tall, strong, slender and good-looking as you are, Makena says with a laugh. Let's go to sleep now. It's getting late."

Muronga wakes up. He feels around in his bed, as if to touch Makena who was with him only a moment ago. She is gone. It was a dream! Just a dream!

The whole day of Saturday Muronga is preoccupied with his dream. When he goes to the meeting in Nakare's room, he thinks about the dream, and whether he should tell his friends about it. No, I cannot tell them about such a dream. They will think that I am not manly if I miss home and my family so much, Muronga thinks before entering the meeting room. But even during the meeting his mind flashes back and forth between the meeting in the compound and his family back home.

"Brothers, let's start our meeting so that we can break up early tonight," Nakare opens the meeting. All the men listen attentively as Nakare continues, "Tonight we are not going to discuss many things. First of all I was asked by the leader of the Native Mine Workers' Consultation Committee in this mine to announce tonight that there are other organizations in the compound that are also meeting secretly as we are doing. The Black Promotion Movement, a very good organization in this country, speaks for all of us in this land, including this compound.

I know the name of the person who is the leader of the movement. He is a good man, brothers. The white people fear this man. He doesn't speak very much, but he knows what our problems are. This big leader, whose name is Archie Bokwe, is calling upon all of us—the workers in this mine—to stay in their beds next Monday and not go to work."

"What? What is going to happen?" asks one man at the meeting. Muronga, who has been absent-minded for a while is awakened by the man's reaction.

"No, don't be afraid," Nakare reassures him. "Every person in the mine, all the black people, are staying away from work. Not only us."

"Why?" Muronga asks quietly.

Nakare looks at him. "Because we blacks are not getting enough money for the work we are doing here. The white people who sit around and give us orders get many, many times more than we in this room get. This man Archie Bokwe knows everything about money. He speaks to the white people and he says that they do not want to listen. Now he wants us all to stand up and speak with one voice. It is very important that we people from South West Africa collaborate with what our fellow workers are doing. What they experience here is also what we experience. We cannot go to work while they are staying at home."

"Yes, we must stand with our brothers," Ndango adds. "We must also remember that if we do what other people are not doing, it is dangerous to us. Remember, this is not our land. We cannot run home if something bad happens to us. We would not even find the road home if we ran away on foot. We have been stolen from our homeland. We have been coerced into coming here to work as contract laborers for very little money when our own families need us. We must stand together and oppose this system."

There is a long silence in the room. This is not the type of meeting the men are used to attending. This is something new—a new situation. There is no disagreement. There is fear and uncertainty, but no disagreement. They look at one another. There are questions on their faces. Nakare is expected to provide them with the sense of security that they need.

"Listen, brothers," Nakare continues after giving them a chance to reflect on what he has said. "What you must do now is keep quite about what you have heard. On Monday morning we will watch what other people are doing. Go where the other people are going, but do not go in this group. This is very important. Now we must go to our rooms and sleep. The other issues about our own group we will pursue after Monday. Sleep well, everybody."

"Sleep well, Nakare," the men respond as they leave the room stealthily. Muronga is confused. He thinks about Monday and what is going to happen, not understanding what all this means. At the same time he wonders if last night's dream would return again.

Monday morning Muronga does not sleep late as he did the day before when he didn't have a shift to do. Before the sun sits above the roof of his barracks, he is awakened by what sounds like an unfriendly kick on the door. He sits bolt upright, wondering what could be happening. Is it somebody, maybe one of my friends, coming to fetch me? he thinks, rubbing his eyes and staring at the door. But we are not supposed to go to work today! he remembers.

"*Puma, pumani, puma,* come out!" comes the sound of a husky voice through the red metal door. "It is the police. Come out all of you. Every one must go to work! Get ready and come out. Nobody is staying in the rooms, come out! Quick, or else you will be arrested. We know that some trouble-makers are telling you not to go to work today. We know it . . . !" The policeman continues to talk to them from outside. Muronga can hear similar sounds by the doors of adjacent rooms—there are many more voices saying the same things.

Oh, my mother, what is going on here? Muronga asks himself, his heart pounding faster and faster. And how did they know that something was planned for today? Did any white people attend any of the meetings? How can that be? Or is it as Nakare said—there are among us those who listen for the white man? What a shame it is if these people—black people—can do such things to their fellow black people!

"Come out, all of you!" the voice continues. Muronga and his roommates are too afraid to open the door. Suddenly the door is kicked open and two uniformed white men, accompanied by four black guards in khaki-green uniforms enter the room.

"Who of you are supposed to work today?" a tall black guard asks loudly.

"I am. But I am not going," Muronga answers softly and slowly.

"Stand up! Go to work!" screams one of the black guards, ready to strike Muronga. He ducks in sheer anticipation of a blow. The other men in the room say they start work later on Mondays. "We are waiting for our shift to start, later," explains one of Muronga's roommates apologetically. "I, I am, . . . was going to work," Muronga stutters, not knowing what to say to them.

"Come, all of you! No one is allowed to stay in these rooms. You think you are clever, and that you are here to hold meetings, meeting, meetings. You will have your meeting at work while your asses sweat at the shovels.

Who told you not to go to work, huh? What's his name, Bokwe? Do you think we don't know your silly plans. Bokwe can have his own men to sleep here today. You are going to work!" the younger white policeman goes on.

They even know the person whose name I only heard the other day. These people are dangerous, Muronga thinks as he leaves his bed cautiously, not knowing what to expect next—both from the police and from Bokwe's group.

The men are hurled out of their rooms by the police. Someone has given their secret away. No meeting. No activity to demand better wages. For the rest of the day, the men go about their usual shifts. But unlike the other times when they go enthusiastically and singing, this time they go by force. The whole day the police escort them to and from the barracks. They are watched at the *pondok* while they eat. After their meal the head police guard announces through a loudspeaker that all of them must go to their rooms and that there will be no meetings in the compound.

The next morning most of the police are gone. On his way to work, Muronga runs into Diyeve, who is coming out of the mine.

"Good morning, Diyeve! Do you work at night?"

"Yes, I started yesterday. I was just thinking about you. How did you sleep?"

"Oh, I slept well. I am now going to start my long day in the hole. Did you spend the night there?"

"Yes. It was very strange. We worked like mice, all night long. And it is dark in there. Is that where you work, too? No wonder you people are so strong. Shoveling all those rocks and filling up those cars! I was very afraid when the white man I work for told me to go and move a rock with a piece of metal. I could see that this rock was loose; it was about to fall down. So I stood by the side and touched it. It fell down immediately, right in front of me. He didn't tell me how to do it right. Is that how you also started?"

"I am happy that you weren't hurt. These white people do not explain things well. They don't think about how dangerous it is to do what you did. It is good that you knew yourself that the rock was ready to come down. You can imagine what would have happened if you had been standing under it."

"Yes, I know," Diyeve exclaims with a shudder. "And yesterday morning I saw many policemen walking behind people on their way to work. Is that how they go to work? And where are they today?"

"No, yesterday was a bad day," Muronga replies.

"A bad day? Why?" interrupts Diyeve.

"The policemen came to walk us to work. If they hadn't come, we would not have gone to work. Listen, I have to go. I will tell you the story later. You need to be here for a while to understand these things. But I will tell you. May your day be good until I see you."

"Yes, then you can tell me everything. I was wondering what was happening; it didn't look normal to me. Work well, Muronga."

After dinner, Muronga walks to Diyeve's room. Diyeve is alone in his room, his roommates are sitting outside in the moonlight.

"*Moro*, how are you?" says Muronga.

"*Moro*, come inside. Sit down on my bed," Diyeve responds. "It is very kind of you to come and visit. I thought you would be too tired to come tonight. I expected you on Sunday and you didn't come. It is nice that you came tonight."

"I wanted to come and visit you on Sunday, but I was too afraid to come to you. I didn't want people to see that you know me. On Saturday I heard that we were not going to do any work on Monday."

"No work?" Diyeve responds, looking frightened.

"Yes, that's why you saw so many policemen. There is a lot happening in this compound. There is a group of people who hold meetings in secret. They call themselves the Black Promotion Movement. They say that we are not getting paid enough money. White people get all the money."

"And who was going to work? The white people? They don't know how to shovel. It is our work."

"This is what I wanted to talk to you about. It is not true that only we, the black people, can do the work that makes your body full of dust. White people should do that, too. They are people; they can do it. Since I have been here, I have learned many things. I am not afraid of the white people any more. They are lazy, too lazy to do what they want us to do. You will meet my friends soon. They speak big words about the people. We also have our meetings," Muronga carries on in a whispering voice. "I will tell you about our meetings later. Just don't say anything to anybody. I am not supposed to tell you all of this yet. But I trust you, and I want you to be safe here."

"Thank you, Muronga. I am so happy to have you here to tell me what is going on. I can see that you know many big people here. You say that you are not afraid of the white people any more! Yoh, you are saying big things now, aren't you? Won't they put you in jail if they heard you saying that?"

"They will, but I am not afraid of that, either. You see, the man who said we shouldn't go to work on Monday has been put in jail many times, I have heard. But he tells the white people the truth. We are people; we are men. My friends say these words all the time. You will see when you stay here longer."

"But people went to work yesterday morning."

"Yes, they did. It is because someone, one of us, a black person went to the white people and told them about Bokwe's words. I myself do not know this man, Bokwe, but I know his words are good. I must go to sleep now. Keep the words that you have heard to yourself. If you have any questions, ask me later. Don't say anything in front of people you don't know. Remember, this is a white man's mine, and the mine has ears."

"Oh, no, I cannot speak about such big things to strangers. I am asking you to tell me because you are my brother. We come from one place. We know each other. You know my people and I know your people. If anything happens to you here, I will carry the message. If it is me, you will carry the news to our people."

"Yes. Sleep well, Diyeve."

"Sleep well, Muronga."

CHAPTER 13

It is Monday morning, nine months after Muronga's arrival in the mine. Monday—the first day of the week—the day for starting work for the week. But this Monday is different. The compound is quiet and the barracks, *pondoks*, and mine shafts are deserted despite the usual schedule of continuous shifts.

At seven o'clock in the morning they heard the radio news. "Archie Bokwe, leader of the Black Promotion Movement, died in detention early this morning. The cause of his death is not yet known." As the words spread, the name "Bokwe" could be heard passing from one man to the next until everyone in the compound had heard the story. Ndango brought the news to Muronga's room. He himself had not known much about Bokwe, but he explained that while Archie Bokwe was speaking to a group of his black brothers and sisters, the whites had arrested him and put him in jail. And now he is dead.

Nakare, who had, like any other morning, silenced the screeching of his alarm clock and then turned on his battery operated radio, heard the news in the white man's language. Immediately alert, he goes looking for his comrade, Ndango, and finds him with Muronga. There, together, the three men look at Nakare's *Rand Daily Mail*. which says in large, bold letters, "*Si kahlela indoda yaMadoda*—We salute the man of men." For a short while Nakare translates bits and pieces of the article that accompanies the full-page picture of Archie Bokwe.

"It says here that Archie Bokwe was a leader of the Black Promotion Movement. He was arrested three weeks ago, for the fourth time, because he was telling people to hate the whites and not to work in their mines. It says that he was a violent man, who wanted to kill white people . . . and kill us, too," he says incredulously. "Can you believe it?" Nakare asks, looking up for a moment to see his companions' reactions.

"Hmm," they respond, nodding their heads in unison, as if this is nothing new.

"Further, it says that the police found some papers in his pockets on which he had written and told people . . . black people . . . to think that the country belongs to them and that they should stand up for what is theirs. He told them that the white people had stolen the land from them."

"And isn't that, ehm, true?" Muronga asks quickly.

"Well, what do you think? What I can tell you is that these people who write in papers can tell lies, yoh!" Nakare skims the rest of the article while the two other men remain silently waiting. "No, I don't think we need to read the rest of this. It says he died of a cold while he was asleep, in jail," Nakare concludes, shaking his head in disbelief, as he folds up the paper. A few moments pass before he speaks again in a hushed voice.

"This is serious, brothers, and I fear that there will be a general meeting organized today or tomorrow. I don't think people will keep quiet about this . . . I smell trouble in the air," he sighs, his gaze penetrating.

"And what will happen then?" asks Muronga nervously.

"Nakare is right. If Archie Bokwe is dead, then there will be trouble soon. I know it," adds Ndango.

"Anyway, let's wait and see. I will tell you if I hear anything. But keep quiet," Nakare replies, preparing to leave. "At times like this, you never know who to trust. Do you understand?" he queries.

Not waiting for a response, Nakare and Ndango leave Muronga's room so that they can get more information about this unpredictable day.

Dressing quickly, Muronga rushes off to the washrooms and then to the eating *pondok*, where he swallows his food practically whole. By this time, notices have been put up in every conceivable spot, most of them written in ordinary ink on thin pieces of cardboard. Messages have been tucked under the doors of the barracks and read, "One of our leaders is dead. We must remember him today!" Later, Muronga and his roommates, like all of the other men in the compound, talk in hushed tones and wait anxiously for their instructions.

Then it comes. As quietly as before, the message passes from one man to the next, from one room to another. But the words ring out loudly and clearly. They hang like weights on the friendly Transvaal breeze. "There will be a commemorative service for our fallen leader, Archie Bokwe, this morning at ten o'clock in the soccer stadium. There will be no work today. Let's show our solidarity by being there. Dissenters will be judged by history."

Before Muronga joins Nakare and Ndango to go to the big meeting, he walks across to Diyeve's room. He finds him getting ready for his breakfast. He has just returned from his night shift.

"Good morning, Diyeve. How did you work during the night?"

"Good morning. I worked well, thank you. But I am not tired this morning. What brings you here so early? Did you see me come in? And what are you doing? Aren't you going to work today?"

"No, there is no work today. I came to tell you that there is trouble in the compound today. You remember the other time we were supposed to stay at home and we went? This time I don't think the white people will stop it. Do you remember the big leader of the black people I told you about, Archie Bokwe? He has died. They say he died in jail. His people want him. We are going to listen, but I don't think that we should all go. I shall go, but you stay here. Nobody knows what is going to happen to us. The white people are very angry. You stay here so that if I don't return, you can take the news home. I will tell you everything that is said at this meeting. You stay in your bed. If anybody finds you there, just pretend that you are ill. I will keep my eyes and ears open for you."

"It sounds like it will be a big thing. You are right. It is important that one of us does not go. I will stay here. I shall wait for the words from you."

Hastily, Muronga leaves Diyeve's room to join Ndango. With the other men, they walk to the playground where the meeting is to be held.

From their armored vans parked atop the sand mounds that encircle the Doornfontein mines, the police can see everything with their high-powered binoculars. In their mottled camouflage uniforms of green and brown, they wait like vipers about to strike at their prey. Swarming now below them, like a colony of black worker ants, the black miners converge on, or appear to be sucked into, the open area that forms the stadium and assemble loosely in front of the covered bleachers. Streaming through the gates of the compound, they ignore the black security guards who, this time, offer little resistance—they were all warned not to "play white" today. The management of the mine told the black miners that they would break the law by assembling, and that there would be trouble, but even so, over a thousand black workers are gathering together for this meeting. Intense energy can be felt pulsating through the crowd.

Elbowing his way to the front of the stadium with Ndango, Muronga eagerly listens to him as he explains what is going on. Ndango tells Muronga about the president of the Native Mine Workers' Consultative Committee, Teboho Maseko, the man who has defied Mister Koekoemoer, the Afrikaner who is the general manager of the mine, and organized this gathering. Muronga has heard that black workers used to get only one meal a day before Maseko bravely argued with the white management for more and better food. Thus, Maseko is well respected by the men in the compound. And the whites know that Maseko has the power to rally the other men behind him. Muronga is excited by the thought of finally seeing and hearing this man whom he has heard so much about. Maseko steps forward and the roaring crowd becomes subdued.

"My brothers," he begins, "we are gathered together here this morning to commemorate one of our leaders, our brother Archibald Nkosinathi Bokwe, who is dead." He raises the picture that appeared on the front page of the newspaper in the sky so that everybody can see it. Upon seeing the picture, the men murmur loudly.

"*Amandla!*" shouts Maseko with his right clenched fist raised in the air.

"*Ngawethu!*" respond the men thunderously, frightening Muronga who has never heard such loud shouts before.

"*Matla!*"

"*Ke arona!*"

"Power"

"Is ours!"

"*Mayibuye!*"

"*lAfrika!*"

"*lAfrika!*"

"*Mayibuye!*"

"Archie Bokwe, as he is commonly known, died while he was being held in the white man's prison. As we stand here today, he is dead, not because he wanted to die, but because he opposed the way the white man treats us in this country. He is dead because he refused to accept or be treated as a subhuman. He is dead because he defied the white man's laws. That is why he was arrested, some weeks ago. I must tell you that we, too, are breaking those laws that Bokwe was against, as we gather here this morning. That means that we may be arrested too, today. The police may come here and take us to prison any time today. They can come now and break up this meeting, because this meeting hurts them. We must remember, brothers, that what the white man wants of us is not our life, but our work. To the white man, we may as well not be here, but for our labor. What this means is that the white man needs us, not as people but as workers, because our work is very important. This is like saying that we build and maintain the house in which the white man sleeps. Then the white man turns around and says we cannot enter in this house. He even says then that he alone built this house, and that we must sleep outside because we were too stupid to build our own house!"

"*Ayibo! Tyhini!*" several men exclaim loudly.

"And Bokwe knew this very well," Maseko continues. "They arrested him because they did not want him to tell our people this truth. We need to understand this.

Our only sin, is the color of our skin. If we go to prison today, it is because of this. . . . "

"Oh, no. Oh, my God!" Muronga says to himself aloud, suddenly afraid.

"Don't panic," Ndango says, patting Muronga on the shoulder. "We are too many to feel the pain, even if the police come."

"If the police come," Maseko continues, "you must not resist them. Do not, I repeat, do not throw rocks at the police or try to run away from them or they will shoot you. Be brave men and stand firm and united. We are proud of what we are doing here today and we must therefore face the consequences of our actions as our leader Bokwe has. Bokwe would not want to see you running away or getting shot. He would want all of us to follow in his footsteps by continuing the work he started. He is asking each one of us, right now, 'How much longer can we continue to suffer?'"

Maseko's last words hang heavily in the air. No one speaks. They are proud to be together like this, to remember their fallen comrade. He speaks again. "If there is anyone among us who would like to say a few words about our leader Bokwe, will you please come forward." No one moves. Muronga, his arms folded across his chest, wonders why no one has anything to say. After a few moments Maseko says finally, "Then let us continue with our service. I know why you are silent, and I understand. But let's sing to pay tribute to our comrade, Archie Bokwe, whom we shall never see again."

Like an echo coming from the back of the stadium it begins. Then, like a gathering storm, a thousand voices join in, rising toward the heavens in unison, singing in isiXhosa,

Senzenina, senzenina   (What have we done?)

Senzenina, se sifa nje?	(What have we done to die like this?)
Sono sethu, ubumnyama	(Our only sin is the color of our skin)

Ndango translates the words of the song for Muronga. "What have we done, to die like that? Our sin is being black." Exhilarated by the words and their meaning, the men clap their hands and stamp their feet to the music. Then they sing,

Mabauyekhe umhlaba wethu	(They must leave our land)
Si khalela lizwe lethu	(We cry for our land)
E'lathathwa ngamabhulu . . .	(Which has been taken by the Boers . . .)

Without warning, it happens like an explosion. The singing disintegrates into panicked cries as the thud of heavy boots is heard rushing towards them. Snarling, barking police dogs and their camouflaged masters close in on the crowd. Shouts of "The police are coming! Don't panic!" and "Stand firm!" penetrate the electrified air. Terrified at the sight of fleshy pink hands resting on the triggers of expectant rifles, the group of men squeeze tightly together. Muronga's senses are alive. The hairs on his head pierce his scalp like thorns; he is aware of every fingertip, of every toe. This is it, he thinks, the white man is going to kill me. I am going to die here, so far away from my home and family.

"Don't shout! We are having a religious service. We are just singing and praying," pleads Maseko, his voice strong and reassuring to the frightened men. In response, the white police commander tells Maseko in *vsvsvsvs* that they are all under arrest for breaking the law. Maseko explains to the crowd, "My brothers, this policeman says that we have broken the law and that we are all under arrest. Please, do not resist arrest. Do not say or do anything."

Police vans move in and encircle the entire assemblage. Vicious brown-grey police dogs pace frantically back and forth, leaping about, straining against their leashes, looking for an opportunity to attack. With shields held out in front of them, the camouflage-uniformed policemen with their rifles and batons approach quickly, pressing the individual black bodies into one massive lump of writhing humanity. Swiftly and efficiently, as more vans arrive, the policemen herd small clumps of offenders into the waiting vans, prodding them like cattle with the butts of their rifles and batons as the mad dogs nip at their shins and heels. Once loaded, the padlocked vehicles speed away to an unknown destination. The men inside are silent, not knowing what to expect. Arrested. Arrested. The words ring in each man's ears. Are we being taken to a jail? they wonder. Will we die there as Bokwe did?

No one knows how much time has passed before the vans begin to slow down and come to a halt. Until the metal doors of the vans are unlocked, the men don't know that they have arrived at a police station. They are herded out of the vans in the same fashion as they were forced into them. Poked and pushed by the policemen, the black men are packed into the open area outside of the police station buildings which is enclosed by a high barbed wire fence. Standing next to Ndango, Muronga waits anxiously, his eyes searching the crowd for the familiar faces of Nyangana, Nakare, and his roommates. The hostility of the policemen is apparent. One man has managed to invoke the wrath of one of the officials simply by daring to look at him too long. The butt of the policeman's rifle comes down on the unsuspecting man's shoulder. He crumples under the blow. Jeering, the brutal man in green and brown says loudly, "Am I too beautiful for you to believe your eyes? Is that why you stand there staring at me—huh? Do you want to buy me, bastard?" Looking up from where he has fallen on the ground, the black man's eyes plead with his attacker, but to no avail. The sardonic policeman mercilessly kicks his victim in the side. Lying motionless now, his eyes tightly closed, the black man holds his cries of anguished pain. This is a warning to all the other offenders to stand silently, their heads lowered, cowed into submission.

The day wears on. The sun becomes hotter and hotter. Hour after hour the men stand in the midday heat staring at the black tips of their shoes, growinq exhausted, almost losing consciousness. but alert to everything around them. Muronga, sweating profusely, is thirsty, hungry, and needs to pee. Some of the other men, unable to hold out any longer, have soaked their trousers with urine while standing there. Unable to move to relieve themselves, they have had no choice. Muronga prays that he will be able to endure. Feeling the sun burning his skin, he moves his tongue around to get rid of the dryness in his mouth and on his lips. To distract his thoughts he thinks about his family and home and wonders if he will ever see his people again. Still disbelieving what has happened to him today, he reruns every moment of this day since it began. As he tries to remember the melody to the song they sang this morning, the words come back slowly. *"Senzenina, senzenina . . . what have we done?"*

Finally the sun begins to set and the evening announces itself with the gentle blowing of a welcome Transvaal breeze. Without moving a muscle, the men breathe more deeply and for a moment feel hopeful. But their mood is quickly shattered by the return of the vile-mannered, rifle-waving policemen, who waste no time shoving the men with their rifles and batons into groups of twenty. Once again they are herded into the waiting police vans and another long journey ensues. In the semi-darkness of the late evening, they see another police station directly in front of them as they hop down out of the police vans.

Pushed into lines, the men are led inside the police station where they are ordered to keep their mouths shut and squat by the office door while they wait to be processed. Again the waiting is painful. After some time in this position, Muronga can hardly stand it anymore. His knees ache and feel stiff, but finally it is his turn to go into the office. He is rudely spoken to by a black policeman who asks him questions while filling out some papers and then he is fingerprinted. The whole activity reminds Muronga of the first time he was fingerprinted when he and Kaye went to the Tribal Community Bureau back home. When the process is finished, Muronga is ordered back into the line again where he waits until the rest of the men are processed. So far as any of the men knows there has been no charge made against them. However, that is of little consequence; the men know that in the white man's world the burden of proving his innocence is on the black man. They were at the stadium, they sang songs, they wanted to know about their fallen leader . . . that was their crime.

Commanded at last to get up, the prisoners follow yet another mean-tempered policeman down a narrow, dark passageway to a small, filthy, stinking, barred cell. An ungodly stench issues forth from a hole in the corner of the room. It fills the men's nostrils as they are thrown into the cell. Revolted and gagging, they cover their noses as best they can. But the function of the hole is obvious and at long last the men are able to relieve themselves.

Not daring to speak to one another, the half-dozen men in the cell look questioningly from one face to the next. Seating themselves cautiously on the dirty, cold cement floor, some of them close their eyes, trying to forget where they are. Still ravenous with hunger and thirst, but a shade more comfortable than before, they hold their noses and breathe through their mouths until a bundle of grey blankets is brought into their cell. Stale smelling from their previous users, the blankets provide little relief for their discomfort. Soon, however, a rotund black warder haughtily marches into the cell and instructs them to go to sleep. Each man spreads his two blankets on the floor and with stomachs growling noisily, each man falls into a deep sleep, exhausted. The horrible experiences of the day are forgotten, . . . for now.

The sound of heavy footsteps and the rattling of keys awakens the men abruptly early the following morning. For an instant, they are not sure where they are, but within seconds everything comes back into focus. Awake and on guard, but unable to move quickly enough, they are still lying on the floor, the blankets pulled up to their eyes, when two white policemen plant themselves firmly outside the cell door as a black policeman enters. In Afrikaans, one of the white policemen starts yelling at them.

Julle slapende gate! Julle het gedink julle is slim, ne? Nou le julle lekker hier by sterk manne. Julle fokken Bokwe het mos die sleutel vir die hemel. Hy moet nou die tronkdeure oopmaak . . . laat ons sien. Kom, waar is julle vergadering en die gesingery nou? Hier het ek die sleutel. Julle le en kak hier!

(You sleeping assholes! You thought you were smart, didn't you? Now you are lying fine here where strong men are. Hasn't your fucking Bokwe got the key to heaven? Let's see now how he opens the prison doors. And where is your meeting and bawling now? Here, I have the key. You lie and shit here!)

Muronga does not understand. But he can see that the words coming from the white man's mouth carry anger and hatred, and his eyes convey a sense of thirst to kill and destroy.

The black policeman inside the cell then shouts, "Now, fold up your blankets and squat neatly in front of me! Two-two!" As the men hastily obey their orders, the policeman struts back and forth, swinging his baton and adjusting his cap nervously. Glancing now and then at his white superiors, he tries to exude an air of authority. He has been ordered to say these things and behave this way. He is pitiful, but no more so than Muronga and his fellow inmates, who are also just pawns in the white man's game.

This is the prelude to breakfast—their first food in twenty-four hours. The men eat the thick brown bread and porridge, trying not to breathe the rotten air as they swallow. The black policeman paces the concrete floor as the men gulp down their food. He glares at them, watching their every move. The guard reminds Muronga of his father's dog, which used to watch people closely when they were eating so as not to miss a single bone that was thrown away. Finally the three snarling humans leave the cell and the men seat themselves on the floor again.

It is later in the day when a group of heavily armed policemen come to the cell and the prisoners are ordered to file out one by one. Outside the jail they are loaded into vans once more to be taken they know not where. In the van, Muronga overhears one of his cell mates whispering to another that this is what they did to Bokwe before he died—they kept moving him around so that it was impossible to keep track of him. The idea is to keep the prisoners guessing until they are finally anticipating the worst, the man said.

The ride seems endless. It is dark and Muronga and the other men in the van cannot see whence they are coming and where they are going. Muronga closes his eyes, trying to fall asleep. But the movements of the van make it impossible for him to do so. Where the road is smooth for the van to run sturdily, the driver deliberately drives in a zig-zag way so that the prisoners cannot be comfortable. This is part of the treatment.

With his eyes closed, Muronga thinks to himself, I wonder where we will sleep tonight. Maybe we will keep going, going, and going until the end of the world.

CHAPTER 14

Suddenly the van comes to a bumpy halt. One of the policemen quickly opens the door while barking a few words at Muronga's group. They are ordered to jump out quickly, but not to talk.

Mfundi, one of the men getting out of the van with Muronga, whispers to Fikile close to him, "We are in Pretoria. You see what's written above the gate over there?"

"Yes, I can see the writing, but I cannot read," Fikile answers. Muronga positions himself closer to Mfundi and Fikile so that he can hear what they are saying.

"We are in Pretoria," Mfundi continues. "And it says there that this is the central prison for black people. It is written in English and in Afrikaans. We are here where Archie Bokwe died."

"Here is where Bokwe died?" Muronga and Fikile exclaim simultaneously.

Again they are instructed not to talk. Then they are divided into groups. This time there are forty men crammed into one small cell. The stench from the hole in the corner of the room is as repulsive as before. The instructions are the same—there is to be no talking; they must all go to sleep now. Muronga and Ndango find places on the floor next to one another in the hope that they will be able to whisper a few words to each other once the dim ceiling light overhead is turned off. A small bed mat measuring about two feet wide and five feet long and two grey woolen blankets are folded together to mark each place. Muronga and Ndango spread their blankets on the mats and lie down uncomfortably. The bedding has a disgusting odor. It reeks of decaying bodies. How anyone can sleep under such things is a wonder. It is like spending a night among the dead, Muronga thinks.

Muronga is awake early the next morning and thinking of the first night he spent next to Kaye in the Rundu compound when he hears a policeman's heavy footsteps approachinq. "Up, . . . up! Get out and run . . . run you fools!" shouts the white policeman. "Line up behind one another! Two-two!" Leaping to their feet, the men form two lines and walk out as the policeman pokes and prods them with his baton as if they were cattle. They have only gone a short distance before they enter an open courtyard-like area and are ordered to stop. Warm sunshine, fresh air, the smell of food, and familiar faces greet them. Still in their lines they are instructed to file past a huge cement table where several guards hand them metal cups without handles, plates, and spoons and then serve them from big steaming pots. As they are waiting, they look for the faces of their friends, many of whom, like Nakare, whisper their cell numbers as they pass by. As they near the end of the table, they can hear a white guard talking loudly in *vsvsvsvs*. Nakare whispers that the guard is saying that if they drop the cup he will teach them how to hold it so they will never forget. When each man holds up his cup to be filled with coffee, the guard purposely misses the cup and pours the steaming hot coffee over their hands. But they don't dare to drop the cup! When Muronga's turn comes, he wraps his fingers tightly around the metal cup. His face contorts and his eyes water as the hot liquid scalds his skin, but he holds the cup, even as the metal burns his palms and the coffee sets in a small pool between his thumb and forefinger until it gets cold. He passes the test, but even then doesn't dare to change the position of the cup to relieve the pain, although he has realized that if he had held the cup with one finger underneath it, and his thumb on the upper rim, the coffee would have run off quicker. The guards are disappointed as not one man drops his cup—they had been waiting for all hell to break loose!

As soon as they have finished their meal of hard brown bread and old vegetable soup, the prisoners are chased back into their cells, a few receiving blows from rifle butts and batons just for good measure. Thus begins a series of days that begin and end inside the same grey drab walls of the prison. During the first few days no one speaks except through sign language. Then, a few words at a time are uttered, but nothing is said about Archie Bokwe in case the cells are bugged. All of the men know that the whites have ways of listening in on their conversations. So, the men have only their thoughts to keep them company. Every morning Muronga thinks about his family and wonders if they have any idea where he is and what he is going through. He keeps track of the number of days that have passed, wondering how much longer they will be kept there, and if they will ever return to the mine, and much later to their homes and families. Daily he thinks about the meetings back in the compound and now of the treatment he is receiving at the white man's hands.

As the days drag on, and uncertainty turns to restlessness, the men become braver, and for a time engage in playing jokes on the policemen who guard their cells. Screaming until one of the policemen would come running, the men would then pretend to be asleep and not answer when asked who had screamed. Once while playing this prank, Muronga was almost in stitches with laughter, trying to cover his face with the stinking blanket, and thinking as he did so that the guard was very stupid, when the black policeman came over to Ndango and him. Tossing his rifle from one hand to the other, he looked at Ndango and said, "I know who you are. I knew your brother. He was an agitator until T. B. got good hold of him. You had better not start that shit with me!" He brought his rifle butt down on Ndango's belly with a thud. Muronga flinched as Ndango stifled a cry. Standing over the two men, the guard then paused for only a moment before deciding to let Muronga feel his strength, too. He gave him a solid kick in the back with his heavy boot before leaving the cell. The thick metal door slammed shut behind him and the clanging of keys turning in the lock could be heard until the door was firmly bolted shut once more. Groaning in pain, Muronga and Ndango could only stare speechlessly at one another with wide, suffering eyes. They had sworn that one day they and their people would suffer no more—neither at the hands of the whites, nor at those of their "white" black brothers.

But it is the situation that has made them the way they are; they have had little choice in the matter. The men's pranks, while satisfying their need for a bit of entertainment, provoke the guard into a dangerous game with them—a game that must, unfortunately, be played if one is to maintain any semblance of self-respect while enduring such humiliation and degradation. In this respect, Archie Bokwe's death becomes more understandable to the men. Confidently and courageously confronting his white oppressors, his mere presence made a mockery of his black brothers' positions within the whites' system. Ruthlessly, they tried to defend it with intimidation. It is frightening to find out how much the guards know about people like Ndango's brother, but it is all part of the way things are done within the system.

Once they had tired of playing their game, there was nothing left to do but sit and stare at the grey ceiling and walls and the one small barred window close to the ceiling that was supposed to let in a bit of light and provide some ventilation for the foul-smelling room. Pacing the floor restlessly on the seventh day, Muronga decides to find out what has been written on the otherwise drab grey cell walls. Cautiously, he approaches one of the men.

"Can you read?" he asks the man, whispering in Sfanakalo.

"Yes, why?" the man replies softly.

"Can you tell me what is written on these walls and by whom?" "Ehm . . . yes. Men who were prisoners in this cell before us wrote the sayings. They are written in isiXhosa, which is my language, and in Sesotho." Squinting, he begins reading aloud. "*Unzima umthwalo*— that means: The burden is heavy. *Banna ba robala mo*— Men sleep here. *Matla ke arona*—Power is ours. *Modimo o kae bjalo?*—Where is God now? *Kuyanyiwa apha*—We shit here."

"These are brave men who wrote these words," Muronga interrupts him.

"Yes. They learned that only men, strong men come here."

"But it is hard here."

"Yes, but it is the best way to learn." Then he continues reading, "*Masilwe, madoda*—Let us fight, men. *Umlungu iligwala, inja*—The white man is a coward, a dog. *Itronko umzi wamadoda*—Jail is a man's home. *A re tshabe*—We are not afraid."

There are too many phrases to read them all. When Muronga nods that he understands and has heard enough, the man stops. Thanking him, Muronga returns to his mat to contemplate what the man has said. He wonders if the men who wrote these words are alive today. Did they suffer greatly while they were here, and were they here for a long time? Or did they die the way Bokwe did? More troubled now than he was before, Muronga's thoughts turn to his own plight and to his fate. He is frustrated at having no control over his destiny. Is there any way to get out of this hell hole? he wonders. Are we ever going to get out of here, or are we going to die here? *Senzenina, senzenina?*

By the ninth day, Muronga is obsessed with death. Rotting away in a filthy prison cell is no longer just a story to him—he can feel it and see it happening. He begins to worry about losing his mind as he watches as one man begins uncontrollably hitting his fists against the cement wall until his knuckles are bleeding. He prays repeatedly to the God of His Forefathers that he and Ndango will not be split up or that he will not be put in a cell alone. The uncertainty wears on him until he realizes finally that he must not, for his sanity's sake, dwell on such thoughts.

Closing his eyes tightly, he tries to imagine himself back in his village as a child. He remembers the way the air smelled after a heavy rain, and the way it sounded as it hit the grass roof of his family's hut. He remembers the evenings when the elders would gather the children together to tell them stories about their ancestors. He remembers how they would also tell the children's favorite story about two brothers, Tjakova and Manongo. Manongo was said to be the lazy older brother and Tjakova the zealous and successful younger brother who slew giants and worked miracles. Muronga always wanted to be Tjakova and would become upset anytime anyone called him Manongo. Calmed at last by his mind's wanderings, he continues to relive his childhood in the days that follow.

Sitting ... thinking ... wondering ... dreaming. Every day it is the same. Every day ... the same tasteless porridge and bitter coffee for breakfast, the same bland soup and beans for dinner. A guard comes into the cell every day and tells the prisoners to squat on their mats while he counts them. Routinely, they are subjected to the tauntings and insults of the policemen who guard the cells. Every day the stench from the hole in the corner gets worse and the daily discomforts and indignities go on. It is a fact of life that one has to submit to the body's demands, but using the hole in public view is humiliating to the men. They are made to feel even more uncomfortable as the days pass and they can smell their own and the other men's foul breath. They have not been able to wash themselves, not even their hands, since before being arrested. Unwashed, their skin begins to feel dry and crusty and their bodies give off a strong, offensive odor. Their clothes are stiff with dirt and sweat.

By the morning of the twelfth day, Muronga has happily recalled many of the days of his youth; finally the time has begun to pass more easily. Dozing after breakfast, his memories and dreams converge, and for a short time he becomes his hero, Tjakova. Finding himself locked in a prison cell, Tjakova uses his magical powers to turn himself into a black mouse, and by crawling through the small window in his cell, he escapes to freedom. But knowing his duty to free his imprisoned comrades, he makes his way to the prison office where, again by using his magical powers, he changes his appearance. Still disguised as a mouse, he then makes himself grow bigger and bigger until he is the size of a baby hippopotamus. The policemen and the guards in the office cannot believe their eyes! There before them is a monster mouse, gnashing its teeth and rolling its eyes at them. Frightened nearly out of their wits, the policemen charge out of the office with Muronga-Tjakova, The Monster Mouse, hot on their heels. Grinning from ear to ear, his whiskers twitching, he chases the police officers from one room to the next until they are exhausted and can find no safe place to hide other than the prison cells. Releasing the prisoners in the hope that they will pacify the hungry mouse, the officers lock themselves inside the prison cells, there to wait, terrified. Free at last, the prisoners are euphoric and fearless in the presence of the giant mouse who they soon realize poses no threat to them. Jubilantly, they all march out of the prison into the bright sunshine, with Muronga-Tjakova staying behind just long enough to change himself into a man again, whereupon he joins the lively procession. Awakening at this point, Muronga laughs heartily at the absurdity of his daydream.

Soon several policemen come to the cells and chase the men outside for their daily calisthenics. Muronga cannot help smiling as he pictures himself as a huge mouse scaring the pompous guards almost to death when they see him. He imagines himself taking a few bites out of the policemen he despises the most and, for the first time since being thrown into jail, he doesn't feel powerless against the authorities. Realizing this, he spends the better part of the afternoon reflecting on the lessons he has learned throughout his life. Closing his eyes, he meditates.

Always in the past I have felt inferior to the white man, but why? wonders Muronga. When I was a child listening to the stories and teachings of the elders, I was taught to have respect for others, for authority, for my elders, but also for my peers. I was taught that respect was given others because they respected me and my rights in return. And I was also taught that laws were not made arbitrarily in favor of one person or group over another. It has been only over time that these lessons have been weakened as more of my people have come into contact with the white man. They have become the supreme authorities to whom we owe absolute obedience and they have assumed the right to take our land away from us. The white man has told us that he has this right because God made him white and he is therefore superior to us blacks. He has gone to school and can read and write and that, too, makes him better. Yes, we have been taught to feel inferior to the white man and to fear him. But are we inferior? I know many things the white man doesn't know, but does that make me a better man? Now that I have gone to the mine school and can speak a new language and will go home to my people a rich man, does that make me better or superior to any other man? I wasn't taught that I am because of what I have. I was taught that I am because of others. No . . . I am not superior or inferior to any man—not even the white man.

Opening his eyes, Muronga sees the four thick grey walls on all sides. So, he thinks, if I am no less of a man than the white man, what am I doing locked up in this cage like an animal? What has happened to my freedom? He ponders this question for a long time. Are my thoughts not free? Am I not free to think, feel, and believe what I want? My body is imprisoned, but the rest of me is free. Surprised by this revelation, Muronga lets his thoughts come rushing together, and a curious mixture of peace and agitation comes over him. It was the same way when I was working in the mine. I couldn't do what I wanted to do, but I could feel what I wanted to. I hate my supervisor even though I know it is wrong to hate. The elders told us this, and so did Pater Dickmann. I am afraid of these white men because they can destroy me and my family. I fear the white man because he has told me that he is superior to me, but now I know better. And after all, there are blacks who are feared by whites, as Musoke told me. They are feared because they have gone to school—and that is what I will do. I will learn to read and write, and I will learn the white man's ways and then I will not need to be afraid of him or hate him. I will not become a slave to him. I will learn everything I can, and when I get out of this stinking hole, I will return to my village with all of my knowledge and tell everyone about the United People's Organization. We must not be afraid of or hate the white man, nor should we allow ourselves to become his slaves. We must fight to get our land back. We must fight for our right to be equals with the white man.

Muronga is happy now, knowing what he must do for his people back home. Suddenly, Pater Dickmann's words come to his mind. "Take care of my lambs." These words are like another revelation, and Muronga wonders if there is some greater reason for his imprisonment. Maybe I have been chosen to bear this so that I can teach my people and help them to be free again. But before I can teach my people to be free, I must be free myself—free from fear, free from hatred, and free from . . . all the things that will make me a slave to another man. My son must be free. When he is old enough, I will teach him the lessons I learned as a child, and I will send him to school. I will send my son to school to learn the white man's skills, but I will teach him to have pride in his own heritage and to have faith, not in the white man's ways, but in the black man's ways. I will teach him to be true to his family, true to his forefathers, and true to the land. Then he, too, will be free. This is what I want for my son, and for my people. This is my duty. I have been born only once, and only once shall I die. I have only one life to live and I cannot wait any longer to be a free man. How much longer can my people wait? Who will help them? There is no one in my village that the white people will fear. Uncle Ndara is wise, but what we need now is not only wisdom. We need to resist and talk day and night in a new language—in a language that the white man understands. Our language alone is not enough. The white man does not fear wisdom, he fears noise. So, when I go back I will teach my people to make noise . . . to sing for our land.

It is on the fourteenth day of their confinement when, not long after they have returned to their cells after breakfast, the men are surprised by the sound of heavy footsteps approaching. They have become so accustomed to the routine in the prison that, as soon as they hear the rattling of keys and the opening of doors, they know that something different is about to happen.

A voice can be heard, and then the sound of many footsteps outside the cells in the dimly lighted corridor. The door to their cell is unlocked and three policemen stand outside while one enters and orders the prisoners to follow him. Obediently the men fall into two neat lines behind two of the policemen, while the remaining two guards bring up the rear. Strangely, this time the guards behind them do not chase them as they always have in the past. Instead they walk quietly and passively. Muronga waits anxiously to hear the "clack, clack" as the guards put bullets into their rifles. But they never do. He and the other men wonder what is amiss. They exchange fearful glances. Change in the routine always suggests the worst. Muronga cannot help thinking about the many people who were said to have died in prison and of how the government didn't tell the truth about their deaths. Feeling the presence of others who have gone before him helps Muronga accept his own fate more easily and he is no longer afraid as he and the other men file past the empty cells. Knowing that he has made his peace with himself and the world, Muronga is ready to accept death.

He feels happy to have been in prison. All the other men feel the same. Muronga feels much more fulfilled and accomplished than when he was baptized by Pater Dickmann. The words on the grey walls of the cell meant more to him than the catechism classes he went through before his Baptism. He is no longer afraid of death. He does not fear the white man anymore. He does not feel as if he is born again. He feels different, stronger, like he felt before Pater Dickmann told him that he was born again. He remembers that he was born only once, by his mother. It is due to this only birth that he experiences all this.

I was born to go through all this, Muronga thinks. All these men here are just like me. We were born to learn through pain how not to fear the white man, how not to fear death.

CHAPTER 15

Out in the courtyard Muronga and Ndango look for any signs of their friends. Silently they communicate their happiness at being together, even if it may be for the last time. With armed guards and mean-tempered dogs surrounding them, the men await their sentences, strengthened by their common experience, more united than ever. Solidarity pervades the air.

For hours they stand waiting until finally they are ordered to form a line outside the office. What they did not know, of course, was that while they were in prison, the mine management was negotiating with the government for their release, since their imprisonment was slowing down production. A sigh of relief can almost be heard echoing throughout the prison courtyard, as the men realize that they are probably going to be released. So they are not going to die today after all. As the line grows shorter and the courtyard empties, voices raised in song can be heard outside the prison walls. Louder and louder the men sing,

Igama lika Archie Bokwe   (Praised be the name Archie Bokwe)

Mali-bongwe	(Let it be praised)
Igama lika Archie Bokwe	(Praised be the name Archie Bokwe)
Mali-bongwe	(Let it be praised)
Mali-bongwe	(Let it be praised)
Mali-bongwe	(Let it be praised)
Igama lika Yesu Krestu	(Praised be the name Jesus Christ)
Mali-bongwe	(Let it be praised)
Igama lika Yesu Krestu	(Praised be the name Jesus Christ)
Mali-bongwe	(Let it be praised)
Mali-bongwe	(Let it be praised)
Mali-bongwe	(Let it be praised)
Igama lika . . .	(Praised be the name . . .)

Waiting impatiently, eagerly, anxiously, Muronga inches his way to the office, trying all the while not to join in the singing which has caught hold of him. At last his turn comes. His personal belongings are tossed at him and a white policeman orders him to "Get out!" He leaves the office feeling like a new man. Ndango is a few steps ahead of Muronga and together they meet Nakare and Nyangana who are waiting for them. They greet one another excitedly and inquire about their other comrades. Fourteen days felt like a lifetime, every day like a full moon.

On the buses that put more and more distance between the free men and that den of deadened, imprisoned souls, the men sing their freedom songs and joke about the arrogant prison warders. Rather than being ashamed of their filthy condition, they are now proud to have endured their imprisonment. They are eager to be united with their fellow miners who are waiting for them in the compound. These are the men who either did not attend the meeting or who were returned to the compound because there was no space for them in the jails.

As was usually the case in the compound, word passed quickly that the imprisoned men were on their way back to the compound. Enthusiastically, almost disbelieving, a group of men immediately began to gather by the gates to the barracks. After waiting for a while they started to sing and sway, beginning the rhythmic movements of the gumboot dance. In synchronized fashion they leaned forward, slapping their heavy black boots in unison. Almost intuitively, those without boots ran back to their barracks to fetch theirs and those of their returning comrades. Gradually, more men joined in the rhythms until two lines of thirty or more men had been formed.

Finally the buses pull into the compound, and the men jump out as if they have just returned from a holiday, their fists raised triumphantly.

"Come! Put on your boots!" shout their roommates, with their comrades, boots held high in the air. Grabbing their boots and pulling them on quickly, the men join the line-up. With the men added to their ranks, there are now seven lines of men slapping and clapping with acrobatic zeal. Their harmonious movements and the thunderous roar of their rhythms even attracts the cynical gaze of their white mine supervisors.

When the bell finally summons them all to supper, the men break into song and move in the direction of their barracks. Muronga, flushed and sweating, goes straight to Diyeve's room. "Do you know where my friend is?" he asks one of Diyeve's roommates.

"You want the man who sleeps in this bed? He is in the hospital. He has been in the hospital for a few days now. Yesterday he came to fetch something and went back. His arm was all in bandages. He said that you would look for him and that we should tell you to go and see him in the hospital."

"Thank you for telling me. I will go there immediately. Oh, I hope it is not serious," mumbles Muronga as he rushes outside the compound to the hospital. I wonder what could have happened, he thinks.

Before he reaches the entrance to the ward, Diyeve, who is sitting in the sunshine outside the hospital, spots Muronga coming.

"I am here, Muronga. Are you looking for me?"

"Yes, how are you? I am coming to see you. Why else would I come to the hospital when I just got out of jail?"

"I knew that you were going to come. You won't like what I have to tell you. I . . . I . . . I got hurt. I have only a thumb left on this hand that is in bandages. It happened at work. The white man that I work for didn't teach me well. I was picking up a rock from the rail like he told me and the truck came and ran over my hand very fast. I didn't even feel the pain, it happened so fast. Now they say that I am going to be sent home."

"All four fingers are gone? How awful! I knew something like this was going to happen sometime. These white supervisors!"

"Don't be too upset about it, Muronga. I am still fine. My hand is still strong. I will just go home and work in the fields."

"That's not what makes me unhappy. It is the laws of the white man. Did they tell you how much they were going to pay you?"

"No, I don't know. They said, a lot. They said they will pay me my money as if I had finished my contract . . . "

"I would like to see that! It's your fingers that are gone. You cannot buy new fingers. They are gone. And it's your supervisor's fault! When did they say you are going home?"

"Soon. Maybe next week. They will tell me tomorrow. I also want to go home now and go through the pain near my people. I am not doing anything here now."

"I will come and see you tomorrow again. I must go and tell my friends about this. And I need to sleep. Jail was a bad place. I am happy that you didn't go to the meeting, . . . and to jail. It is unfortunate that this happened to you. Stay well, Diyeve. I will see you tomorrow."

"Go well, Muronga. And thank you . . . "

Diyeve is discharged from the hospital the following day. He is given some cash, and told that he will get the rest of the money for his accident when he gets to Shakawe.

"Keep the bandages on and go to the nearest hospital when you arrive home," the attendant in the hospital tells him. "And give these papers to the doctor or nurse in that hospital."

Before going to his room, Diyeve looks for Muronga to let him know that he is no longer in the hospital and that he is to leave for home soon.

"Before you leave, I should buy something, . . . clothes for my family. Will you take them with you, Diyeve?" asks Muronga.

"Yes, why not? It would be good for me if I took clothes to them. Then they will see that you are fine here and that we were together. Get the clothes quickly. They said I might leave today. They don't want people to know that I was in an accident, I heard my supervisor say to the nurse in the hospital. Now that the people who were in jail are back, they want me to leave as soon as possible."

"If that is so, then I cannot buy any new things. I have to go to work this afternoon. But I do have some clothes that I bought before I went to jail. I think that's enough for you to take to my family."

Muronga pulls a trunk from underneath his bed, opens it, and takes out a few items. "This dress is for my wife. And this skirt, too. This hat is for my father. This blanket give to Uncle Ndara. And these small clothes and the toys are for my son. Tell them that I am fine here and that I am learning to name things. Tell them that I am going to learn to read and write. Tell them that one day I will also teach Mandaha how to read and write. Tell them that we are trying to work here so that one day we will tell the white man to get out of our land and off our backs. But don't say too much about it. It is too dangerous."

"I heard about what you are doing here while you were away. Many people know you here. They told me that you are going to help us. Why didn't you tell me that you are one of the big people here?"

"No, I am not. We are only trying to do something to help our people. I am helping the others, those who have been here a long time and who know how to speak. I am still learning . . . you see."

"I must go to my room. Maybe they are looking for me. I will come and say good-bye when I go, if you are here. If you are at work, I will just leave and trust that you are fine and that we will see each other when you arrive back home."

"Yes, we will be together, at home. Tell our people that I am fine and healthy. And that I will see them soon."

When Muronga returns from work late in the evening, he goes to Diyeve's room. He is not there. He has left on a truck that took him to the railway station. He is on his way home . . . without his fingers.

In no time the men learned the news of the past two weeks. Archie Bokwe's funeral was delayed, supposedly until tests could be done to determine the cause of his death, which still had not been divulged. The funeral was held the previous Sunday in a small town some distance from the mine and the mine management prohibited everyone from going to it. One evening, as the bright red ball of fire descends on the horizon, the men honor their leader by singing softly and reverently,

Igama lika Archie Bokwe

Mali-bongwe

Igama lika . . .

PART IV:
DIFFICULT DECISIONS

CHAPTER 16

Six months have passed since the men were released from prison. The mine management took no direct action against them upon their release, but in the following months the white supervisors have been encouraged to become even more brutal with those men who have now been labeled "troublemakers". But the experience of being in prison has made the men stronger and more impervious to the insults and kicks of their nasty white bosses. Muronga has beoome more involved in the United People's Organization, having spoken twice at meetings. Every other night he goes to evening classes to learn to read and write. He has learned the alphabet, he can write his name and the names of his wife and son. In fact, he can write most names. He has even learned some *vsvsvsvs* and knows now that it is called "Afrikaans". He takes his lessons seriously—more so than any of the other men in the class, and perhaps even more than the teacher himself, who closes the book as soon as the bell rings.

One evening, just after class, Muronga writes his first letter to his wife.

"A letter to my wife, Nyina-Mandaha . . .

How did you sleep? How did Mandaha sleep? How are the others, Uncle Ndara, Mama Rwenge, *Nyina-Karumbu*? How are the rains? I work well. Here we do men's work. There are problems here in the mine. White people make the problems. But we are strong. All about problems.

Good News. These words on this paper are mine. I put them here. With my own fingers. I hold the pen. I go to school like a boy. Now I can read and write words. I am very strong now. I will teach you and Mandaha to hear the words on the paper. It is good to hold a pen. It is like a gun. White people know it. Did you see Diyeve? He was here. But went back. His fingers stayed in the mine. The bad spirits were on him. I gave him words and clothes.

I will write again. Greet all the people. And Mandaha. Your husband. *Wiha-Mandaha* who can write."

For two days, Muronga reads his own letter every night before he goes to sleep. Then he asks Nakare for an envelope. Nakare explains to him how to send a letter home. Muronga does as he is told. On the envelope he writes:

Mariamagdalena Makena

Catholic Mission Andara

Post Office Rundu

Village Kake

Chief Dimbare

Headman Shamashora

Kraalhead Ndara

Early the following morning, he takes his letter to Nakare. "Here is my letter. I wrote it all by myself! I put the stamp you gave me on it."

"Very good, Muronga. Your people will be very happy. You are a very clever man."

"Can you send it?"

"Yes, I will send it today. Yes, everything is written well. It will get there."

"Will it? Are you sure? My letter?"

"Yes, it will go there. Letters travel fast."

"I hope that they will write back."

Flopping on his bed at the end of one more long, tiring day of working in the mines, Muronga lies motionless, his legs spread wide apart and his hands folded together on his chest. Yawning loudly, the other men in the room share their fatigue. More frustrated and bored than usual, Muronga, without realizing it, mutters aloud, "What am I doing here? I want to go home to my wife and son, and instead I am stuck here forever. I have earned enough money and have learned many things, too. I can even read and write. So what am I doing here? I want to go home and use what I have learned to help my people before it is too late." His voice trails off so that his roommates can barely hear his last words.

His words catch the attention of one of his roommates, who sleepily asks, "What is that you are saying, Muronga?"

"I want to go home to my people," replies Muronga with a sigh filled with pain.

"Wouldn't we all like to," groans another roommate.

"Yes, I know. But you see, I want to go home now so that I can do something. I want to help my people," replies Muronga.

"Help them how?" asks the first roommate curiously.

"I want to help them to understand the white man."

"Understand! Ha! Yes, and then what?"

"And then show the white man how much we understand him and how little he understands us."

"But we already know that we are suffering at the white man's hands. So what? It doesn't change anything. It doesn't make any difference."

"No, understanding does matter. Once you can understand evil, you know how to deal with it. Once you know that you are suffering, you try to avoid it. Once you know what hurts and where it hurts, you don't touch there. The white man doesn't know how much we suffer. We must show him that we are aware of our own suffering. We must show him, together."

Silence follows in the darkening room. Then, slowly, one of the men says, "Yes, you are right. I hadn't thought about it that way before. Did you learn this lesson in prison?"

"No, but being in prison brought me closer to understanding my pain. We learn a lot through suffering, but I don't think that I have suffered any more than anyone else here."

"You are right. We all suffer here—more than we realize."

"That is what I am talking about. We ... "

The dinner bell rings and abruptly ends the conversation. The men roll out of their beds and walk at a quick pace to the eating place. Muronga and Ndango meet as usual, having almost made a ritual out of eating together ever since they came back from the "home for men".

Musoke, the Nyasa, joins them, his mouth bulging with food. He can barely keep his eyes open as he ravenously chews his food. They have all gotten used to the food by now and don't care how it tastes, as long as it doesn't kill them. The three of them smile wryly. "Here we are, being fed so that we can be put to work—like a bunch of domestic animals," Musoke says. Ndango and Muronga wait until he has swallowed his food before they speak. They don't want to make him talk or laugh, lest he spit his food out on them.

Finally, Musoke, with his plate of food held tightly in his left hand, motions with his right hand as he bolts down some of his food. Clearing his throat he begins, "*Madoda*, it is good to see you. We have not spoken with one another for how long now. Two weeks? Either you or I have come to eat earlier these days, I guess. But, how are you both otherwise? Any news from home? Have the rains come yet?"

"We are both fine, but there is no news from home. How about you? You must be getting lots of news from home?" replies Muronga.

"Yes, I receive letters often. We are getting a lot of rain in my country now."

"That is good," reply Ndango and Muronga together. Ndango continues, "I have received some news . . . bad news. I was just about to tell Muronga when you came."

"What is it? What has happened?" the two men ask anxiously.

"Well, you remember Natangwe . . . he recently finished his contract and went home."

"Yes. What has happened to him?"

"Nakare received a letter from him yesterday. He arrived home safely, but he was no sooner there when he was arrested and thrown in jail. I don't know how the whites found out that he is one of us. Apparently they knew about our meetings and that Natangwe had been sent to begin telling people about the United People's Organization. The police somehow knew and they simply went to his house, confiscated all of his belongings, his tax papers, and our papers. They were then able to read everything about us. So the next day they arrested him and put him in jail. Nakare says that Natangwe must have gotten the letter out through our Lutheran Church contacts. I suppose we can only hope that he will be able to do some work while he is in jail. After all, prison is the best place to tell people about the white man's laws; it is the best place to tell them that the white man is a menace in our land."

"They have caught him already?" exclaims Muronga softly, shaking his head despairingly. "I hope his fate will not be like Archie Bokwe's."

The men are silent for a moment until Muronga says to Musoke, "You people who live in countries where your own people govern you are lucky. The God of Your Forefathers loves you."

"Yes, but in many ways things have not changed that much," replies Musoke. "People are still suffering in my country. Anyone who is caught saying things against the President and his men will end up in deep trouble. There the men in government can understand every word you say, whereas here you can say whatever you want to say in your own language and the white man doesn't understand. Because the black men in the government are often black and white combined they are really black "white" men. They see you as different from themselves— like the whites see us—and they thus become more dangerous than the whites. Yet, in some ways, they are good men. They tell the white man to sit down and listen, so even if they are not the best men, or in some cases even worse than the whites, it is better to be governed by one's own people than by total strangers."

As Musoke finishes speaking all three men suddenly become aware that they are the last ones in the *pondok*. Wolfing down their food, their mouths bulging, they stare at one another like rivals in an eating competition. With broad smiles covering their stuffed cheeks, they wipe their plates clean. Chewing vigorously, they nod their heads in greeting as a husky but tired-looking man enters the *pondok*. He doesn't greet them, but only stares back. When a white man in blue overalls follows him in and orders him around, the men realize he is the man who does slave work for the white man who comes to the compound to collect leftover food for his pigs. He gets one meal a day and a pittance for wages. That is why he looks enviously at those who have food in abundance—so much that they can throw what they don't want to the pigs. Exchanging knowing glances, the three men look at one another. "You see, our sin is the color of our skin," Ndango says.

Finally rising from their seats, they leave the *pondok* and Ndango, after clearing his throat, says to Muronga, "Nakare is coming to my room in a short while, when it is dark. There are important things that we need to discuss. Can you come?"

"Yes, of course. I want to hear what is happening," responds Muronga. With a nod and a handshake the three men part company.

Shortly thereafter Muronga, Nakare, and Ndango are seated together in Ndango's room. After greeting one another, Nakare begins speaking in a low tone of voice. "As you both know, I have just received a letter which says that our brother, Natangwe, has been arrested and imprisoned. The letter came from the church in Oniipa and was signed by Bishop Iihuna. Fortunately, Natangwe first met with the church leaders in Oniipa and told them about what we are doing in the United People's Organization. They were very interested in what he had to say and so, when they heard that he had been arrested, they took the trouble of telling us what happened. Bishop Iihuna of the Lutheran Church writes that no one knows where Natangwe is being held, and he goes on to say that the police are searching everyone who is coming home after having been away for a long while. He says that the police are particularly suspicious of men who arrive home in clean clothes. Some priests are also suspicious about people who like to speak. This is a sign that there will be more trouble ahead for us."

"But what I don't understand," interjects Muronga, "is how the whites back home knew about us and our meetings."

"It is easy for them to know what we are doing here," responds Ndango. "Their friends here in the mine could have told them, or it could have been one or more of our own brothers who told them. Those of our brothers who are willing to be informers are paid big money for every name and word they give. People want the money. That is our weakness. And the white man knows how to use our weaknesses."

"Yes, of course," sighs Muronga."We cannot expect it to be otherwise."

"No, but in spite of the dangers involved, I believe that we are all committed to our organization, to fighting for what is rightfully ours—and to suffering the consequences, if we must," replies Nakare, as he looks from one man's face to the other as they nod in agreement.

"Good," he continues. "I think you both agree with me that we have now done enough groundwork. In our meetings we have been speaking about uniting with one another in the struggle for humanity, justice and peace. I believe the time has come for us to call upon all of our brothers to stand with us. We must speak out now. We can only talk now, but one day we will act. We will talk less and do more."

"Yes, I agree," says Ndango. "As I told you yesterday, the time has come for us to go beyond just sitting on our beds and speechifying to each other. Our country is going to the lions—the Boers. If we just sit and sit and sit, things will go on as they are now, or even get worse. Our country and our people will not be liberated by anyone but ourselves."

Muronga, who has been listening attentively, has absently fixed his gaze on the insects that are swarming around the light bulb that hangs from the ceiling. As more insects are attracted to the light, they block its illumination and the white bulb becomes dimmer. Pausing for a moment and looking back at the faces of his friends, he says, "I, too, have been thinking such thoughts. Our future is in our hands, but there will be no future if things do not change, and things will not change unless we, the people, change them. But we cannot change anything unless we are willing to take risks, to stand united, to speak out, and to do something. I want to do something to help our people and our country. As it was, instead of fighting the white man and his system, I believed him when he said that what was mine by birthright was actually his. I came here to earn money to pay the white man's taxes, but the money I will take home will only be enough to pay the taxes for one year. Then what? What about the land—our land—that is being taken from us by these people? I agree with you that we must do something, but what and how? By being here we have merely bought the white man's chains with our labor." Nakare and Ndango glance at one another, listening carefully to what Muronga has to say as they nod their heads in agreement now and then. "We must tell our people how other black people in Africa have shaken off the yoke of oppression by the white people. We must motivate our people to unite behind our United People's Organization and in so doing, be united in our struggle for freedom. But we also must tell our people honestly that the road to freedom will be hard. We have no guns, we have no cars, we have no airplanes. But we have the will. And with this will, this strong will to be free, one day we will be free . . . free to determine our own future and free to rule ourselves."

For a few moments there is silence in the room. While Nakare and Ndango have heard Muronga say similar things before, this time they are even more impressed with his ability to speak with conviction and sincerity. He is truly speaking from the heart.

Another moment passes before Nakare says, "Yes, that is exactly what we must do. And we must begin at once—here in the mine—to unite our people. The time has come to organize a big public meeting of all our brothers here in the mine. The three of us can begin planning it tonight. So, what do you think?"

Both Ndango and Muronga nod in agreement.

"We will need enough time to make all of the arrangements. This Saturday would be too soon, but the next Saturday should be fine. Does three o'clock in the afternoon sound like a good time?" Again the two men nod. "Good. Then we will need a place to hold the meeting. I have already talked to our brother, the policeman, who is going to ask his supervisor if we can use the big classroom. He said that his supervisor is a very reasonable man—actually almost too reasonable for a white police-man. He thinks we can get the room."

"But won't the white policeman be a danger to us?" asks Muronga.

"No, not necessarily. Our brother trusts him. He is white, yes, but he is one of those whites whose blood flows in the right direction. Even if he is like the other whites, we cannot worry about such things anymore. They can do what they want."

"That is true . . . very true. We cannot wait any longer," responds Muronga.

"I will begin the meeting by welcoming everyone and giving a short speech. Ndango, I think you should then say a few words, after which I think you, Muronga, should give a speech also."

"But . . . but," says Muronga, obviously surprised. "But what will I say?"

"All you have to say is just what you said here in this room a few moments ago. Muronga, both Ndango and I have heard the other men talking about you and saying very good things. They are very impressed by your sincerity and humility. They respect you because you have learned to read and write while you have been here and they know how committed you are to our people, our country, and our organization. They see the three of us as the leaders of the organization."

"The two of you are certainly our recognized leaders, but I am not sure that I am thought of in the same way. But I do want to be a servant of my people. If they think that I can say or do something useful—anything—that will help in the cause of liberating our people and our country—then I will do it."

"Good. I was hoping you would say that. Now, after the speeches I think we should hold elections. We are already seen as the leaders of the organization, but we want to be sure that everyone's voice is heard. Ndango, can you organize a group of men to make the preparations for the elections? Then I think we need to have some songs—liberation songs—to sing. Muronga, can you organize another group to write some songs for us? I will organize another group to make signs and begin spreading the word. What do you think?"

Muronga and Ndango are excited by the idea of the meeting and nod their heads vigorously in their agreement with Nakare's plans. It is only at this time, as they are concluding their long trio *indaba* when Ndango's roommates burst into the room after having seen an often played cowboy film, that they realize how much time they have spent together this evening. They break up quickly and Nakare and Muronga go to their rooms, there to fall asleep on dreams of the big meeting and the words of the songs.

During the week that follows the three men are constantly busy. Every possible moment is used to spread the word around. Signs begin to appear here and there and eventually, even those men who cannot read or write know what is written on the pieces of cardboard. As word travels to all corners of the compound, increasing anti-white feelings begin to surface among the members and would-be members of the United People's Organization in response to mounting pressure from the white mine workers who oppose anything that appears to them to bring about unity and solidarity among the black workers.

For his part, Muronga devotes all of his free time to working on the songs. He and three other men translate a few of the known freedom songs from South African languages into their own. In RuKavango, Otjiherero, Oshiwambo, Nama and Setswana they say,

Nda ninga shike	(What have I done)
Mbaungura tjike	(What have I done)
Yinke na ninka	(What have I done)
Nye yi na tenda	(What have I done)
Tae a di ha	(What have I done)
Kedihileng	(What have I done)
Nda ninga shike	(What have I done)
Mbaungura tjike	(What have I done)

They translate the African Anthem, which they practice singing over and over again. Softly and slowly they sing together,

Karunga tungika Afrika	(God bless Africa)
Nonkondo dendi di zerura	(Let her power be lifted)
Zuva makanderero getu	(Hear our prayers)
Hompa tu tungika	(Lord bless us)
Ose vana woge	(We, your children)
Indjo, Mbepo	(Come Spirit)
Indjo, indjo	(Come, come)
Indjo Mbepo	(Come Spirit)
Indjo Mbepo Ondjapuke	(Come Holy Spirit)
Hompa tu tungika	(Lord bless us)
Ose vana woge	(We, your children)
Mwene endifa po Oshiwana shetu	(Lord lead our Nation)
Hulifa po oita nomahepeko	(End war and oppression)
Mwene endifa po Oshiwana shetu	(Lord lead our Nation)
Hulifa po oita nomahepeko	(End war and oppression)
!Khutse ore sida !haosa	(Save our Nation)
Sida !haosa	(Our Nation)
!Khutse ore sida !haosa	(Save our Nation)
Sida !haosa	(Our Nation)
Sicaba sa luna	(Our Nation)
Sicaba sa Afrika	(Our African Nation)

CHAPTER 17

Every night they rehearse the songs after dinner, after which Muronga tries to decide what he should say at the big meeting as he drifts off to sleep. He sleeps restlessly, feeling anxious about standing up in front of such a huge group of his comrades, but gradually he works out a plan of what he wants to say and each day as he is working in the mine he goes over it. He is still refining his speech when the day of the big meeting finally arrives.

Muronga, Ndango and Nakare are up bright and early on Saturday morning to make the final arrangements. "The South West Africans are having a big meeting today," is the talk of the day throughout the compound. As the three men bustle about the compound they are greeted with friendly words and smiles from all of their black brothers. Everyone knows who they are by this time. By two o'clock everything is ready. They have only to go to the white policeman to get the key to the meeting room. He is waiting for them when they arrive at his office at the entrance of the compound.

Handing the key to Nakare, he says deliberately, "I am doing you a big favor, you know? I shouldn't be doing this. My white friends would kill me if they ever caught me talking to you as if you were people. It isn't done, you understand? So, behave yourselves. Don't break anything or shit in this room, you understand? And no noise . . . no *nyakanyaka* here, okay? And if anything wild happens in which I am implicated, I will go back into my white skin and deny that I have ever spoken a word to any of you!" He stares sternly at each face before turning and walking toward the compound.

With the key in hand, the three men walk the short distance to the classroom and opening the door, they survey the interior of the room. Everything looks like it is in order. Going back outside, they wait by the door with the black policeman who procured the room. Soon the men begin arriving and the policeman smiles as he shakes their hands and shows them to the entrance. It was decided before the meeting that the policeman's presence would make everyone feel more comfortable. At first there are only a few men who come, then more arrive, and more, until men are streaming into the room. All of the chairs fill up and the only space left is at the back of the room. There must be at least two hundred men in the room by the time the last few arrive. Only Nakare, Ndango and Muronga remain outside with the policeman. Finally, they enter, smiling broadly, their fists raised high above their heads as they walk through the seated crowds and take their places at the small teacher's table at the front of the room. A few clenched fists appear above the many heads as a few hands can be heard clapping.

While Muronga and Ndango seat themselves, Nakare remains standing and welcomes everyone. Although he is smiling, his tone of voice is serious. The men listen respectfully to his words. "As you know, many of us here today have long been concerned about the future of our country and people. We have learned how black people in other countries have worked together to liberate themselves from the greed and oppression of the white man. They had to fight hard to gain their freedom, but now they are the masters of their own lives.

"But are we? No! Our task today, brothers, is to interpret the past, analyze the present and determine the future of our country. We must ask ourselves here, today, what kind of future we want for our people and country. Are we willing to work together to liberate ourselves and become the masters of our own lives? If so, then what message are we going to take home to our people when we leave here—a message of misery and hopelessness, or a message of liberation and hope? We believe that the time has finally come for us to realize that we must do what some of our black brothers have already done—we must stand, united, against the whites. A slave will remain a slave only as long as he allows his master to be master..."

There is thunderous applause as Nakare finishes his speech. Ndango's speech is even more emotionally charged. He calls upon his countrymen to ask themselves what they can do for their country and people—now. He ends his speech by saying, "Only we can make the white man see, know and believe that he is not our master!" This time the thunderous applause is accompanied by loud whistling and foot stomping.

At last Muronga's turn has come. Rising to his feet, he coughs a bit to clear his throat and then begins, hesitantly, "My brothers, our presence here today is a testament to our suffering and to our desire to be free. We are suffering here in the white man's mines, even though we came here to work so that our people back home would not suffer. We came here to earn money, but money will not relieve our suffering. It is not money that will set us and our people free. Money cannot buy our freedom." Muronga pauses for a moment, then goes on with greater confidence. "Every day the white man takes more of our land and claims it as his own. If we do not stop him, he will keep taking it until we haven't even a place to lay our heads.

But how can we stop him? you ask. I say to you that we must unite behind the United People's Organization. There is strength in unity. We must be willing to make sacrifices and take risks, for there is no gain without risk.

"And we must begin at once. I call on you now, to stand with me as we demand our land and our freedom from the white man. Our children will have no land and no future unless we do our duty to them and to our ancestors. We have only one chance to demand our freedom—for we will walk on this earth only once. Each one of us has been born only once and will live only once—as a slave or as a free man. The time has come. It is now or never!"

For a brief moment, there is total silence in the room. It seems as if no one is even breathing, when suddenly the silence is shattered by clapping, whistling, and shouting. The words *"Viva, viva, viva"* beam through the hall. Muronga is taken aback by the crowd's response and can only sit humbly in his chair until Nakare stands up and motions to the men to calm down, be seated and listen.

The men heed Nakare's plea and sit down. Folding his hands, he clears his throat and continues, "My brothers, we now have some serious business to attend to. The time has come for us to elect our leaders. It is necessary for us to have some people who can act as spokespersons on behalf of all of us. The people we elect will be responsible for making decisions for all of us in the organization when we cannot all be together. They will be the ones to whom questions, suggestions and concerns will be directed. They will act in our best interest always. They will be responsible for representing us and leading us. They must be people we can trust. So, do any of you have names you would like to put forth?"

A humming sound rises from the crowd as the men consult with one another. Several hands go up, but

Nakare's eye rests on the face of an older man in the far corner whom he recognizes. The elderly man stands up slowly and walks ponderously to the front of the room. The other men sit quietly and respectfully. With wisdom and conviction he speaks slowly in his coarse voice.

"I don't have many words to say. I would only like to tell you young people that a good idea could be lost if it is not acted upon swiftly. Now that we have assembled here and heard these mighty words that have moved my heart, let us not waste time with doubts and fears. In my opinion, the three sons who have spoken here today should be the ones to lead us. During all of the years that I have been in this world, no one has spoken these words until now. I do not think we need to elect other people whom we do not know. We support this organization and know that we need to take action now, so let us go ahead without further ado. I, an old man with grey hair on my head, can only say here today, let the God of Our Forefathers show you the way on the road to freedom so that we might live long enough to see the liberation of our country."

The applause is steady and confident. As the gentleman walks slowly back to his seat, and the applause dies down, Nakare says, "Thank you . . . now, who else had his hand raised?" His eyes slowly scan the crowd for raised hands as a few heads in front turn to look toward the back of the room. When he sees no raised hands he goes on, "Is there anyone else who would like to speak at this time?" Again there is no response. Finally Nakare asks, "Does this mean that you are all in agreement that the three of us should be the leaders of our United People's Organization? There is thunderous applause, shouts of "Yes!", whistling and foot stomping.

Muronga, a bit bewildered by this sudden confidence in him, stands up when Nakare motions to him to acknowledge the crowd. Together the three men nod their heads, and in unison, raise their fists in the air. There are more shouts and applause. Someone in the crowd begins singing,

Karunga tungika Afrika

Nonkondo dendi di zerura . . .

The applause fades as more and more voices pick up the tune and the men struggle to catch the words. Inspired beyond words, Muronga sings exuberantly. They sing the song over and over again, once, twice, three times, until virtually everyone knows the words and melody. The air is charged with energy as the men sing the other songs, until at last, Nakare looks at his watch and, shouting over the voices, declares that the meeting is over, that everyone will be kept informed, and that everyone should be careful not to say too much in the presence of their supervisors. Dispersing in different directions, the men leave the meeting room as if they were leaving a dining hall after a huge feast—they feel full and well satisfied. Muronga, Ndango and Nakare stay behind for a short while to put the room back into order. Then, accompanied by their policeman comrade, they lock the room and return the key to the white policeman who gave them permission to use the room. As they thank him and assure him that everything is as they found it, he looks at them pensively and questioningly, but chooses to say nothing.

It is dinner time when the three men return to the compound. They walk straight to the food *pondok*, where their appearance invites approving nods and stares. Muronga's arrival, in particular, is greeted with smiles of respect, to which he is not at all accustomed. As he goes through the line to receive his food, he tries to ignore the attention he is getting—he really does not feel comfortable being elevated above the rest. Tired from the day's excitement and aware that everyone is watching them, the three comrades eat silently, avoiding any discussion of the meeting until they have finished and are walking back to the barracks.

"I am actually very pleased that the three of us have been chosen to lead our organization," begins Nakare, "because I have great confidence in you both. With the three of us charting the organization's course and steering it in the right direction, I am sure that our organization will grow and become a force to be reckoned with. I know that we all take this challenge seriously, and we must not let our people down." With nods of agreement and handshakes from Muronga and Ndango, the three men bid one another, "Good night," and disappear into the darkness.

Back in his room, Muronga undresses slowly. Crawling under his blanket, he lies motionless, instantly falling into a deep sleep. The following morning, sleeping lightly, he dreams about being home with his wife, Makena, in their hut with their little son who is grwoing bigger every day. As he becomes fully awake, he thinks about how much he misses them and how anxious he is to be with them again. But he reassures himself that it will not be too much longer yet. He continues to think about his family, his people back home, and his new role as a leader of the United People's Organization, when the breakfast bell rings. Not being very hungry, he decides to stay in bed and continue his meditations. More interested now, than ever before, Muronga spends the rest of the day reading from his books. By the end of this quiet day, he has seen neither Ndango nor Nakare—not even at the eating place. He goes to bed early, knowing that the work week begins again tomorrow.

CHAPTER 18

Muronga starts this day like any other. After dressing and eating breakfast, he rushes through the gates to the compound toward his mine shaft with the other men. Passing by his supervisor, who is already at the entrance to the mine shaft, Muronga's routine greeting is returned with nothing more than a cold stare. Muronga notices the difference in his response, but it doesn't tell him much. These people are funny, he says to himself. They change moods as quickly as the weather changes in this place. He shrugs his shoulders and ignores the incident, carrying on with his work until the end of the day. As he is leaving the mine for the compound, his boss again stares at him coldly. It only then occurs to Muronga that this man's changed attitude must have something to do with the meeting on Saturday. Surely he has heard something. It amuses Muronga to think that he has now been labeled a "troublemaker" who must be watched extra carefully, lest he open his big mouth and start putting wild ideas into the heads of good workers. It is about time we gave these whites some trouble. They need to taste a bit of their own bitter medicine! he says to himself with a smile.

Near the gates to the compound, Muronga senses that there is tension in the air. Like an animal that is suddenly aware of impending danger, he scans the area in front of him with a quick eye. Up ahead he sees several uniformed white policemen all gathered tightly around the entrance to the compound. Keeping his head down, but his eyes focused on the policemen, he keeps step with the other men, trying to maintain a relaxed stride. *"Daar's die ander tsotsi, die donner,"* shouts a hefty policeman in Afrikaans. Hearing the word *"tsotsi"*, Muronga is certain that he has been recognized. Fear quickly overtakes him. His eyes dart in every direction as he looks for any possible escape. But before he can move he is rushed by two large, heavily armed policemen. Grabbing him from both sides with their muscular white hands, they force his arms together behind his back and handcuff him. It is only as he is led to a waiting police van that he sees Ndango and Nakare being taken under guard and handcuffed to the same place. The three men are hurled into the van with strict instructions not to talk to one another. As the van speeds away from the compound, Muronga is reminded of the first time he was arrested a few months ago. Leave it to the whites to wait until we "trouble-makers" have completed our day's work before arresting us. The white man has done it again.

After a short while, the van begins to slow down and come to a halt. Moments later, the doors of the van are thrown open and the prisoners dragged out. As before, they have been delivered to a police station, only this time they don't have to wait before being flung into separate cells. Surely this time will be worse than the last.

With his hands still handcuffed behind his back, Muronga stumbles a bit as he is thrust into the cold dark cell. He stands still for a few moments until his eyes have adjusted to the darkness. A tiny bit of light shines through a hole in the high ceiling. He walks across the room and, leaning against the wall, feels the cold concrete through the fabric of his uniform. Standing back from it again, he kicks at the wall softly with his shoe before walking around the perimeters of the room. In one of the corners he finds a stack of blankets. Assuming that it is for him, he sits down on the pile and makes himself as comfortable as possible.

He barely has a chance to think about what is happening to him when he hears the sound of keys grinding in the cell door lock. Feeling trapped, he inches his way further into the corner as a white policeman accompanied by two black guards enter the cell with flashlights in their hands. Flashing the fiery wands in the corners of the cell, they soon spot Muronga. By the light of their flashlights Muronga sees their angry black and white faces. As the white policeman shouts obscenities at Muronga in Afrikaans, one of the black guards translates into Sfanakalo.

"South West, you bastards think you are clever assholes, right?" begins the white guard in an abusive manner. "What is this organization that you have told people lots of shit about? Who told you all this shit about freedom?" he continues in Afrikaans. "What do you want to be free from anyway, from the white man's help and guardianship? Do you want to kill yourselves? Where would you be without the white people, in the bush eating roots and insects? Now, tell us, do you know big terrorists like Mandela? Do you know about Nkrumah, Kaunda, Banda, Lumumba, or Kenyatta? Tell me now who they are! Did they teach you all this nonsense? Did you know that they are cheeky *kaffirs* and that they think they are like white people just because they speak English? You South West boys are beginning that shit here, aren't you? Assholes! Do you see this policeman here? He is cleverer than all of you and all of the stupid black presidents in Africa put together, because he doesn't fart around and disturb the peace and order like you ... *kaffirs*! Do you understand, you pumpkin? Who taught you how to make a speech?" the questions rain.

Before Muronga has a chance to respond, he is ordered to get up. One of the black guards yanks his handcuffs off, and then orders him to take his clothes off and run around the room. As he runs around naked, the policemen scream at him, "Now, show us how strong you are. Let's see how you baboons run around in the bush in South West! Quickly! Faster! You stupid bloody communists! Here you have to reckon with us!" Defenseless, Muronga has no choice but to follow the orders. As he tries to run around faster and faster in the darkened cell, he trips and falls to the floor, where the two black guards descend upon him with fury. Kicking and beating him with all their might, they pass him back and forth between them as Muronga cries out softly in agony. Like professional boxers, the two black guards go at him as if he were a punching bag. Oblivious to his pleas for mercy, they continue to hit him.

"No, you want to be big, so we will teach you how to be big! Let's see you free yourself now!" ridicules one of the black guards. "Tell us the names of everyone in the compound who told you about the difference between whites and blacks!"

"I don't understand what you mean."

"You do! Who are your leaders? Come on, be quick!"

"I don't know. We worked together. We stand together."

"We know that, but who are the ones who told you that you were suffering in this country? Tell us! Your friends in the next cell have told us everything. We just want to know how honest you are so that we can let you go. If you tell us the truth, we will let you go. Now, tell us!"

"I don't know," answers Muronga, wondering if his friends have really told the policeman the truth. *How can Nakare and Ndango tell these people who we are? I don't believe it,* he says to himself.

"Tell us what you are planning to do, you cheeky bastards. Kill the white people? Then what?"

"Who told you such things?" Muronga answers with a question.

"Don't ask stupid questions here! You are not here to argue. You are here to answer questions! Your friends already have. You think you are clever, hey?"

"Which friends?"

"Listen, we told you not to ask questions here!" shouts the black guard, hitting Muronga with his baton.

Muronga tries to escape the blow, but falls to the floor.He manages to pull himself to his feet just in time to answer the next question. At the same time, he hears someone being hit in the cell next door. That must be Nakare or Ndango, he thinks, his fear increasing. He looks around to see if there is a way out. No way. He is trapped.

"And now clever man, did you heare your friend next door talking to the wall? You are next, if you don't tell us eveything you know."

"There is nothing that I can tell you that you don't already know. If you didn't know, we wouldn't be here.... "

Before Muronga finishes his sentence, he is shoved up against the wall by the other black guard. Holding him tightly by the neck, the guard continues to threaten him.

"Do you feel these hands around your neck? They have held many stupid people like you. Now tell us the truth— who is Nakare? What is the United People's Organization? Speak!"

Pinned to the wall, Muronga chokes out, "Nakare is my friend who is next door. The United People's Organization is our organization."

"Now you are talking. And who gives you clever ideas? White people?

"No, no white people," answers Muronga, struggling to breathe.

"What is he saying?" asks the white policeman. "Is he saying that there are no white people giving them these communist ideas? Let me show him what a white man can teach him. You keep asking him questions while I talk straight to his dirty body."

Muronga is hit several times by the white policeman. The questions come like an avalanche from the two black guards. He can barely feel the pain as he tries to hear what the black guards are saying and wonders if they have any sympathy for him.

Engrossed in their cruel pastime, the three policemen do not hear or see their supervisor, Major Nougat, opening the door and entering the cell.

"Who is this baboon you are playing with?" asks the Major, sarcastically. "Is he one of the big men who just came in from the Doornfontein Mine . . . the three who want terrorism in South West?"

"Yes, he is one of the bastards," replies the white policeman. "We are teaching him a bit of manhood. . . ," he says with a punch, knocking Muronga to the floor. One of the black guard grabs Muronga by his scrotum and forces him to his feet again. "*Nawe ne tate!*" Muronga cries out as if his mother and father could help him. Being stronger, faster, and also black, the black guard's blows hurt Muronga more than the white guard's—he is by far more ruthless than his white counterpart. The black policeman continues beating and kicking Muronga nonstop as if he is paid for every single blow he unleashes onto his own kin. He goes on until he is finally stopped by Major Nougat who commands, "Leave him to me now. I haven't had any fun of late."

With his arms poised in front of him and the weight of his body on the balls of his feet, he descends upon Muronga like a confident boxer. Both of his sharp knuckled fists land on Muronga's jaws. With the punches, Muronga loses his balance and his already bloodied head hits the wall. Stunned, he falls to the floor. "That will fix you, you asshole terrorist!" Muronga tries to inhale. The Major's shining, polished shoe kicks Muronga, leaving a black mark on his exposed knee. "Get up, you bastard. Take this baton! Hold it over your head and run in a circle. Show us how you communists run around like assholes with your guns in the air!" Dazed, near collapse, Muronga has no choice but to start to run. Major Nougat charges at him with clenched fists. Still holding the baton overhead, Muronga makes a feeble, instinctive attempt to defend himself. The Major punches him in the gut, his body crumples slightly, and the baton catches Major Nougat right between his big blue eyes. "*Eina, eina!*" shouts the Major, more surprised than pained, glaring at Muronga. The two black guards immediately fly at Muronga for the felony he has committed. With a few punches from each of them, his exhausted body begins to give out as he is sent to the floor again. Thinking quickly, he lies motionless, pretending to have fainted. "Get up!" shouts one of the black guards in Sfanakalo. But Muronga barely breathes. The four officers stare at one another for a moment. Then, looking as if to lay blame on each other, they back away from Muronga. Muronga's plan works. The Major orders the three police guards to leave the room and not to return until further notice. Making no attempt to revive Muronga, he also leaves the cell and appoints another black guard to watch Muronga and feed him as usual.

His body deathly still, Muronga sighs deeply as he hears the door slam and the keys turn in the lock. Fearing that someone may return, he doesn't dare to move. Bruised and bloodied, he feels his head begin to swell, his body begin to ache. The cold concrete floor feels good against his hot skin, and Muronga drifts off to sleep, awakening only when he becomes chilled and feverish. Dragging himself to his feet, he stumbles to the pile of blankets. Crawling under them, his whole body racked with pain, he falls into a fitful sleep. Throughout the long night, he relives the beating in his dreams. At the slightest move, he involuntarily groans in agony, waking, then drifting into the nightmare again.

Early the next morning he is rousted by his cell guard who brings a pail of water and a cloth and orders him to clean himself off. "Here, you! Wake up, clean yourself!" shouts the guard. Although he is terribly weak, Muronga is glad to be able to wash off the dried blood. The guard then brings him some porridge which he eats without thinking. The guard says nothing, but watches Muronga and leaves the cell as soon as he has finished eating. Slowly, and carefully, Muronga crawls back under his blankets and falls asleep. He sleeps deeply this time and awakens only when the guard brings lunch. He eats it in a daze, falls asleep again, eats his dinner when it is brought to him, and goes to sleep. Sleeping soundly throughout the night, he wakes up early the following morning before the guard comes. Feeling the cut in his head, he begins to take stock of his wounds. He hurts all over, but especially feels the pain in his ribs and jaw. His lips and eyes are very swollen. No doubt I look quite horrible, he thinks. I wonder if anyone would recognize me if they saw me like this? And Ndango and Nakare . . . do they look like this also? Or are they dead, perhaps? Muronga thinks back to that terrible night and he silently thanks the God of His Forefathers for giving him the idea of pretending to faint. But were his comrades as lucky?

Muronga's thoughts are interrupted when the guard brings breakfast, but afterward he resumes his meditations. What will be my fate, here at the hands of the white man? I am all alone here. No one would know if I died here in this prison, not even Ndango and Nakare. Muronga thinks back to his earlier imprisonment, when his greatest fear was being separated from Ndango or of being put in a cell alone, in isolation. Like now. Alone. Alone. The word and the feeling sink deeper and deeper into him. What will they do to me? Will they torture me some more, or just leave me here until I go crazy? Muronga imagines every possible form of brutal treatment he can. But the worst punishment of all would be to be kept alive forever in this stinking hole. I would rather be dead. Better to be free and dead than imprisoned and alive.

The day wears on. Muronga barely moves. His mind wanders. He asks himself the same questions over and over again. As the evening comes and goes, Muronga realizes that the only person he has seen for two days has been the guard.

His thoughts are broken when he hears the sound of heavy footsteps approaching. His body stiffens and his nostrils flare at the sudden awareness of impending danger. But the footsteps stop before reaching his cell door. At first he strains his ears to make out what is being said, but as the voices raise and he hears a loud thud against the wall, he stops wondering. He grimaces as he listens to someone being thrown against the walls as if he were a child's ball. He hears a shrill cry. It is more than Muronga can take and shaking, he covers his ears tightly. Oh, my mother, it is another man being beaten, he concludes wearily. The beating goes on for quite some time. Muronga can only hold onto what strength he has left until, after hearing a very loud bang against the wall, the sounds stop and he hears the door slam.

"Good!" he hears a guard exclaim. "These communist terrorists! They think they are clever, and that they can get power and take our white women. We will show them what they will get before that, these shit! This is not fucking America where slaves want to be white. I feel like finishing

off this bloody *kaffir* right now. If I had it my way . . . "
Muronga hears the guard mutter as he locks the door
and walks away down the corridor.

Muronga awakens early to the sound of the cocks
crowing. He thinks of his family. Makena is already up
and about, tending to the fire as she chatters softly and
sings to Mandaha, who is growing bigger every day. Idly,
tenderly he watches his wife and son from where he lies
on his flat wooden *kafungo*. He decides that he, too, should
begin the day's work.

Throwing back the blankets, he sits up and wipes his
hands over his face. It hurts. With his eyes fully open
now, he looks at the four concrete walls that surround
him. Makena and Mandaha are gone. The fire and the
kafungo are gone. Blinking his puffy eyes, Muronga stares
sadly into the grey space before him. They were so real.
I could almost feel them. He feels weary. Why have they
left me?

Closing his eyes, he lies down again on the bed of
blankets on the cell floor. If only Makena were really here,
he thinks. I wonder how she looks these days? He realizes
that his memory of her has grown dim. Straining his
feverish mind, he tries to recall every detail of her—how
she looks, how she walks, her voice, her smile. He tries
to remember how it felt to have her lying next to him
at night. His aloneness is stronger than ever. His throat
tightens as he tries to choke back tears that begin to well
up in his eyes. Will I ever see my wife and son again?
he wonders. The walls of the cell seem to be closing in
on him, strangling him. "Oh . . . God of My Forefathers,
please get me out of here!" he prays aloud. "Take me
home to my people . . . to my wife and child."

His sorrow cuts deep, like an open wound. He can barely
breathe. The vision of Makena returns softly. Oh, Makena,
how did I end up here, so far away from you and our

son? Muronga asks himself. I left you to go to work in the mines, to earn money to pay the white man's taxes— taxes on our land. Did I make the wrong decision? Should I have stayed with you and my son? I could have. I didn't have to go to the mines. There were others who could have gone. Why didn't I simply refuse to pay the taxes? But I didn't know then what I know now.

No, I did what I had to do. My duty was then, and is still, to protect and provide for my family and my people. I had no other choice. I did the only thing I could.

Muronga's thoughts drift back to the time when he and Kaye decided to climb the lorry. Kaye, he thinks with a sigh, my dear friend. I wonder how he is these days? I wonder if somehow my ancestors are telling him what is happening to me? Muronga recalls the days they spent together before they were separated and sent east and west. Would Kaye also have joined our brothers in the United People's Organization if he had been in my place? Muronga ponders this question for a while and finally decides that, yes, Kaye would have. Maybe he is also in prison at this moment.

The thought is not at all pleasant, but it gives Muronga a sense of not being alone in his misery. Somewhat relieved by his memories, he relaxes and his composure returns. Reassured in his convictions, his courage begins to return. Surely my fate cannot be to die in this prison. All I have ever tried to be is true to my family, true to my forefathers, and true to my land. How, then, have I ended up being so far from them?

He hears the familiar sound of the keys rattling outside the cell door. The guard hands the usual breakfast to Muronga, then leaves again without saying a word when Muronga has finished.

Over and over again Muronga asks himself how he got here. Morning becomes afternoon. What is the purpose of my being here? Am I to become another Archie Bokwe? Maybe . . . but . . . no . . . no. My fate cannot be to die here, Muronga says to himself with determination. No! I must live to see my people again . . . my son. I must go home and teach him everything I have learned. Nothing else matters . . . nothing . . .

Again he hears rattling, but this time he also hears voices. Alert and on his guard, he waits. What can it be? Are they coming to beat me again? Or maybe they are going to interrogate me again . . . or torture me . . . Muronga tries to take deep breaths as he braces himself, anticipating the worst. In a moment the cell door opens and a uniformed white policeman enters, followed by the black guard. The white policeman looks more senior than the four guards who beat Muronga. He surveys Muronga and the cell with a quick eye and then relays a command to the guard. "Tell the prisoner to get dressed and then handcuff him." Hurriedly, Muronga dresses. When the handcuffs are securely fastened on his wrists, he is led down a corridor.

A police van is waiting outside. "Get in and put your ass there, you terrorist!" a guard bellows. As Muronga is shoved into the van, he sees the familiar faces of Nakare and Ndango. He can hardly contain his excitement—they are alive and well, although obviously still bruised from beatings. The three greet one another warmly with their eyes, having been instructed not to talk to one another or they will be shot by the two black guards who accompany them in the van.

It is dusk as the van speeds along. Is this the road to the compound? Could it be? Maybe they just put us in prison to frighten us . . . or maybe we aren't going back to the compound after all. Muronga remembers the stories about how they moved Archie Bokwe around so it was impossible to keep track of him. Apprehensively, Muronga stares down at the handcuffs on his wrists. He tries to be hopeful about his fate, as he looks up at the reassuring faces of Ndango and Nakare.

The van slowly turns and comes to a stop. The door is flung open and a black policeman orders them to get out. There before them is the compound. The prisoners' hearts leap at the sight as they are escorted through the gates at the entrance by three black guards and one white one who orders them to go to their rooms and collect all of their belongings. "Go get your things and come back quickly. Or I will come and burn your asses!" he says. "If you have too many things, then only take a few of them and leave the rest. Quickly!"

Puzzled, the three men do as they are told, each one going to his room accompanied by a guard. It is dinner time, so the other men are not in their rooms and do not see the three being smuggled into and out of the compound.

While Muronga assembles his belongings, he notices an envelope with his name and a stamp on it lying on his bed. In a great hurry, he sticks it in his shirt pocket. He collects a few of his things and carries them in a large suitcase towards the gates.

With their personal possessions in hand, the three men pass through the entrance again and are given small parcels. "These envelopes have your money. The money you worked for. Ask no questions, you hear?" the guard raves.

The van ride begins again. Muronga remembers the envelope with his name and address on it that had been lying on top of his bed when he entered the room. Pulling it carefully out of his shirt pocket, he opens the letter— his first letter ever—and reads the words in it.

"A letter to *Wiha-Mandaha.*

How did you sleep? Did you wake up well? Are you working well? This is *Nyina-Mandaha,* your wife, writing this letter with the help of Uncle Ndara. Your cousin, Andreas, who is in school at the mission is writing this for us. You have been away such a long time and we are all having bad dreams in our sleep about you. Your young friend, Diyeve, came here some time ago. He brought us the clothes you sent us. Now Mandaha is the best-dressed baby in the village and I am sure he knows his father sent these clothes. Diyeve told us all about you, too. He says that you are a big person there. He told us that you can read and write words like a teacher. And that you speak *vsvsvsvs* and other people's languages. The other people fear you.

We have received your letter. It has good words. You are almost a teacher now. Uncle Ndara is afraid you will get lost and not come back. He went to ask *Muruti* if he could help us reach you, but *Muruti* said he should ask the commissioner. So Uncle Ndara went with *Muruti* to Rundu to speak to the commissioner. Uncle Ndara wanted to come and fetch you and bring you home. But the commissioner told Uncle Ndara that the law would not allow him, an old man, to follow you. He only gave him the bag for the letter and the stamp on it. He told him we can put our words inside it and give it to *Muruti.* The lorries will pick it up and bring it to you.

The news here is little. We have rains and the cattle are fat. Uncle Ndara and everyone in our kraal help me and Mandaha, but we all need you. We begin to forget how you look. Mandaha asks when you are coming home. He speaks of you in his own tongue. He says ta-ta-ta-ta. You can see from his foot that he is a big boy now. I feel like I am not a married woman anymore. Please come back soon . . . now. Uncle Ndara says you have worked enough, and should come home now . . . before you are hurt like young Diyeve. You will take over Uncle Ndara's work for him. He says his back is hurting more these days. We need you here. Please send me more words. Everybody greets you. This is the end of our letter. Your wife, *Nyina-Mandaha.*

On the next page is a child's footprint . . . powdered charcoal pressed on white paper. Overwhelmed with joy and longing to see his family and friends, Muronga thanks the God of His Forefathers that he can now read words by himself. Closing his eyes tightly, he imagines how his wife and son must look, and wishes more than ever that he were on his way home.

Muronga looks questioningly at the faces of Nakare and Ndango, but they seem to be equally perplexed and only shrug their shoulders cautiously. What can possibly happen to us next? they wonder.

CHAPTER 19

Every time the van slows down slightly, the men think the trip is coming to an end. They try to figure out where they might be, but the van doesn't stop—it keeps going and going. All through the night they sleep uncomfortably as the van bounces along the rough roads. Just before dawn, Nakare, who has been awake for a short while and looking out the small barred window of the van, sees a sign with a name written on it reflected by the van's headlights. Excitedly, he carefully nudges Ndango and whispers, "Francistown. We are being taken to Botswana, and maybe home!" Ndango excitedly pokes at Muronga to wake him. Sleepily, Muronga asks, "Hm . . . what . . . what is it?" From what Ndango says to him in a soft whisper he can only make out the "Francistown" and "taken home". Stunned awake now, he blinks his eyes, trying to comprehend the words. Can it be true? he wonders. Is Ndango right? Are we really going home? The word "home" washes over and over Muronga like a huge wave. Home . . . home. . . , he thinks. Home to my people . . . home to my wife and son . . . home to my land. I am going home at last. A shudder runs through his body as he realizes that his dream may soon be coming true.

Unable to sleep anymore, the three men sit impatiently watching the sun rise through the back window, waiting for the van to reach its final destination. Finally they arrive at the South African Embassy, where they are taken to a room to wait.

"Good morning," one of the two South African policemen greets his Botswana counterpart who opens the door for them. "I am Captain DeKok and my colleague here is Sergeant Venter. We spoke with you earlier, and these are the three terrorists that we are sending home. We would like you to transport them further, please."

"Oh, yes, I remember you phoned. Just leave them here. We will take care of them."

"Please send them off soon. They are dangerous. Here are their papers."

"Okay, we will handle them. Thank you."

Some time passes before they are escorted by two Botswana policemen to another police van for a short ride to the main prison in Francistown. As they are being led to a large cell with several other black prisoners in it, they are told that they will be kept here until tomorrow afternoon when they will be taken to the airport.

"You will stay here until you get on the plane to Shakawe," one of the policemen explains. "You are not allowed to speak too much. Your government has given you to us."

As soon as the cell door closes behind them, Muronga, Ndango and Nakare see that this prison is different from the ones they have known in South Africa. The prison guards here seem to sympathize and have some respect for the prisoners. The prisoners in the cell greet Muronga and his comrades and show them to their beds. Each thick cotton mattress is covered by two heavy grey blankets, and a pillow rests at the head of each bed. Not even in their compound barracks did they have decent bedding like this. To them, this is luxury.

"Things are better here," Muronga whispers to Nakare. "Not like the prison we were in before."

"Yes, it is different. Even the prisoners smile and look like people, the way we look. None of them has a swollen face."

As Muronga surveys the cell and its inmates, he is reminded of Musoke's words—that it is better to be governed by one's own people, no matter how bad they are, than by total strangers.

It is just after they have introduced themselves and are beginning to tell their fellow inmates about why they were arrested and brought to this prison when the cell door opens and a black warden enters. He greets the prisoners in Setswana and they return his greeting before he says in Sfanakalo, "The three of you from South West Africa, come with me, please." Not knowing what to expect, Muronga and his companions look at one another, but do as they are asked. They follow the warden to a small secluded office. He motions to them to sit down on the bench opposite his desk while he closes the door securely. Taking a seat behind the desk, he talks to them calmly and decently. "You need not be afraid of me. I only want to ask you some questions. First, is it true that you were involved in political activities in the mine, and you have an organization that wants freedom and independence for your country, South West Africa? Tell me."

Hesitantly, Nakare answers for all three men. "Yes, we are the leaders. All our comrades are still in the mine. We don't know what will happen."

Then the warden asks each man about his family back home and his plans for the future. Each one answers briefly, still not knowing how much to tell this man. They are too suspicious of him. I wish we had a chance to talk about how much we should tell this man, Muronga thinks. They glance at each other to exchange their fears and suspicions. But the warden's manner is friendly and he seems sympathetic and concerned about them. When it appears that he has asked them every question he can think of, he stops, and sighing audibly, taps his fingers on the desk top while he stares into space.

Finally, he speaks. "My brothers, I must commend you for what you are trying to do for your people and your country. Not long ago we here in Botswana were in the same situation you are in in South West Africa. We were oppressed by the white man, too, and we had to struggle for our independence. In most African countries it has been the same story. Many African countries have had to fight for their independence, but they have finally won it and now they rule themselves. They lost many lives in the fight, though—many comrades."

He pauses momentarily. Then, with a sigh, he continues, "They lost other comrades through exile. I am sure you have heard of Nkrumah, Lumumba, and Kenyatta—men who have led their people to freedom in other African countries." The three men on the bench nod, listening attentively.

"They, like some of our people, had to lead the struggle from outside. Because of their convictions, they were forced to choose between their families and their freedom. At great personal cost they chose to work for the liberation of their people's hearts and minds.

"I have listened to your plans for the future with both hope and fear. People all over Africa are waiting for your country's liberation, but it will not be that easy. Especially for you. You are marked men. The South African authorities in your country no doubt know everything about you, including when you are due to arrive home. They will watch you constantly. At the slightest move, they will arrest you or try to kill you. You will not be able to speak about the United People's Organization without risking your lives.

"As you may remember, not very long ago, some brave men began to confront the whites in your country. They decided to use the barrel of the gun to try to get your country back. These men went through our country. We gave them shelter and helped them to get strong so that they could go back and fight. Now, some of them have been killed and some put in jail. They need more people, like you. We didn't have to shed very much blood for our freedom. We got our independence last year, and as you can see, things have changed. That is why I am able to speak to you in this way. But your freedom is still a long way ahead of you. You will have to fight very hard for it and a great deal of blood will be spilt, I am sure, because you have a different kind of monster to reckon with. I know what I am talking about and I know that there are many people in my country who want to see you free. The decision, however, is entirely yours . . . Do you understand?"

The three men think of their meetings and of the fate of their comrade Natangwe and begin to believe that the warden is speaking the truth. He sounds as if he knows what he is talking about and he looks sincere. For a long while, they barely breathe. They stare at him, at each other and at the ceiling as if to obtain some instant wisdom from an external force.

"You must make a choice . . . now . . . and quickly," the warden continues after a pause. "I can help you to escape from this prison and get to a safe place in Botswana where you can work for your country's liberation. But you have only until dawn tomorrow morning to decide. And if you decide to follow my plan to escape, you must realize that you may never see your families again." The word "never" rings in the air.

For several moments silence hangs in the room as the three men try to digest the warden's words. The only communication between the three comrades is through coughing and deep sighs. They are too scared to express their suspicions. And they don't feel like talking. They wish they could believe him.

"Once you have decided, either to go home or escape, there will be no turning back. Either way you will have to make a sacrifice. The price is high ... very high." Again he pauses, waiting for the three men to grasp what he has said.

"Now, this is the plan. Tomorrow morning I will come to your cell very early and unlock the door. Whoever of you decides to escape must come to the door immediately, but you must not make a sound. If anyone hears you or sees you leaving, we will all be in deep trouble. You will be severely punished. So will I." He sighs, rubbing his face.

"Opposite the cell door is a black metal door. As soon as you are out of the cell, you go straight through the black door. It will lead you to the light outside. A friend of mine will be waiting there to take you to your destination. You can trust him, believe me. He will explain everything to you. And he will take good care of you. But remember, once you go through that door, there will be no way to turn back.

"So, now you must go back to your cell before anyone misses you and gets suspicious. You have a lot of thinking to do and I wish you well, my brothers. No one, least of all I, will find fault in what you decide. Go well ... stay well," he says as he shakes their hands and opens the office door. The three men mumble, "Thank you ... thank you," as they leave the office and are led back to their cell.

Back in the cell the three men resume their places and the discussions they were having with their cellmates before the warden came in, as if nothing had happened. For the rest of the morning they try to avoid thinking about what the warden told them by talking to the other prisoners about life in the prison.

"Do you think that man wants to help us?" Muronga asks eventually.

"I think so," Nakare replies. "He sounds like a good man. His eyes are trustworthy."

They are still busy talking when a guard comes to usher them all to a large dining hall. They go through a line to get their food, just as in the compound, but here they sit at long tables and eat with the other inmates. Returning to their cell, the men rest on their beds or sleep a bit. Muronga, Ndango and Nakare still do not speak about their meeting with the warden, but they hardly need to— they know each other so well that they can communicate their feelings without words. Each one knows what the others are going through.

Lying on his bed, his hands clasped behind his head, Muronga stares at the ceiling as he recalls the words of the warden. "Once you have decided, there will be no turning back." What shall I do, he asks himself. I must decide . . . and quickly. Again Muronga hears the warden say, ". . . You may never see your families again." He repeats the sentence in his mind. Never see Makena again. Never see Mandaha again. Never see my people again . . . He shudders and closes his eyes tightly, trying to block out the emptiness that wells up inside him. No . . . I must see my family again. Nothing else matters. Without them there is nothing to live for. I left my people in order to help them, but where has it brought me? Am I helping them by being here? By going around making speeches, am I helping them? Or am I just inviting the wrath of the white man?

No ... no. Our organization has done some good already. We frightened the white man—we made him think of us as people. Now he thinks of us as troublemakers and not merely followers of his orders. Yes ... in a way, we taught him.

Somewhat satisfied that his work with the organization has been worthwhile, he stretches his sore arms. But is that worth giving up my family? Is teaching the white man more important than teaching my people . . . and my son? Muronga imagines himself with Uncle Ndara, with Mama Rwenge, Makena, and Mandaha, as they sit around the fire and he tells stories about his adventures. Closing his eyes, he daydreams that he has arrived back in the village. Everyone in his *kraal* comes to meet him, and in the evening he sits by the fire with Uncle Ndara and others. They are happy to be with him. With his son in his lap and his wife next to him, he begins to tell them: "It was good to work in the mine, but it is also good to be back amongst you. I learned so many things while I was away from home. Now I understand why these white people come here to get us to work in the mines. They want to enslave us. They are also afraid of the black people in their land, because the blacks there are educated in the white man's ways. They understand the white man's laws and they know how to use those laws against him. They are fighting for what they think is theirs now. This is why we were in jail."

"You were in jail? What happened?" he hears Uncle Ndara asking him curiously.

"An important leader of the black people, a man who always spoke in the name of his people against the white people, was put in jail for a long time. This man died in jail and most people in the mine and everywhere in the country thought that the white people killed him. I also believe that they killed him. If they treated us so badly in the mine because we asked questions, how much worse would they treat a man who told them where and when they were wrong. I have learned that the white people do not want to hear the truth. They have no truth. They have no hearts. They love themselves too much to see that we are as human as they are. I just don't know what makes them like that."

As Muronga continues to tell them about his experiences away from home, other people in the *kraal* join them by the fire to hear Muronga. For the first time Muronga gives an account of his life in the mine to his own people. One, two, three, four and more men and women come to listen enthusiastically as he transports them through his life there.

"When I arrived in the compound, I felt very lonely. I did not know the people that I was put with there, to sleep and to work with. I missed Kaye all the time. I missed home, Uncle Ndara, my parents, my wife, my son Mandaha, and all of you. It took me a while to get used to the idea of living with strangers, all strangers. Like all the other people there, I had to accept that life there was different for everyone. So it was for me. I made friends and started to learn new things, new ideas, and later I learned how to read and write. The language that is spoken in the mine everyone there knows, as Uncle Ndara and other men here used to tell us.

"I began to like being busy all the time, working and learning. I also learned there that it is very important to work together with other people who are not necessarily from your *kraal*, because many people have the same problems and want to work together. This is why we went to jail. It was important for us to work with other people. In jail, I was taught many things. I began to understand that many black people are dying because of the laws of the white people. And the way the white people treated us while we were in jail was bad. It was as if they were dealing with animals. The worst thing was to see how the people who are working with the white policemen have ceased to be our people. They are more cruel and more dangerous than the whites themselves. They beat us and abused us. They did it more than the whites because they know where it hurts most. I don't remember crying before I left home, because my mother used to say to me that girls cried, not boys. But in jail, I cried. Not because the policemen were beating me. That I could not cry about. I cried because every time a black man struck me, it felt like I myself was striking my son Mandaha, or any of you . . . Oh, it hurt!"

"Oh, yes, it must have hurt!" interrupts Uncle Ndara. "Who are those black people? Are they black like us?"

"Yes, they are. Life in the mines was better before we went to jail, because Diyeve arrived and told me a lot of news about home and you. I felt much better again. When I came back from jail, I found him in the hospital. He had lost his fingers. Again, that was a white man's fault. His white supervisor did not explain to him how to do his work without hurting himself. I was very bitter about that. The money Diyeve got for his fingers was very little. If a white man was hurt that way, he would have received money that would not fit into his hands.

"I learned to read and write because I wanted to be able to stand up and work to help not only myself, but my people—all of you. You have power in your hands if you can read the words that are written on paper and if you can put them there. Now the white man cannot lie to me. I can read his words. The words will speak to me. Words do not lie, but people's tongues lie.

"I was not happy to be in jail. But I am happy that I was there. It made me strong. It made me see the white people and their black police as people who fear us. They fear black people. They are not happy. They think we are against them. They always fear truth, because they know deep down in their stomachs that they are wrong, not those whom they beat and kick.

"I thought of you all the time. In times of happiness like when Diyeve arrived, and in times of pain like when I was beaten, when I was bleeding through my nose in jail. I missed you. I missed the children, the cattle, the fowls. I missed the cool waters of our river. I dreamed of going in the *wato* with Mandaha. I thought of the birds in the trees. I wondered who was sick, and felt sad when I thought that if you saw me in jail, you would have cried, too. Now I am happy to be with you. The God of our Forefathers and your good wishes brought me home safely. Before I came home, my friends and I were selected to be the leaders of our organization, the United People's Organization. The white people hated us. They abused us. They decided to send us home with little money. When I got your letter, *Nyina-Mandaha*, we were on our way back home. It was a very bad experience. Very bad. My two friends, Nakare and Ndango are in a foreign land right now. They decided to go away for us."

"For us? Where are they?" asks Uncle Ndara.

"Yes, for us. They are in Botswana. They will fight for our liberation."

"What is that, liberation?" Mama Rwenge asks."What will your friends liberate us from?"

"From the laws of the white man. He is taking our land away from us. And if we do not stand up for it, we will have no land."

"Why didn't you go with them if the white man is taking our land away? You are the people who know these things!" Muronga's father adds.

"I was torn between going with my friends and returning here to tell you all of this. And I thought that together we could do something here. I also wanted to see and be with my son, Mandaha. It was very hard for me to decide otherwise . . . "

He sees Makena and Mama Rwenge crying upon hearing his story. He also sees one old man holding back his tears. He wakes up. He is still in jail. With Nakare and Ndango next to him.

"Oh, my mother, I was dreaming! It was a dream! A dream!"

Awakening some time later, he is sad and disturbed, remembering how he felt in his dream when he had to explain to his people about why he was sent home. What will I tell them? What can I tell them that won't land me in prison? How can I explain prison to them? he asks himself. In the midst of pondering these question a guard comes once again to escort the men to the dining hall. The whole afternoon has passed and he has not yet made up his mind.

Returning to their cell after dinner, the men converse before going to sleep for the night. Muronga and his comrades join the discussion, but their hearts are not really in it. Before the lights are turned out, Muronga shakes hands with Nakare and Ndango, saying, "Good night and good luck." Each one knows that he has a long road to travel before the night is over, but that his friends are with him in spirit. All night Muronga thinks of his friends and their families back home. I wonder what I will say to their families to explain why I came back and they didn't?

None of the three men manages to sleep at all. They toss and turn all night long, thinking and wondering what to do. Each one would like to consult the other two about their decision, but even if they could, they know that no one can help them decide. They will each have to decide for themselves. While Muronga's mind is nearly made up to go back home to his family, he agonizes over what it will mean to him to give up his newfound cause. Will he be able to accept bondage now that he understands what freedom is and knows how he and his country can liberate themselves? It is the road to freedom that is hard— this he has learned, too. As the night grows older, Muronga agonizes. He must choose between his love for his family and his duty to them, and his love and duty to his people and country. He must choose between yesterday and tomorrow . . . between known misery and uncertain joy. Between oppression and liberation. More confused than ever, Muronga turns fitfully in his bed. Vacillating, he becomes very tense. He tries to sleep, but cannot. He wonders if his friends have decided. They are older than he is, their children bigger, and they have more experience in the world than he has. Muronga is sure of his commitment to the liberation of his country, but he lacks the strength to give up his family. Hearing Ndango tossing in his bed beside him, he rolls over and carefully whispers, "I have decided to go home. I will try to do what little I can do there. If you decide to go through the door, remember that I am with you in spirit. I will pray to the God of Our Forefathers that we will be together again one day." Reaching out and grasping Muronga's hand tightly, Ndango whispers, "I understand, my brother." Nakare, who is lying head-to-head with Ndango, overhears the two men and, stretching out his arm, he joins hands with them and whispers, "I have heard what you have said and I also understand. Tell our people what we are doing, but be careful." Squeezing their hands tightly he says, "Go well . . . stay well."

Having announced his decision to his comrades, Muronga expects to feel relieved, but as their hands pull away from his, he feels the emptiness within himself again. He struggles against this feeling by thinking about going home. Yes . . . I will go home and tell our people what I know and teach my son what I have learned. I will teach him to be proud of himself and of our ancestors. I will teach him to be a free man—free from the white man's bondage. He persuades himself that everything will be fine once he gets home. But he cannot teach his son to be what he is not—a free man. How can I teach Mandaha that he has an obligation to his people that he must fulfill if I cannot do so myself? How am I going to explain to him and to my people why I chose them instead of my convictions?

Torn between his love and his convictions, Muronga's grief overwhelms him. Tears begin to well up in his eyes. Through the tears, he sees the first glimmer of daylight enter the room. The cell is still dark inside, but he can begin to see the walls. Looking around at the sleeping men, he is reminded that people do not become heroes because they suffer imprisonment, but because they are willing to give up the joys of ordinary life. It is the sacrifice they make that makes them heroes, not the comfort they cling to. Freedom comes only through hardship and sacrifice. Muronga's tired, wet eyes rest upon the grey metal door of the cell. By choosing to remain here, behind these bars, I accept oppression and the restriction of my soul for the rest of my life. But if I choose to go through that door, I accept the responsibility of going through life determining my own fate.

Ndango and Nakare are awake and ready to go as soon as the warden comes. Muronga shakes their hands one last time and then turns away so as not to see them leaving. Lying quietly on his bed he closes his eyes and tries to find some peace of mind by thinking of Makena and his son. His vision of them is of the last time he saw them before he left with Kaye to climb the lorry. "To me, you are always here, even if you go far away to other countries," Makena said then. "Go well . . . Work well . . . We will all wait for you." The keys turn softly in the cell door lock. As he hears his friends stealthily walking to the door, he quickly pulls himself from his bed and stands with his back to the door, his right hand pressed to his chest. Bewildered, he turns around quickly to have one final look at Ndango and Nakare. His eyes half closed, he makes one . . . two . . . three . . . four quick steps behind them—through the door!

GLOSSARY

African words used in this story come from black South African languages Sotho, Xhosa and Zulu, Namibian languages Herero, Damara/Nama, Kavango and Owambo, and Tswana and Sfanakalo, used in the mines in Southern Africa.

Amandla   A term meaning "power" in Xhosa and Zulu, its equivalent is *Matla* in Sotho, and *Nonkondo* in Kavango.

Ayibo   An exclamation of incredulity in Xhosa or Zulu.

Baas   An Afrikaans word for boss, literally meaning owner.

Baasboy   An Afrikaans word for an African mine worker who has been given extra responsibility as an overseer.

Calabash   A South African word for a dried gourd emptied of its seeds and used as a container.

CDM   The abbreviation for Consolidated Diamond

	Mines, a De Beers mining company that operates in Namibia.
Dagga	A South African word for hashish.
Dinongo	A Kavango word for black beeswax that is put on drums to make the sound lower.
Dominee	An Afrikaans word for a minister in the Dutch Reformed Church.
Ghutara	The Kavango name for a grass-roofed canopy shelter held up by thick sticks.
Indaba	A Zulu/Xhosa word for a serious discussion.
Kaffir	A derogatory South African term for a person of African descent, equivalent to "nigger" in American English.
Katekete	A Kavango word for a lay catechism instructor.
Kerrie or kierie	A South African word for a fighting stick, baton or scepter.
Madoda	A Zulu or Xhosa word for men.
Magayisa	A Sfanakalo term for men who have completed their contract labor and are returning home.
Mahangu	The Kavango name for sorghum, which forms the staple diet in northern Namibia.
Manyowani	A Sfanakalo term for new recruits, or those men who have not yet started their contract labor.
Marewu	A Sfanakalo word for a yogurt-like drink that is made by letting *mealie meal pap* ferment overnight.
Matanyuna	A Sfanakalo and Kavango term for "sexual intercourse" between men.

Mbukushu	The root word for a Kavango tribe in northern Namibia. MuMbukushu means a member of this tribe, haMbukushu means members of the tribe, and Thimbukushu is the language spoken by the tribe. Kwangali is the root word for another tribe, hence, muKwangali, vaKwangali and Rukwangali refer to a member of the tribe, members of the tribe, and the language of the Kwangali, respectively.
Mealie meal	A South African term meaning meal made from maize (or corn).
Moro	A common greeting in Kavango, regardless of the time of day.
Muhindi	A Kavango term for a man assigned to serve drinks, usually because he is known to be fair and has a good memory for faces.
Munuko ghothikuwa	The Kavango term for a synthetic smell associated with white people.
Muruti	The Kavango word for a preacher or pastor.
Ndandari	The Kavango name for a traditional male game played by throwing long wooden spears to hit a discus-like plant root.
Ndjambi	A Kavango term used to describe a system of rotating communal labor, especially planting, harvesting and construction.
Nganga	The Kavango term for an African traditional healer.
Ngoma	A Kavango word for drum.
Nyakanyaka	A Zulu/Xhosa/Sfanakalo word for disorder.
Nyambi	A Kavango word for the God of Ages,

worshipped in Africa before the arrival of western missionaries.

Nyina	A Kavango word used as a prefix for a child's given name which means "mother of". It indicates the greater respect given to a mother. *Wiha* is the prefix used for the father of a child.
pap	An Afrikaans term for a very thick, stiff, almost bread-like porridge.
Pikinini	A Sfanakalo word for small.
Poephol	An Afrikaans word meaning "asshole".
Pondok	A South African word for a shelter made from a piece of corrugated metal placed on metal poles.
Rand	A unit of South African currency.
Rondavels	Pseudo huts, usually found in white people's camps.
Sibonda	A Sfanakalo word for a black overseer in the barracks.
Sfanakalo	A South African mine language composed of words taken from African and European languages added to corrupt Zulu to facilitate communication between the people working in the mines.
Skelm	An Afrikaans word meaning cunning or foxy.
Stimela	A Zulu word for train.
Thidhira	The Kavango term for prohibited or taboo behavior.
Thishongero	Catechism in Kavango.
Thivanda	A Kavango term for the far-away places

where men went to work.

Tickey	Threepence.
Tshetshisa	A Zulu word meaning "make haste".
Tshotsholoza	A South African mine work-chant.
Tsotsi	A South African word for a black thug.
Tyhini	An exclamation of dismay or consternation in Xhosa.
Vsvsvsvs	The term Kavango village people used to describe strange-sounding European languages.
Wato	The Kavango word for canoe or dugout.
WENELA	The abbreviation for Witwatersrand Native Labor Association, a South African agency that recruits African migrant laborers from the countries in Southern Africa to work in the gold mines in South Africa.
Wera	The Kavango term for a traditional game played by men in which twelve or more small holes are dug in the ground and stones are used as playing pieces. The stones represent cattle, and the object of the game is to win the opponent's cattle.
Yithima	A Kavango word for a traditional staple stiff porridge, originally made from millet.